"Porter writes with honesty, warmth, and compassion about the uncomfortable issues that may arise in one's life. Anticipate a good series as each sister explores different paths and different outcomes that are challenging and real." —*Library Journal*

"[Porter's] characters are compelling individuals who quickly grab your heart . . . This beautifully written story sends readers on an emotional roller-coaster ride that twists and turns right to the end."
—*RT Book Reviews*

She's Gone Country

"I've always been a big fan of Jane Porter's. She understands the passion of grown-up love and the dark humor of mothering teenagers. What a smart, satisfying novel *She's Gone Country* is."
—Robyn Carr, *New York Times* bestselling author of the Virgin River novels

"A celebration of a woman's indomitable spirit. Suddenly single, juggling motherhood and a journey home, Shey embodies every woman's hopes and dreams. Once again, Jane Porter has written her way into this reader's heart."
—Susan Wiggs, #1 *New York Times* bestselling author of the Bella Vista Chronicles novels

"Richly rewarding." —*Chicago Tribune*

"Strongly plotted, with a heroine who is vulnerable yet resilient . . . engaging." —*The Seattle Times*

Easy on the Eyes

"An irresistible mix of glamour and genuine heart . . . *Easy on the Eyes* sparkles!" —Beth Kendrick, author of *New Uses for Old Boyfriends*

"A smart, sophisticated, fun read with characters you'll fall in love with. Another winning novel by Jane Porter."
—Mia King, national bestselling author of *Table Manners*

Mrs. Perfect

"With great warmth and wisdom, in *Mrs. Perfect* Jane Porter creates a richly emotional story about a realistically flawed and wonderfully human hero who only discovers what is important in life when she learns to let go of her quest for perfection."　—*Chicago Tribune*

"Porter's authentic character studies and meditations on what really matters make *Mrs. Perfect* a perfect summer novel."　—*USA Today*

"The witty first-person narration keeps things lively in Porter's latest. Taylor's neurotic fussiness provides both vicarious thrills and laughs before Taylor moves on to self-awareness and a new kind of empowerment . . . a feel-good read."　—*Kirkus Reviews*

Flirting with Forty
Basis for the Lifetime Original Movie

"A terrific read! A wonderful, life- and love-affirming story for women of all ages."
　—Jayne Ann Krentz, *New York Times* bestselling author of *Trust No One*

"Fits the bill as a calorie-free accompaniment for a poolside daiquiri."
　—*Publishers Weekly*

Odd Mom Out

"Jane Porter must know firsthand how it feels to not fit in. She nails it poignantly and perfectly in *Odd Mom Out*. This mommy-lit title is far from fluff . . . Sensitive characters and a protagonist who doesn't cave to the in-crowd gives this novel its heft."　—*USA Today*

"[Porter's] musings on balancing work, life, and love ring true."
　—*Entertainment Weekly*

"The draining pace of Marta's life comes across convincingly, and Porter's got a knack for getting into the heads of the preteen set; Eva's worries are right on the mark. A poignant critique of mommy cliques and the plight of single parents."　—*Kirkus Reviews*

Berkley Books by Jane Porter

THE GOOD WOMAN
THE GOOD DAUGHTER
THE GOOD WIFE
IT'S YOU

It's You

JANE PORTER

BERKLEY BOOKS, NEW YORK

R

B
BERKLEY

An imprint of Penguin Random House LLC
375 Hudson Street, New York, New York 10014

This book is an original publication of Penguin Random House LLC.

Library of Congress Cataloging-in-Publication Data

Porter, Jane, 1964–
It's you / Jane Porter.—Berkley trade paperback edition.
pages ; cm
ISBN 978-0-425-27715-7 (softcover)
1. Loss (Psychology)—Fiction.   2. Life change events—Fiction.   3. Self-realization in
women—Fiction.   4. Self-actualization (Psychology) in women—Fiction.
I. Title.   II. Title: It is you.
PS3616.O78I87 2016
813'.6—dc23
2015001531

PUBLISHING HISTORY
Berkley trade paperback edition / June 2015

PRINTED IN THE UNITED STATES OF AMERICA

10   9   8   7   6   5   4   3   2   1

Cover photos: "Woman Swinging" by Brooke Pennington / Getty Images; "Vintage background of
old photos with keys on a table" by Neirfy / Shutterstock Images; "Beautiful vineyard landscape"
by Mythja / Shutterstock Images; "Vintage Wallpaper" by Irtsya / Shutterstock Images.
Cover design by Rita Frangie.
Interior text design by Kristin del Rosario.

Penguin
Random
House

It's You is dedicated to my family who came before me:
the Gansneders, Mullendores, Platzs, Schneiders,
Riedls, Wertzs, Venemanns, Brotts, and Cutsingers.

To my late father,
who took us to live in Nuremberg for a year
so we could see the world.

To my mother,
who made sure we understood that it is important
to know where you come from,
so you know where you want to go.

To my sister and brothers,
who journeyed with me.

To my husband and sons,
whom I love dearly.

To all who live, hope, and dream.

Let us not just remember. Let us do better.

Courage. Unity. Love.

Peace.

ACKNOWLEDGMENTS

Thank you to the wonderful, generous German editor Iris Paepke, who had a conversation with me in Berlin on May 23, 2014, at the CORA/ MIRA Taschenbuch dinner that stayed with me, giving life to the Berlin in this story . . . and who then, months later, took the time to read the manuscript and give me feedback. I am deeply indebted to you. Thank you.

Thank you to the founders and organizers of the LoveLetter Convention, Kris Alice Hohls and Katrin Grassmann, for inviting me to join you in Berlin and making me fall in love with Germany and Berlin all over again. Also huge thanks and hugs to Meghan Farrell for attending the conference with me and making it so fun.

Talia Seehoff, thank you from the bottom of my heart for reading this story in chunks and giving me feedback and encouragement. I never forgot how my story is also tied to "your story." Thank you for keeping it real.

Thank you to my agent, Holly Root, for believing in me and supporting me, and a huge thank-you to my brilliant editor, Cindy Hwang, for understanding what I was trying to do with Ali's and Edie's stories and helping me get there.

Lastly, thank you to my family for loving me even when I'm a mad, creative disaster. You keep me sane.

ONE

Ali

For over a year following Andrew's death I showed up and performed and executed perfectly.

I handled that horrible year and the next few months so well that I'd begun to think the worst was behind me.

And then I got the note.

I'd left the office on my lunch, dashing to the Nordstrom at the Scottsdale Fashion Square for a pair of shoes for Dad. He has a birthday coming up in late June and I'm hoping to see him Memorial Day weekend. I'd meant to go north for Easter but Dr. Morris took time off and I was needed. Dad was fine with it but I think he'd appreciate a new pair of Clarks, even if he doesn't do as much walking in his retirement home.

I'd zipped into the shopping mall, made the purchase, and was hurrying back to my car, pleased that I'd still have time for a quick bite of lunch at the office before my first afternoon appointment, when I noticed the scrap of paper on my windshield, pinned to the glass by the windshield wiper. I tugged on the paper, sliding it free and reading the blue scrawl.

Learn to park. <u>Asshole</u>.

Dumbfounded, I set the paper shopping bag at my feet and flipped the note over. The back was blank and I read the scribble of blue ink again.

Learn to park. <u>Asshole</u>.

"Asshole" had been underlined.

The *A* was huge. The two *s*'s looked almost like *z*'s.

For a moment I thought it was a joke, or a mistake. And then I was hit by a wave of nausea.

It wasn't a joke.

It was just a mean note.

Sickened, I crumpled it up and shoved it into my purse. I don't know why I put it in my purse but I was suddenly and deeply ashamed.

My car was on the white line, on the passenger side. Normally I park exactly between the painted lines, but when I pulled in the car on my left was a little bit over, and so I parked and dashed into the store.

Driving back to the office, I mentally reviewed my parking job. I was *on* the line. I probably was parked too close to the car on my right. But I wasn't *over* the line. And the car on my left was crowding me. My car isn't a big car. It's not as if I drive a big SUV. I slid out of my driver side without dinging the car next to me.

Maybe I shouldn't have parked there.

Maybe I should have kept looking for a spot.

I'm still obsessing—rationalizing—my choices as I reach the office. I can't let it go. I don't know why I have to defend myself.

The person who wrote the note was rude. It was a rude note by a rude person. *Let it go.*

I try.

I try as I park—carefully.

I try as I enter the modern marble and glass building with the tinted windows and open the door to Morris Dental & Associates, catching a whiff of the distinctive smell unique to dentist offices. The odor wafts from the back. It's a mix of chemicals. Formocreasol. Cresatin. Eugenol. Acrylic Monomer.

Oh, and teeth.

The office is cold, chilled to sixty-seven degrees, the temperature Dr. Morris prefers for his own comfort. He doesn't like being warm when he works. His hands are steadier, his concentration better, when it's cool, and it is his office.

Normally I don't smell the chemicals but I do now. Maybe it's the shock of the note, a shock I can't shake.

I'm still unsettled as I open my yogurt in the staff room. But I can't take a bite. Instead I hold my yogurt and spoon and stand at the window staring out at the taupe and gold Camelback Mountain.

Learn to park. Asshole.

"Dr. McAdams, you've a patient in exam room three," Natalie, one of the practice's two dental assistants, announces from the staff room door.

I thank her and put the yogurt back into the refrigerator. My legs feel funny as I walk. Like I'm walking in wet cement. If Andrew were here right now he'd make a joke and tease me about being an asshole and my horrible driving skills, and I'd laugh and it'd be okay. But he's not here because he'd rather be dead. He's not here—

I enter the sunlit exam room holding my breath, keeping the pain bottled inside as I glance at the chart on the counter. Leah

Saunders. I quickly wash my hands, and face her, forcing a smile. "I'm Dr. McAdams. How are you today, Leah?"

"Not good."

"No?"

"I was just telling your dental hygienist that I hate the smell of dentist offices." Leah is immaculately dressed and groomed, the blue paper bib covering an ivory silk top that only accents her fit frame. Her dark blonde hair, carefully highlighted and blown out, frames a face that is smooth for her age. I know by her chart that she's early forties but she appears years younger. "The smell makes me sick," she adds.

I give her a quick, reassuring nod. "I hear that a lot." The smell doesn't bother me. It never has. Andrew never liked it, but for him, it was the smell of his childhood. He grew up visiting his dad at the office, working here in the summers.

"I've never understood my fear. It seems so irrational. It's not like I'm going to die here—" She breaks off, laughs nervously, her fingers twisting in her necklace. "Right?"

"Nope. No dying. No suffering. It's going to be okay." I roll closer to her side on my stool.

"That's what my husband says. He doesn't understand my fear. He doesn't know why I make such a big deal out of it. I tried to explain that it's the smell that makes me nervous. The moment I open the door to the office it hits me—and I want to run."

"But you're here."

"Only because my tooth hurts so much. The pain just keeps getting worse, and it's not going away anymore, not even with Advil."

"Which side?"

"Here." She touches her upper right jaw. "It aches all the time now."

"Let me take a look."

Her eyes meet mine, the hazel irises bright. She's terrified.

I touch her arm. "It's going to be all right."

"I don't know why I'm so scared."

"There is nothing to be afraid of. I'm not going to hurt you. I promise."

"But what if the tooth has to come out? What if I need a root canal—"

"Root canals get a bad rap. They don't usually hurt any more than when you have a filling replaced."

"I don't like those, either."

"The good news is that we can fix this. Whatever the issue, we'll get it sorted out, and you won't have to live with more pain. The worst pain is always before you come in." I hold her gaze, firm, confident. Dentistry isn't torture. We help people. We don't make it worse.

Fortunately, it doesn't look as if Leah needs a root canal yet. She's come in time. Natalie returns to assist with the procedure.

I'm just wrapping up with Leah when Helene from the front desk appears in the doorway, letting me know I have someone on the phone holding.

"Can you take a message?" I ask, checking my annoyance at the interruption. Leah is the last person I want to feel rushed.

Helene grimaces. "Apparently it's an emergency." She drops her voice. "Your dad."

He's all I have left. Mom's gone. Andrew's gone. He's it. I apologize and excuse myself, taking the call in the staff room. "Dad?"

"I'm fine," he answers brusquely, his voice unsteady with the Parkinson's quaver. "Took a little fall but nothing too serious."

"You wouldn't call if it weren't serious," I retort. My dad and I aren't very close. My mom and I were. My mom and I were thick as thieves. I got into dentistry to impress my dad. It didn't work.

"It's not serious," he repeats, even as I hear voices in the background. Two women talking. He's not alone. "Just a little fall, but they wanted me to let you know. A broken wrist and a couple scrapes, nothing much."

"Oh, Dad."

"It happens."

"I'll come up."

"No need—"

"I want to."

"There's nothing you can do."

"You're my dad."

"Doesn't make sense to lose work time."

"It doesn't make sense to lose you."

"I'll be here when you have vacation time—"

"I'd like to take that vacation time now."

He says nothing but the silence is tense. I hold my breath, battling my frustration, bottling the confusion. He doesn't want me. I don't understand it. It was easier when Mom was alive. She was our buffer. She made us a family. "You're important to me," I say quietly. "I want to come see you. I need to come see you. Please."

The silence stretches again.

"Fine," he says, exasperation in his voice.

I tell myself not to be hurt. There's no point in being sensitive. This is Dad. It's how he's always been. It's how he'll always be. "I'll fly up tonight, and if I take tomorrow off, that will give us a three-day weekend."

"Your front office will have to reschedule."

"It happens when there's an emergency."

"Alison, I don't want a fuss."

"That's good, Dad, because I don't fuss. That's not my style." My tone is brisk. I mastered professional crispness long before I graduated from dental school. It was the only way to survive life with my father. Now I'm grateful for the training. Grateful I'm not easily crushed.

He sighs. "No. It's not your style. I'll give you that."

High praise indeed. "I need to book a flight, Dad, and I'm not sure when I'll land, but I imagine it'll be late, so plan on seeing me tomorrow. If not for breakfast, then by lunch."

"Don't rush. Tomorrow morning is duplicate bridge."

"How will you hold the cards?"

"I'll manage."

I'm sure he will. Dad is remarkably resourceful. "Do I need to talk to a nurse? Is there someone with you waiting to speak to me?"

"No. I think I've handled it just fine."

"Then I'll see you tomorrow."

"You know where to find me."

I need a second to compose myself after the call. I use the time to make a list of all the things I need to do. Clear my schedule. Book a flight. Get a rental car or shuttle to the house. Maybe I should drive. Twelve hours driving. Too long. Book a flight. Get a car. Make sure I pack Dad's new shoes.

In the next exam room I see the mother in the corner first, and then the little boy in the exam chair, blue paper bib around his neck. His eyes are huge. His lower lip is trembling. He's afraid.

"I'm Dr. Alison McAdams," I say, introducing myself before washing my hands at the sink. "But most of my patients call me Dr. Ali."

The boy says nothing. The mother gives me a grim smile. Maybe she had to take time off work, or maybe she has children at home, or maybe she's not a fan of dentists.

I dry my hands on a paper towel and sit down on my stool and roll towards the child. "What's your name?" I ask.

He glances at his mom, brown eyes huge.

"Tell her," the mother says.

"Brett," he whispers.

"James," his mother adds. "That's our last name. We've been patients of Dr. Morris for years."

I register the mother's comment. That means she knows me. Or she knows about Andrew and me. Or just knows about Andrew.

"Brett James," I repeat, forcing myself to focus. He's little. Can't be much older than five. "That's a nice name. And how old are you?"

"Five."

"And that's a good age."

He just looks at me. I keep smiling at him even though I suddenly want to cry and I never cry at work. Never. Ever.

"So what are we doing today?" I ask, even though I already know. I glanced at the chart on the counter even as I was washing my hands.

"I have a cavity," Brett whispers.

"Well, I'll fix that up for you."

"Will it hurt?"

"No." I pat his arm. He's warm. His arm is small. I want to protect him. When you are a child you have no control. Everyone makes all the decisions for you. I can't imagine not having any control.

"Are you a kindergartener?" I ask.

He shakes his head.

"He's going to be," his mom answers from her chair in the corner. "In September. He's in pre-K now."

"You're going to love kindergarten," I say.

He shakes his head. "I have to wear a uniform. And a vest." His sadness has changed to despair. "I hate vests."

"Why do you have to wear vests?"

"Because it's a Catholic school," his mother says. "The children wear vests on Mass days."

Brett looks at her and then me. "I'd rather wear my Ninja Turtle shirt," he whispers.

"I would, too," I whisper back.

He smiles at me but there are tears in his eyes.

I smile back because if I don't smile, I'll start crying.

Brett leaves the office with thick cotton tucked between his cheek and gum and a shy smile for me.

He has beautiful eyes, golden brown with long black lashes.

Andrew had lovely lashes, too. So long they didn't look real. I used to touch them lightly, wonderingly. *What did you do to get eyelashes like these?*

And then suddenly I remember the note.

Learn to park.

Asshole.

And I want Andrew back. I want him to make fun of the note. And me. I want him to make things better. He knew how to make everything better . . .

Suddenly I can't be here, in this office, anymore. I can't handle the frigid temperature or the whir of the drill, or the sweet eugenol with its clove oil scent.

Even though I have yet another patient waiting for me, I walk down the hall, out the door into the warm Arizona sunshine, squeezing my hands into fists, digging my nails into the skin to keep from making a sound.

My heart is broken.

It will never be the same.

None of it will ever be the same again.

Dr. Andrew Morris finds me outside. Andrew, my Andrew, was named after his father. My Andrew is the third. His father, the founder of the dental practice, is the second. Andrew

Morris the first wasn't a dentist. I don't know what he did but he isn't spoken of in hushed, reverent tones. He isn't spoken of at all.

"Helene mentioned something about your father taking a spill," Dr. Morris says, hands buried in his white coat. Unlike the new generation of dentists that prefer suits and ties and collared shirts, Dr. Morris still wears a white buttoned coat over his shirt. He's old-school, and proud of it. "Is he okay?"

I nod once. "A fractured wrist. He says he's fine."

"Are you okay?"

I nod again, more slowly, but no, I'm not okay. I'm not sure what I am.

For a moment there is just silence. I want to go see my dad. Not Memorial Day weekend—two weeks from now—but now. I want to go *now*. Tonight. I need to. I need someone and something that is mine.

"I think I should go see him," I say quietly. "I would feel better if I could check on him personally."

Dr. Morris hesitates for just a moment and then nods. "That's probably a good idea. When would you go?"

"I'd like to go tonight—" I break off, take a quick deep breath. "I'll be back in the office Monday morning. It'll mean cancelling the rest of the week's appointments."

"I could probably take some of them."

"You don't mind?"

He shakes his head. "It's good that you're heading up to see your dad. But maybe you shouldn't rush back. Maybe you need more time up there. Maybe you need more time for you."

"I'll schedule some time this summer—"

"I don't know that you can wait."

I lift my head and look up into Dr. Morris' face. His expression is focused, his eyes sad. We are all still sad. I've secretly begun to think we, who loved Andrew, will never be happy again. His father, his mother, me . . . we're functioning, but not living, not the way one wants to live.

A lump fills my throat, making it ache as I swallow.

"Do you need a ride to the airport?" Dr. Morris asks, changing the subject.

I shake my head, even though I haven't actually thought that far. Can't seem to think clearly right now. There's so much white noise in my head. And this unbearable weight on my heart.

"What time is your flight?"

"I haven't booked it yet."

"I imagine then that you probably won't see your father until tomorrow."

"I'm hoping to join him for lunch."

"That'll be nice."

"Hope so."

"When was the last time you saw him?"

I have to think. Since I didn't make it Easter it was . . . it was . . . "Christmas."

It's been too long. I've not been an attentive daughter. I should have been up to see him several times since. But Napa isn't home, and his senior retirement home isn't where I want him to be. After mom died, I thought he'd want to come live with me, in Scottsdale. He didn't, choosing to move into the retirement home instead. It's not close or convenient for my work. I'd give up my practice here, but that would leave Dr. Morris alone.

I look up into Andrew Morris II's eyes and see things I don't want to see.

He misses Andrew terribly. Andrew was his son, his heir. The future. Not just in life, but the next generation to run the dental practice. From the time Andrew was a boy, he was going to be part of the Scottsdale practice. It was going to be Morris and Morris.

Instead it's Morris & Associates.

I'm the associate. Andrew's fiancée.

I'm able to book a flight out while still at the office, and once home, I quickly pack for two weeks. Dr. Morris is taking me off the books for the first half of June as well, but I can't imagine being gone that long. I'm not someone who likes to sit around. I prefer working. I need to be active.

Andrew used to say I loved nothing more than a long to-do list. I'd make a face at him, rolling my eyes. But he was right. I'm most comfortable being busy, making plans, having places to go, even if it's just to the grocery store. I have an ongoing list for that, too.

Add on.

Cross off.

Accomplished.

I'm all about the doing. And now Andrew is gone and I'm cracked. Broken. So broken I can't even make a single list.

Don't know what to do anymore.

Don't know where to go.

The shuttle picks me up on time but traffic is terrible on the way to Phoenix International Airport. I'm panicking that we're not going to get to the airport before they start boarding. It shouldn't be this long of a drive. I close my eyes, stressed. Eyes closed, I focus on just breathing.

Inhale to a count of ten. Exhale to a count of ten. Inhale . . .

As I breathe my thoughts drift to Dad. I have his shoes in my suitcase. I hope he'll like them. I hope I got the right size. I'm pretty confident he's a size eleven. Or a ten and a half. Maybe he's a ten and a half, and in that case the elevens would be too big, particularly with his balance issues.

In the past I could have texted my mom and she'd text me back right away, giving me his size. She was good about getting back to me right away. Always. Mom was a former teacher turned principal. She died five months after Andrew. Had an aneurysm in August. It happened in her sleep. So glad she didn't suffer. But nobody saw that one coming, either.

To lose both Mom and Andrew in less than six months . . . Still trying to wrap my head around life. How it happens. How it ends.

I don't even feel as if I'm grieving. I'm not sure what grieving is supposed to feel like. I've no one to talk to about this. Certainly can't discuss it with Dad and I don't have friends who have lost anyone other than a grandparent yet, and now I've lost my fiancé and my mom in short order.

Maybe the fact that I am just here, present, but not able to feel a damn thing is grief.

If that's the case, I'm good with it. I don't want to feel more pain. And being numb has actually allowed me to be a very good dentist.

God knows patients are nervous enough coming in as it is. They don't need me weeping as I drill and fill their teeth.

The airport is cordoned off when I arrive. The shuttle can't even get close to the terminal entrance. I pay and grab my bags and join the crowd outside. Police empty the terminal and everyone mills about the parking area while a bomb squad goes through an abandoned backpack found inside.

A businessman next to me said all flights will be delayed hours, if they even go out tonight. No flight has been allowed to land for the past hour.

I take this in without comment, watching the swarming police and SWAT team, but not seeing the SWAT team. Rather I see Andrew. I'm back there on that last day.

I'd gone to the store to get ice cream.

That's where I was when he did it.

The police, his parents, his sisters, his friends, they all wanted to know what had happened that week, that day, in the hours leading up to Andrew's death.

Everyone had the same question—had there been a fight? Were you two quarreling?

No.

And then immediately the other questions: *Was he unhappy? Had he expressed concerns about the wedding? Were there money problems?*

No, no, and there is always debt and bills after college and dental school, and we had just bought our first home so things were really tight, but not the kind of tight finances that make one want to die, the kind of tight that means one must work, and save, and plan.

For the record, Andrew and I never fought. You had to know Andrew to understand. He wasn't argumentative. There wasn't a mean or petty bone in his body. He was kind and thoughtful. Sweet. *Funny.*

He'd be goofy just to make me laugh.

He loved to make me laugh. I loved it when he did.

We were good together. We fit. His mom used to say we were two halves of a whole, and I agreed.

So why would the love of my life take his own life?

And just weeks before our wedding?

I don't know.

I've spent the past year analyzing the last year we had. I've pulled the months apart, examined each week, each day, and I'm still no closer to an answer. What went wrong? And when did it go wrong? And why did I—of all people—not know?

I would have done anything for him. I would have been there—Hell. I *was* there.

We lived together. We worked together. We drove to work together. We trained together. Worked out together. We were together pretty much twenty-four seven.

And it wasn't enough. I wasn't enough . . . not to keep him here, anchored to earth, to life.

He would have rather died than be with me.

A muffled boom comes from across the street.

The bomb squad has blown up the backpack. False alarm. There was nothing inside.

People around me cheer.

I've been told it's wrong—selfish, narcissistic—to make Andrew's death about me, but what else could I do? I was his partner, his lover, his best friend. I was going to be his wife and the mother of his children. If he was so unhappy, why couldn't he tell me? Why wouldn't he?

Why couldn't he give me a chance to help him? I would have.

Now all I'm left with is that last day.

It had been a perfect day.

We'd just recently moved into our new house. We'd gone for a long run that morning, waking early to beat the desert heat. It was a good run, seven miles, which was a lot for me, but nothing for Andrew, since he was already running marathons. I'd agreed to run my first marathon after our honeymoon so we'd been training together, getting me used to the distance.

After running we worked on the house, and then walked to Fashion Square where we ate a late lunch—or early dinner, depending on how you'd call it—at the Yardhouse, our favorite place since we both loved the ahi dishes. Then we walked home, holding hands, talking about the wedding and the future and a couple hours later, I had a craving for ice cream, and I ran to the store.

So why did he do it?

Why, when it had been a good day? Why make me be the one to discover him in the entry, hanging from our new reproduction Spanish Colonial Revival chandelier, to match our authentic Spanish Colonial Revival dream home?

Why take one of the best days of my life and make it the worst day?

Love is supposed to be patient and kind.

It's not.

TWO

The flight to Oakland ends up being delayed nearly three hours, but it looks like we're still going to be able to get out tonight.

I'm sitting by the gate flipping through one of the professional journals I never have time to read when Dad calls. He's heard about the bomb scare through CNN and he's phoning me to see if I've been blown up. Those are, mind you, his exact words. As a little girl I was baffled by my dad's dry humor. I've finally come to understand it.

"No, Dad, I'm fine. A lone backpack was blown to bits, but everything else is intact."

"That's it?" He sounds disappointed.

"That's it. Well, and my flight's delayed a couple hours, but all the excitement is over and I'll still be there in the morning."

"Maybe this is a sign that you're not supposed to come."

"Maybe you need to just embrace my visit."

"I just think it's a mistake for you to take time off work because *I* made a mistake and tripped over my own big feet."

"Me not coming up would be the mistake. And humor me, Dad. This way I can pretend I'm a dutiful daughter."

"So this is really about you."

I answer as sweetly as I can. "Did you ever doubt it?"

He barks a laugh. "Now you sound like your mom."

I smile, pleased. He doesn't laugh often. "She was the one who taught me to kill 'em with kindness."

"As long as you don't kill them in your chair."

"That would be bad," I agree.

"So what time do you land in Oakland tonight?"

"Around eleven."

"Need a ride from the airport?"

"You offering to get me?" I retort, knowing he's given up driving.

"I could probably do all right."

"And whose car would you steal?"

"Mom's car is still at the house. Haven't sold it yet."

"What are you hanging on to it for?"

"It's a nice new Audi. Why sell it?"

"Because you don't need it and it's just going to go down in value the longer you hang on to it."

"So why don't you take it?"

"I have a car."

"An old one. Your mom's car is less than two years old—"

"I can't . . . drive her car . . ." My voice fades away. I'm suddenly tired. I don't have words to explain. Dad wasn't supposed to be in the senior home yet. Not for a couple more years. Mom wasn't supposed to be gone. She was the young one. "I mean, I will, once I'm there. I've got a shuttle reserved to get to the house. Is the key still under the flower pot on the porch?"

"Yes. And you remember the code for the alarm?"

"My birth date backwards."

"That's it. There won't be any food in the house but all the utilities are still on, and things should be clean. I'm paying for a housekeeper each month, so it better be clean."

"I'll let you know."

"So I'll see you at lunch."

"Yes." I hesitate, wanting to say more, but not knowing what to say. There is so much pressure in my chest. It's heavy and immense. The weight makes it hard to breathe. "I've missed you."

Silence stretches. I don't think he's going to say anything. And then he surprises me. "It'll be good to see you," he says gruffly.

A lump fills my throat. "It's going to be a treat."

"Be safe."

We say good-bye, and I hang up feeling better.

And worse.

Because I don't remember what safe feels like anymore.

The woman seated next to me on the plane has two very large carry-on bags that are bursting at the seams. She struggles to make both fit—one above us and one beneath the seat in front of her. I pretend not to notice as she repeatedly shoves her platform sandal into the top and side of the carry-on at her feet to make it fit beneath the seat. It takes quite a few kicks and jabs before it's under.

"There," she says, exhaling and sitting back.

She looks to be about my age. She has dark curly hair, brown eyes, and tons of freckles. She also has very straight white teeth. I always notice teeth.

For the first hour of the flight we don't speak, but then during the beverage service somehow the handoff of the plastic cup between flight attendant and the woman to my right doesn't go well, and the diet Sprite spills on me. The flight attendant hands over napkins and pours another drink while my seatmate apologizes profusely and dabs at my tray and leg. I tell her I'm fine, but she keeps dabbing and apologizing and in the end, we start talking, sharing about where we are each going and why.

Her name is Diana and she's a florist, heading back to Napa after a weekend home in Phoenix to see her mom for a belated Mother's Day visit. "I couldn't make it for Mother's Day," she says. "Way too much work. I'd been warned that it's one of the busiest weekends of the year but wasn't prepared."

It turns out she's still in her first year owning her own business, taking over the small florist shop in downtown Napa last fall. She does everything, but specializes in weddings and special events.

"How did you decide to become a florist?" I ask. "Did you study it in school?"

"Nope. I always thought I was going to go into medicine and then during college decided dentistry would be a good fit. I'd even taken the DAT and had applied to dental schools—got into two, too—but at the last moment, I couldn't do it. I was sick of school and couldn't imagine being stuck inside all day."

I drain my water and look at her. "I'm a dentist."

"Do you like it?"

I nod. "I think I'm good at it."

"That's so cool. Where did you go to dental school?"

"University of Washington."

Her eyes light. "I went there as an undergrad. Go Huskies!"

"What did you study?"

"Psych." She laughs. "And boy it comes in handy when working with brides, moms, and wedding planners. People really do go crazy when it comes to planning a wedding." She glances at my left hand, checking for rings. "Are you married?"

I stopped wearing Andrew's ring on the one year anniversary of his death. Every now and then I put it on, but it doesn't feel right anymore. "No. You?"

"Men are too much work." Her eyes crinkle as she smiles. "But I could change my mind if I met the right one."

We end up talking the rest of the flight to Oakland, and as the plane touches down and taxis to the gate, Diana struggles to get her bag out from beneath the seat and then riffles through it for her wallet. She hands me her card just as we reach the gate. Diana Martin. *A Napa Bouquet*.

"Wait," she says, taking it back and scribbling her cell number across the top. "That way you can call me direct."

I pocket her card and give Diana mine. She studies my name and the address of Dr. Morris' office. "That's a nice area. Is it a new practice?"

"No. It's been around for about thirty years."

"That's awesome. Good for you."

We gather our things as the seat belt light goes off. Everyone bolts to their feet but there is nowhere to go yet. We stand in the aisle making small talk after Diana frees her second bag from the overhead.

"So how long will you be up in Napa?" she asks.

"A couple of weeks," I answer.

"Well, if you get bored or want to head out one night, give me a shout. My shop's in downtown Napa. I'd be happy to meet up for a drink or dinner."

"Sounds good."

Thirty minutes later I've got my bags. I'm the only one tonight in the back of the big passenger van. The driver is quiet, and I check my phone for messages—there are none. My life for the last year has been work and work. It'll be good to use these next few weeks in Napa to relax and rest and figure out how to be a little more social again.

I did enjoy talking to Diana on the plane. Chatting with her made the flight pass quickly, and I liked her. She was fun. Effervescent. I'd forgotten what positive girl energy feels like.

Need more of that. Didn't really have that in dental school, either. There was so much pressure. That first year, especially . . .

But I don't want to think about dental school. Don't want to think about Dr. Morris. Don't want to think about anything at all.

Staring out the van window, I gaze up into the sky. The young moon is three quarters full. Waxing gibbous.

I only know this because Andrew loved the moon. He loved the stars and the night sky and owned a telescope from an early age. In the desert you can see the stars better than you can in a city. The sky is bigger, and the stars are brighter. Andrew loved the sky. He, my independent Aquarius, wanted to make the world a better place. He was full of ideas and change. He had such a good heart, and even better intentions.

I don't understand how he could just go . . . just . . . *leave.*

I don't—

I rub my eyes with my fist. Can't do this now. Not sure I should do this anytime. Can't keep going to these places in my head and heart. But I don't know where to go if I don't go there. Don't want to lose him. Don't want to forget him. So afraid that if I let go too much he'll disappear completely.

And yet he was too good to be forgotten.

Too kind to become nothing.

There must be another way to love. To remember love.

I'm in the hills of Sonoma County now, hills rolling, rising, moonlight whispering to me in slivers and sighs.

I know why Mom and Dad wanted to retire here. It's beautiful. But it's too quiet for me tonight. I need a city. I need urgency and energy.

Or at the very least, I need something to do.

• • •

E ven though no one lives in the 1910 farmhouse on Poppy Lane, the house isn't dark when the shuttle pulls up.

It's almost one thirty but the front porch light is on and two more glow inside, soft yellow lining the edges of the living room curtains. The lights are on timers and every week the housekeeper, who sweeps the front porch and collects the free local community newspaper that lands in the driveway Wednesday afternoons, adjusts the timer so that different lamps turn on and off.

I pay the driver and shoulder my bags and head for the house. It takes me a moment to locate the key and get the alarm off, and then I enter the house, say good night to the moon, and Andrew. I like to think of him happy, there in the sky and stars, and once inside the house I say hello to my mom. I wait to feel her presence but she's not here. This house never had time to truly become her home, and my footsteps echo on the hardwood floors, the interior hollow and empty.

I walk around, turning on and off lights, chasing away the shadows that linger in a house devoid of people. I take in the furniture that is still new and unlived in, furniture bought for the home that was supposed to be a dream house and never came to anything. I open the refrigerator. It's cold and empty, save for an open box of baking soda on the top shelf.

Dad should sell the house. And Mom's car. He should move down to Scottsdale with me and we should become a family again.

I pass through the house a second time, now turning out lights, ending in the master bedroom with the new king bed and new big highboy dresser. The old set with the full bed had been demoted to the guest room, but when Mom died and Dad went to Napa Estates, he took the old master bedroom set with him. It was familiar and he said it felt like Mom.

Mom died so suddenly there were no good-byes.

And Andrew . . . he did say good-bye. He'd kissed me, so very sweetly, before I drove off to get the ice cream.

Damn him.

He didn't even give me a chance to fight for him.

I had no idea that such a kind man could be so cruel.

Sunlight pours through the windows waking me. I hadn't drawn the curtains last night, and I open my eyes, bemused. Everything is foreign. The windows, the light, the pale grass green walls.

And then I remember.

Mom and Dad's.

Well, Dad's.

I've only just woken up but I suddenly want to cry. I want Mom.

And then I can't do it, can't bear being sad, thinking thoughts like this. I'm almost thirty. It has to change.

I toss back the Pottery Barn duvet cover with its green-and-white botanical fern print fabric. There are matching towels in the master bath. Dad didn't take any of them to his new apartment at Napa Estates. He took the old sheets and towels, the ones that he'd shared all those years with Mom. Dad might keep me at arm's length but I've never doubted his loyalty to Mom.

I shower and search the kitchen for coffee. There is none. There is no food in the house at all. Even the Tupperware containers of flour and sugar and salt are gone. The house is ready to be sold. I have no idea why Dad is hanging on to it.

I haven't been to Napa Estates Senior Living since December when I flew up to spend the holidays with Dad. Last December I'd made all these plans for us and our first Christmas without Mom. I'd imagined that Dad would come "home" to the house on Poppy

Lane, and we'd have a small, intimate Christmas, the two of us. I'd gone and done a big shop and had even purchased a small tree and decorated it. But when I went to the retirement home I was dismayed by his reaction.

He wasn't in college and had no desire to go anywhere for "the holidays." I was welcome to join him for meals and activities at Napa Estates, but there wasn't going to be this cozy family Christmas. He had no desire for a family Christmas. Not without Mom.

I cried in secret. I was hurt. And confused.

Dad wasn't the only one who'd lost Mom. I'd lost her, too. And Andrew. I'd lost two people and now it seemed as if I'd lost Dad as well. He didn't feel any need to be a family with me. He didn't want or need the traditions. He didn't want or need the past. I didn't like his idea of the future . . . not for us.

I still don't.

As I park at Napa Estates today, it reminds me all over again of a sprawling, swanky country club in the South. The green lawn flanking the columned main "house" is so perfect I'm tempted to see if it's real. The building's glossy white paint and pale cedar shingles contrast nicely with the sparkling large multi-paned windows that show the elegant, gleaming lobby, with its high ceiling and pale, low-pile carpet—suitable for both wheelchairs and walkers.

Mom and Dad had looked at a lot of retirement homes in Sonoma County before choosing Napa Estates as their future home. They liked that the facility had a couple tennis courts and a large swimming pool even though they never played tennis and rarely swam. It was the idea of having the facilities there, just as they liked Napa Estates' dining room, large gym, library, and movie theater, plus the monthly meetings for Bridge Club and Book Club and Wine Club.

Napa Estates wasn't just a "place" for seniors, but a community. Their brochure boasts that they create a "microcosm of society that brings successful, mature adults together, recognizing their strengths and gifts." I think the language of the brochure is a little overwritten but back in December I was impressed with how the retirement home has been designed to cater to all stages of senior living—independent living, assisted living, and memory care—with its focus on healthy living. I admire their goal to keep seniors fit, active, and independent for as long as possible. Of course there's a financial impetus—healthy seniors' expenses are less than those of seniors with chronic conditions—but there's also the quality of life issue. Healthy seniors are happier.

Dad is in the independent wing, with a one-bedroom apartment. He has several friends who have two-bedroom apartments so that guests can stay over. Dad didn't want that. Said he had no one he'd want to stay. I refused to have hurt feelings. Because I'm not sure *I'd* want to stay over. Dad is fine in three- or four-hour increments, but beyond that, he gets short and sharp. I love him, but don't enjoy his company when he gets snappy.

Fortunately, despite Parkinson's, Dad has been able to stay in the independent living wing, but now that he's had a fall and needs more help, I'm wondering when the staff will want him to move. Where he is now he gets to live with his own furniture, but apparently that changes in assisted living. I don't know the specifics. I only know that this morning, in an empty turn-of-the-century farmhouse, I became determined to convince my father that he should move to Arizona to be with me.

It takes me ten minutes to find Dad after arriving at Napa Estates. It's a big place and he's not in his apartment, or the Game Room, or the restaurant. I eventually track him down in the Reading Room where he's not reading but playing bridge with another gentleman and two ladies. Dad is resting his hand of cards on his splint, using a Scrabble tile holder to keep the cards from sliding down, and drawing and discarding cards with his good hand.

I knew he'd figure out how to play one-handed. He's always enjoyed bridge, but he's become very serious and competitive since arriving here, playing two to three days a week now.

In between deals he introduces me to Edie Stephens, his partner; they are playing against Bob and Rose Dearborn, a married couple.

I've barely been introduced before Edie raps the cards against the table. She's not happy with the interruption. The game isn't over.

Everyone quickly quiets and focuses on the game as Bob deals the next hand.

I don't remember any of these people from Christmas, although Edie looks familiar. Or maybe it's just because she's very old and has that dour look of older women in early photography. Unsmiling, pursed lips, flat stare.

She glances up from her cards, and her gaze meets mine. Her eyes narrow ever so slightly and her expression makes me feel as if I haven't quite measured up somehow. I smile at her. She doesn't smile back. And perhaps it's impudent, but I just keep smiling. There's no reason for her to be so unfriendly. It's my father after all, and I've just dropped everything to rush up here and be with him.

But she's already dismissed me and is focused on her cards.

I get a chair and pull it towards the table, sitting just behind Dad so I can see his cards and follow the game.

Edie shoots me another sharp look as I settle into my seat, her eyes bright blue against her pale, thin skin. Her wispy white hair is twisted back in a severe knot. She must be in her late eighties, but as I soon discover, she plays a mean game of bridge, making calls coolly, crisply, not a hint of a quaver in her voice.

I started to learn bridge years ago when Andrew and I were in dental school so we could play with my parents, giving us a pleasant way to spend time together, but Andrew didn't enjoy the game—it's not a game you learn overnight if you want to play well—so we stopped our lessons. But I'd grown up listening to my parents play on weekends with their friends—card tables up in the living room, the clink of ice in cocktail glasses, and the murmur of voices as they made their bids. And even though I don't know how to really play myself, just sitting in one of the club chairs behind Dad, flipping through a magazine, I am lulled by the sound and rhythm of the game. The dealer, the opener, the responder . . .

My mother always laughed when she was the dummy.

I loved her for that. I loved that she was so warm and easy. She had an ego, but it was about education and excellence and schools. Never herself.

Now Dad, partnered by the formidable Edie, is the dummy, but he doesn't seem to mind. As the game progresses it's obvious he's fond of Edie, almost deferential. But then, he does like winning, and they are winning now. From the quiet, sporadic banter around the table, to the winning of tricks, it's clear Dad and Edie are the team to beat.

Thirty minutes later the game finally ends, and Dad rises carefully, using a cane to assist him to his feet. Bob offered an arm but Dad wouldn't accept the help.

Now Dad leads the way to lunch, walking slightly ahead of me, working the cane as if an aggressive sea captain on the deck of his ship.

He's thinner than when I last saw him, noticeably thinner, but his mood is ebullient after the win. His voice isn't steady but it's impossible to miss his confidence. "Bob and Rose arrived in March and everybody started saying they were the best bridge players at the Estates. But that was before Edie and I started playing together on Tuesdays and Thursdays."

"That makes you happy."

"It's fun to win."

"She seems a little bossy."

"She's almost ninety-five. She's entitled to have a few opinions." He glances at me over his shoulder. "You don't like her."

It's a statement, not a question. I shrug. "I don't know her. But she's not exactly warm and friendly. Whenever she looked at me she seemed to be giving me the evil eye."

"Oh, she was. She doesn't tolerate stuff and nonsense—"

"I'm not stuff and nonsense."

"But you were interrupting our game."

"You told me to meet you for lunch. I was here at noon. That's lunchtime."

"She's very smart, Edie. She was raised overseas, speaks a half-dozen languages, and could have worked for the State Department but chose to become a teacher instead. I enjoy her company a great deal. There aren't a lot of women here like her. She reminds me of my aunt Mary. Mary was brilliant. She wanted to be a doctor but her father, my grandfather, wouldn't hear of it."

We'd reached the large dining room just off the entrance atrium. The dining room's longest wall was lined with tall French doors overlooking Napa's rolling hills covered in trellised grapes. It's a picturesque view and the May sunlight spills into the room, streaking the hardwood floor and dappling the place settings.

The lunch hostess takes us to a table for two near the French doors. Dad is still leaning on his cane, but taking smaller steps to match his small talk with the hostess as she leads us to our table. I think the hostess isn't there to seat us as much as to make sure Dad and the other seniors don't topple over.

I'd been worried that Dad and I would have nothing to talk about but he's cheerful as we study the menu, recommending the taco salad which comes in a big tortilla shell, shaped like a bowl. I consider his recommendations but end up ordering the Chinese chicken salad.

We have ice tea with our salads and I have to pretend it's not difficult to watch Dad struggle with his meal, hand shaking, as it takes him two, three attempts to get lettuce and ground beef onto his fork. He shouldn't have ordered something with ground beef. It doesn't clump. The salad and cheese and beef fall off the tines before they reach his mouth.

"Need help?" I ask.

"Nope."

Why did I know he'd say that? But his good mood wanes as he battles to get his lunch onto his fork and up to his mouth.

I feel a pang.

I haven't seen him enough. Haven't talked to him enough. The phone call every couple of weeks (is it even that often?) isn't enough. I know it's not enough. And more confusing is that I don't know this Dad, not without Mom. Dad's quiet. Never has been much of a talker. And now without Mom, we struggle to communicate.

"You look nice," I tell him, trying to fill the silence.

He's wearing a plaid shirt, blue and burgundy, and his thinning hair is combed neatly, the medium brown fading to gray, but I could see his scalp if I stood above him. I don't want to see it. It makes my heart hurt. I wish Mom were here to take care of him. I'm not going to be able to give him the love he needs. I'm not able to do much other than make small talk and maybe play some cards and kill some time before I head back home. Unless he comes to live with me. And then I could be there every day. I could make dinner for us and plan outings . . . movies or a visit to a play or museum.

Not that he ever wanted to do any of those things.

What would he do in Arizona, living with me?

The thought is uncomfortable and I push it away.

"I should have ordered soup," he says a few minutes later, dropping his fork and irritably tossing his napkin onto his plate. "Or pudding. Pudding would have at least stuck to the spoon."

• • •

Dad seems tired by the end of lunch and we head to his "apartment" with its miniature living room, where we settle onto the small couch and Dad turns on the TV. For the next couple of hours we stare at the small flat-screen TV, watching a program neither of us cares about, letting the commercials and show fill the silence and provide entertainment.

I see Dad wince a couple times as he shifts position. "Are you hurting?"

"I'm fine."

I lean forward, concerned, but can tell from his expression that he doesn't want to be babied. Dad served in Korea before finishing school to become a veterinarian. I know he saw combat but he's never talked about it. And I actually have no idea of what he did in Korea. Or what he was.

We watch the next show and when that ends I look at him. "Do you like it here, Dad?" I'm desperate to find something we can talk about, something to bridge this distance between us.

"If I didn't want to be here, I wouldn't be here."

Good enough. "You don't miss the house?"

"I don't want to be there without your mom. And I can't be there without her. I need assistance, and so here you go."

I hesitate, choosing my words carefully. "You wouldn't want to come live with me?"

"We talked about this already."

"At Christmas, but it's been a while and I thought maybe we should revisit the discussion."

"No."

"Don't you want to be near me?"

"I'm a native Californian. I lived in Washington for a number of years, raised you there, but it was my dream—and your mom's—to return to California one day. I have no desire to live in the desert."

"But you'd be able to be near me."

He shoots me an odd glance. Hard to decipher his expression. "You could always move here. Be a dentist here."

I picture Dr. Morris and his sad eyes and his plans for Andrew. All those hopes and dreams.

I take a deep breath, dangerously close to tears. "I don't know that I can leave Dr. Morris yet. I don't know that he could continue his practice. Knowing him, he'd retire and sell the practice."

"Maybe that would be the best thing for him."

I frown. "Why? He loves his practice, loves his work."

"Maybe he puts too much emphasis on his practice."

Dad is very black and white. He doesn't do ambiguous, but he's being plenty ambiguous now. "What does that mean?"

"Everyone always talks about what Dr. Morris wants, and what's best for him. But what about you? And what about Andrew? Was working in Scottsdale for his dad the best thing for him? I don't think so."

I suddenly can't remain seated and jump up to cross the room to the sliding glass door. I look out the door onto a courtyard with a fountain surrounded by white roses, lavender, and neat green boxwood. It could be the courtyard of a hotel. Pretty and manicured but also very empty.

"Does anyone ever go out there?" I ask, noting the stone benches that look terribly uncomfortable.

"No. But it's a nice view."

"Mmm." I stand there another moment but I'm not looking at the roses. I'm thinking about what Dad said regarding Dr. Morris. "I like Dr. Morris. I love him. He's like my other dad." I turn to face my father. "And he's a good dentist. A really good dentist."

"Not saying he isn't. And I think you were cut out to be a dentist. I don't know that your Andrew was."

My Andrew.

The heaviness in my chest is back. It's a weight that never completely lifts, but sometimes bears down, relentless. Crushing. It feels crushing now.

And beneath the grief is anger. Terrible, terrible anger.

I keep my back to my dad so he can't see how much his words hurt, and infuriate, me.

My Andrew was laughter and light and he made the world a beautiful place. A better place. What was he thinking leaving me here without him? What was he thinking taking the easy way out?

It's hard to love.

It's hard to live.

It's hard to keep one's courage and optimism . . . to keep believing when life slams into you, wave after wave of pain and disappointment. I know. I've been underwater for months here, and yet I just keep swimming and swimming even though my eyes and throat and nose burn with salt and the sharp tang of love lost. Love gone.

But how to stop swimming? How to give up?

There's no part in me willing to accept defeat. Silence.

What kind of message would that be? What kind of woman would I be to quit now just because it's hard?

Of course it's hard! It's life. It's not a carnival ride. It's not something one signs up for. It's something you're thrust into.

"He was a nice young man," my dad says from behind me. "I liked him."

I press my lips together and squeeze my eyes tight, holding all my emotions in. Dad means well. He's trying to comfort me. He's trying . . .

And yet it suddenly enrages me that he's waited all these years to reach out to me. That all these months when I'm down in Scottsdale trying to carry on that he doesn't feel any need to connect with me, or comfort me. He's just assumed that I'm fine. He's assumed I'll manage.

And yes, I'm managing. But my God it hurts.

And I'm lonely. And scared.

Scared that I'll always feel this way. Numb. Dead.

Angry.

I dig deep, bearing down on the anger, pressing it down, burying it where it can't hurt me. Or Dad. I don't want to be rude to Dad but I'm so confused. He's spent his whole life immersed in his work and his thoughts and interests. He had thirty years to learn to love me and he never bothered to do it very well.

He could take care of all those animals but he couldn't take care of me.

He couldn't find time to spend with *me*.

But no sooner do I feel the anger, than I'm consumed by guilt.

I shouldn't need more than I do. I shouldn't need anything more than what I've got. I shouldn't expect anything at all. I wasn't raised with expectations. Neither my mother nor my father taught me that I was entitled to anything; every opportunity was to be seized, every advantage taken. And I have worked hard. Very, very hard.

"You're angry," Dad says now, breaking the silence that has stretched far too long.

I shrug and glance at him. His narrow face is weathered and deeply lined. He's not a young man. I don't know how resilient he really is. He says one thing but I can no longer trust that his words reflect reality. It would be easy to remain angry, but it's not me. It never has been. I prefer moving forward. Not much of a fan of treading water or remaining in place.

"What was Mom's secret for dealing with you?" I ask huskily, managing a faint wry smile.

"She liked me. And she knew my limitations."

"I like you, and I've a good idea about your limitations. You enjoy your routine, you have no patience for idiots, and you don't like small talk or cocktail party chatter."

"I'm short on patience and have a quick temper."

"Except when it comes to animals."

He lifted a trembling hand. "They don't talk."

"And they can't help themselves when hurt or injured."

His head, with its steely strands of gray, nods. "Your mother never minded that I preferred animals to people."

Clearly I'm nothing like my mother, because I do.

Leaving the retirement home, I go grocery shopping before driving back to the house on Poppy Lane.

The cream-colored house looks lavender and yellow in the twilight. Once upon a time the picket fence was bordered by cheerful perennials. The flowers are gone, replaced by some shrubby-looking hedge. I wonder who replaced the flowers. Probably the same gardener that mows twice a month.

There's a big oak tree in the backyard and it's home to a variety of birds. In the morning you hear the jays and mockingbirds. Now crows caw. I pause with the bags of groceries to watch a large black bird swoop from the gnarled tree limbs to a power line, joining the lineup. They screech a welcoming. Or perhaps a warning. The newcomer flaps his wings. He doesn't care.

As I juggle the bags and unlock the front door I glance back at the car. The car and street are bathed in gold. The temperature is still warm. You can smell summer coming.

From the time I was a teenager, my parents talked about their retirement plans. They wanted to return to California, where both had been raised. They wanted a small town. They wanted charm.

They wanted good weather. They discussed small beach towns like San Luis Obispo and Santa Maria, just north of Santa Barbara. They talked about going to the wine country: Sonoma . . . Calistoga . . . Napa. If they'd had a couple drinks, they'd dream bigger—maybe they could have both. Maybe they could split their time between the two: a small house on the coast and a place in the wine country, too.

It was the dream, the thing that kept them working and saving and looking forward. They'd raised me—their only child—in Tacoma, Washington. Dad had his own practice and Mom worked her way from being a teacher to a vice principal, and then a principal, bouncing around the Tacoma Unified School District, taking promotions and advancements when they came.

They both worked hard so they could be secure in their retirement.

They worked hard so they could be free.

Dad was the bigger earner. A good vet, and affordable, he had built a very loyal customer base, and even though he was ten years older than mom, he'd intended to work until she retired and then they'd pool their resources and move.

But Dad's health changed. He developed tremors, couldn't operate, nor did he trust himself during exams. He ended up selling his practice to a young veterinarian who'd been working with him for the past couple of years. The young vet was enthused. Dad suddenly found himself with far too much time on his hands.

It was this house on Poppy Lane that ultimately sold my parents on Napa.

They came to Napa for this house. They loved its history. They loved that it sat on a full acre, with most of the space stretching luxuriously in the back, the yard not filled with a pool but a small fruit orchard and a generous vegetable garden.

They loved the hundred-year-old house and Mom wanted the garden.

I was happy for them. I knew it was their dream, their house. It wasn't mine. It wasn't ever meant to be mine. I was already dating Andrew, and in my second year of dental school. I'd already hitched my star to Andrew's. Wherever he wanted to go, I'd follow, and I knew he planned on returning to Scottsdale after graduation to join his father's dental practice. He was clear about that. He wanted to work with his dad. He wanted to be like his dad . . . a good dentist, and a great father.

I was on board.

My future was his family, people who had a little more energy, activity, and opportunity than I'd been raised with. My mom and dad were homebodies. Dr. and Mrs. Morris were active on the Scottsdale social scene; their large home host to numerous parties and high-profile events. It seemed like the ideal life to me. Dry desert winters and blistering summers where you worked in an adobe-tiled building and then cooled off after work and on weekends in your backyard swimming pool.

I didn't need more. Didn't want more. Work, home, family, that was enough for me. I am apparently too easily entertained and I've always found something to engage my mind . . . something to focus on.

School, studies, exams, career. Whatever I do, I do well and there is satisfaction in excellence. Success. I naturally assumed I'd be a good wife, a devoted mother. I didn't see problems with the plan.

The plan.

The plan is gone.

I wake up in the middle of the night in a cold sweat and stare at nothing, heart pounding, skin clammy.

What is the plan now?

What do I do now?

I don't know.

It's been over a year since Andrew died and I still don't know. Will I ever know again?

It takes me forever to fall back asleep and I sleep heavily, waking to sunlight and the twittering of birds in the oak tree not far from the master bedroom.

I don't get up right away. Everything is heavy inside me. Wet cement. A future I can't see—

Not true. I can see it. Work, work, work. Possibly being promoted to Dr. Morris' partner. Morris & McAdams Dentistry.

But suddenly I'm resistant. Suddenly the idea of sitting so still, mask firmly in place, staring down into open mouths for the rest of my life horrifies me.

Is this what Andrew had thought?

That he'd rather die than sit on that stool and gaze down into open mouths day after day after day?

Dentistry is a science, and an art. It's about perfection. In dentistry, the work is exact. There is no room for error. The quest is for perfect, and perfection is how one is judged in dental school, and the standard continues into one's practice.

I don't even mind the intense focus. At least, I used to like the focus. Now I can't focus on any one thing. I don't know that I can focus on anything. The future is as impossible as the past. It's beyond my control.

I don't know what I want.

I don't know where to go.

Something has to give.

I just don't want it to be me.

THREE

I reluctantly park at Napa Estates, and even more reluctantly walk to the entrance, feeling like a horrible human being for dreading spending the day there.

I don't want to spend the day here today.

I want Dad, not the retirement home. It's depressing being surrounded by so much old age and decay. Not that Napa Estates smells like decay, but you see it in the older seniors' faces and bodies, the ones whose bodies have shrunk, the frail seniors who are in danger of disappearing.

Dad's waiting for me in the main hall. He's sitting in a winged arm chair, holding court with a half-dozen men and a lone woman.

I watch him for a moment, astounded. Dad, the introvert, suddenly seems to be an extrovert. I know he'd told me yesterday that he takes all of his meals in the dining room with everyone else, but it's jarring seeing him surrounded by people. Dad and Mom weren't social. Dad and Mom pretty much just stuck together.

I greet Dad and he introduces me to his circle—Harold Zuss and Bill Malone. Walter Jordan and Graham Durkee. There's a

Floyd and maybe a George, and the woman, LuAnne somebody.
I thought I was doing all right with the names in the beginning
but by the end, I know I won't keep them straight.

Then as Dad gets to his feet, he invites everyone to join us for
lunch.

I blink, shocked.

He's not the dad I know, which makes me wonder if I ever knew
him. Was Mom perhaps the introvert? Would Dad have enjoyed
more social activities when they were married?

I walk next to him into the dining room. It's open seating. He
chooses a round table set for ten and as we take our seats he leans
towards me and says under his breath, "A couple of the guys are
having a hard time. This is good for them. They need to belong."

I nod and sit, thinking, since I obviously don't know him,
perhaps it's time I did.

I return for dinner and "game night." Apparently we're playing
bingo later. Dinner is another group date. Harold and Walter
join us. So does George. But Graham is having a real "dinner date"
with Eleanor Babcock, and Bill Malone was rushed to the hospital
earlier in the day. He had a heart attack and is in ICU now. The
men are subdued. We have quite a few seats empty but then others
slowly fill in, always asking, *Can I join you? Is this seat free?*

The meal is relatively quiet. Everyone has Bill on their mind.
They're worried about him, but there is nothing they can do.

"It's where we are," Walter says gruffly. "This is what happens."

The others nod, solemn, resigned.

This is what happens when you age, I think. You accept your
mortality. You acknowledge one's lack of control.

I'm just not there yet. I'm still fighting for what I want and
need.

To distract myself, I turn to the man on my left. He was one of those who arrived after we were seated. "You said your name is Jerry?" I ask, wanting to draw him out as he's been mostly silent throughout the meal, listening to the others.

"Yes. Gerald or Jerry. It's all the same to me."

I hear an accent. He's not a native Californian but I can't place where he's from. "Where were you raised?"

He smiles. "Philadelphia. But after the war, I worked in Detroit, and then ended up here in California twenty years ago with my Betty."

There was something in the way he said *my Betty* that made my chest tighten. "Is she here?"

"She died six months ago. First Christmas and Easter without her." He looked me in the eye. "Had fifty-eight years together. I consider myself a lucky man."

"Sounds like you were happy."

"She was a catch."

Again, that tug of emotion. I like him, this Jerry. "Where was she from?"

"Met her in Michigan. She had dark red hair, and legs. Amazing legs. And she could dance. Boy, could she dance." His smile faded. "I miss her."

Dad leans in. "But the girls here won't leave Jerry alone. They're shameless. They chase him like you wouldn't believe."

"What?" I glance from Dad to Jerry and back again. "The ladies chase you?"

"He's fresh meat. He's only been here a few months—how long, Gerald? Two months? Three?"

"Almost four. Moved in January." He nodded and folded his napkin neatly, setting it by his plate. "Sometimes seems longer than that. Time is different without her. Can't keep track of it the way I used to."

After dinner, as I walk with Dad back to his apartment, I mention Jerry and what Dad had said during the meal, about Jerry being fresh meat.

"Do women chase you, Dad?"

"Yes. All the time."

"But the ladies here seem so old . . ."

"Not all of them. There are quite a few young ones here, women my age. Phyllis. Linda. Sheila. Dinah. Just to name a few. But they're not hanging around the dining room at lunch. They're out playing golf or tennis or off shopping. We have a courtesy van that takes the ladies downtown." He reaches into his pocket for his room key. "But I'm not interested and they know it."

I wait for him to unlock the door and push it open. "But you might be. One day."

"I might be," he agrees calmly. "Or I might not. I'm not there yet, and even if I was, I'd never marry again, and most of the ladies would like a proposal, and a ring."

"Seriously?"

"You wanted a proposal and a ring."

"Because I'd never been married or had kids—"

"The proposal and ring isn't about kids. It's about the commitment." He closes the door behind us and it shuts with a bang.

FOUR

Edie

That girl is back. Bill's daughter. I can't remember her first name, but she's sitting with him at the table for Friday Night Bingo. I rarely come play. Bingo is a mindless form of entertainment but I don't want to sit alone in my room tonight.

I make my way across the dining room ignoring the table of silly women on my left who've come out tonight wearing too much perfume and red lipstick. You'd think that once a woman is a certain age, she wouldn't need to try so hard, but no. Here the ladies are, talking loudly and laughing, trying to catch the old men's attention.

There is room at Dorothy's table but I couldn't handle listening to her grating voice all night. The only ones who can tolerate her are the seniors who are hard of hearing and don't have on their hearing aids.

Nancy and Louisa have space at their table but Nancy constantly passes gas. I know she can't help it, and she tries to ignore it, but it is so uncomfortable to pretend you don't hear.

Across the room is Grace. She's sitting with four men and she's just fast. She is constantly chasing men, as she's always looking for another husband. I can't even tell you how many times she's been married. Four? Five? More?

I sit down at an empty table on the edge of the room and line up five cards in front of me. We're allowed to play up to ten at a time, but I'm not in the mood tonight. I'm not even sure why I'm here.

I straighten my cards, spacing them half an inch apart, lining up the edges and corners.

There isn't a very big crowd tonight, but I am sure more will come in right when the game begins and then we will have to stop and wait while the latecomers get seated and arrange their cards and get ready to play.

Back when I taught, you knew to be in class on time. I don't have patience with those who dally and expect others to wait.

I drum my fingers on the table, and look out across the room. I'm less interested in the old people. It's Bill's daughter that interests me.

In the last few years I've found myself paying extra attention to the young adults, especially the girls. I'm fascinated by the way they dress and talk and walk.

Was I ever like that, so lithe, so free?

I don't remember being young, not like that. I don't remember . . .

I turn away from the girl, and no, she's not really a girl, she's a young woman in her late twenties with straight blonde hair and what should be a pretty face, but her expression is tight. Flat.

I know that expression. It's the face of disappointment. *Pain*.

I tip my dauber, mixing the ink, and tip it again.

And for some reason I don't understand, I push up to my feet, gather my five bingo cards, and make my way to Bill and his daughter.

• • •

In between games, and when the caller checks someone's card—inevitably in this group there are those who like to shout bingo long before they have anything because they've misheard or they simply can't follow the calls anymore—Bill's daughter asks me questions.

"I like your name," she says as we wait for confirmation on the latest bingo. "Is Edie short for Edna or Edith?"

Does she really care? Or is this her attempt at making small talk with an old person?

If so, I've no desire to encourage her. I'm not one for chatter and I have no need to hear my own voice.

"I like both names," she adds. "They're quite literary, aren't they?"

I look at her, and lift my brows. My grandnephews would call it my "quelling look" but the girl isn't paying any attention, she's just rambling on about Edith Wharton and how she'd read her in high school, but didn't love her, too depressing, women trapped by society into suffocating, rigid roles.

"Only if you happen to be born in the upper class," I answer tartly, because women in the middle class and the poorer classes can't afford to be trapped by anything. "Wharton was wealthy. She could afford to complain."

"She must have done something right. She won a Pulitzer Prize."

I bite down, vexed. I wish she'd stop talking.

Bill turns to us, and he smiles at me. "Edie's a linguist," he says to his daughter. "She speaks five languages."

"I wouldn't say I'm a linguist," I demur. "I was a language teacher, but yes, I do speak five languages. Or at least, I used to. I'm sure my Russian is quite rusty now."

"Which languages did you teach?" Alison asks.

"French, Spanish, and German at the high school. And then

German and Italian for the Monterey Institute in summers. The Russian was for government work. There was a need during the Cold War, but later there were others who were younger and better educated who were used."

"That's amazing."

"Many Europeans speak four or more languages."

"You're European?"

"No. But I grew up overseas. My father worked in the Foreign Service."

The girl's eyes are wide. "That really is impressive."

I don't know why but her admiration unsettles me. I don't want it. It's unnecessary. "Languages are easy if you learn them young."

"I've heard that," she agrees. "But who taught them to you? Did your parents hire language teachers?"

"The nannies always spoke a foreign language to us. Spanish in Mexico City and Chile, German in Austria, French in Morocco, and then I picked up Italian easily after learning Latin in school. And Russian . . . that just happened."

Not true. It didn't just happen. I intensively studied Russian to aid the US embassy in Berlin during the eighteen months I worked there.

Just as I learned bits of Dutch and Hebrew.

I learned everything I could to help our government. And Franz.

"I wouldn't call myself fluent in Spanish," Alison confesses, "and yet I studied it for years."

"You'll never become fluent if you don't immerse yourself in the language. You must live somewhere and read it and speak it. It's the only way the ear will pick up the proper cadence and accent."

"You must be good at music, too. Apparently the same part of the brain processes music and language."

"I'd heard it was music and math."

She flushes but doesn't reply. Another game is about to begin.

We line up new cards in front of us. We're all now playing ten cards at a time and there's no time for conversation, but at the end of this round, won by Eunice, Alison again turns to me.

"So, Edie, your father was an ambassador?"

"No," I answer, always amazed by how little Americans actually know of the Foreign Service and diplomatic core. "Nothing so high ranking. He was a consular, and every four or five years we'd be in a new place."

"With your language ability and your background, I'm surprised you didn't work for the government."

Others have said the same thing. But that's because they don't know that in 1942 I gave up my citizenship to become a German, and was immediately classified a traitor, and quite possibly, a spy.

I reach for fresh bingo cards, my hand shaking. I don't like to remember. The memories have never gotten easier; the anguish is buried so deep that when it resurfaces it poisons all over again. The knowledge that what we did—all our efforts—mattered naught.

That the struggle has been largely ignored.

That people prefer not to remember the good Germans, because it's not politically correct. I'm not sure if it's just an American phenomenon or something global, but most of those in the American middle classes prefer things black and white. Good and bad. Germans bad, the Allies and Jews, good. But it wasn't like that, not living through it, not in Germany, for those who were German.

It's easy for historians and critics to dissect those who were part of the Resistance. I don't even like to refer to my friends—and my love—as the Resistance. They weren't a group. Barely organized. No, they were teachers, lawyers, artists, aristocrats, intellectuals, pastors, ministers, Jews, soldiers, party members . . . people. They were all real people with lives and dreams and consciences.

But the years since the war have silenced virtually all. Those who survived the war will soon all be gone.

There are books about the German Resistance, but they are far and few and rarely discussed. The German Resistance is mostly forgotten.

My friends are forgotten.

How does the death of 5,000 or 6,000 Germans resisting the Nazis compare to the deaths of millions?

How can the deaths of 6,000 teachers and lawyers and students compare to the murder of six million Jews?

So I've been quiet. I've remained silent. I look away and close my eyes and pretend I can't hear when the news or radio discusses the war.

I don't want to remember the war.

I don't want to remember how I lost virtually everyone. I'm not sure how I survived. Not sure why I wasn't one of those hanged at Plötzensee. Three thousand were executed there during those years. And that was just the one prison.

Good people, my friends.

Eyes closed, I can see them.

Peter.

Klaus.

Adam.

Hugo.

Hans.

Robert.

Helmut.

Marion. Marion survived. Thank God. But the others didn't. Most of those who demonstrated resistance didn't. Most of those close to those rumored to be part of the Resistance didn't.

Good people, all of them, and there are more, so many more I haven't named but virtually all believed something had to be done.

I think it was Helmut, Freya's husband, who said that "only by believing in God could one be a total opponent of the Nazis." But faith is hard tested when evil seizes power.

Late the next morning, after a fitful night's sleep and an uneaten breakfast of coffee and toast, I discover that Bill's dentist daughter, Alison, is back. Apparently she has nowhere else to go.

I'm beginning to feel a little sorry for him. How can he relax with that inquisitive girl tagging after him everywhere?

"Edie."

I turn from Alison and focus on Ruthie on my right. Ruth is fidgeting with the buttons on her blouse. She's trying to unfasten them. I'm glad it's a blouse that doesn't open in the front. The pearlized buttons are decorative. She doesn't know. That's fine. They keep her busy and soon she'll forget why she wanted to undo them.

See? She's already forgotten. "Yes, Ruth?"

"Edie," Ruth repeats, reaching for my hand.

"Yes, dear?"

"What are we doing today?"

"Having a nice lunch." Saturday and Sundays are my days with Ruth. She joins me for lunch in the dining room and then we spend the afternoon together. Some person somewhere made a fuss about me breaking the rules, having Ruth come to me. The rules say that the dementia patients stay in their wing where they can have proper supervision, but it's too disturbing for me, being locked inside Memory Care. I can't be locked in anywhere.

"But after lunch? What are we doing?"

"Just relaxing today, dear."

"We're not seeing a show? We haven't seen a show in a long time."

"We could see a show. It's Saturday, movie day."

"I mean to the theater." Ruth draws her hand back, her fingers returning to the button, twisting one again, worrying it needlessly. "We don't go to the theater enough."

No, not often at all, I think. "Maybe we can see if they have a guest speaker today—"

"I want to see a show." She looks at me, brow creasing. "Why, why don't we see plays?"

Because you can't follow them anymore, I want to tell her. *And you'd talk the entire time.* But I don't. She'd be hurt. And she wouldn't understand. "That's a good question."

Ruth beams, pleased. "You know my mother was a dancer, in Warsaw."

"Yes."

"A ballerina." Her smile fades, her expression growing pensive. "I'm sure she was a dancer."

"She was, dear."

Ruth tugs anxiously on the button on her blouse. "How do you know? Did you see her dance?"

"No, but we've been friends a long, long time and you've told me about her."

"I have?"

"Yes. And from what you've told me, she was a beautiful dancer."

Today, much to Ruth's disappointment, there is no movie, as the projection equipment is broken, but Kathleen, the activities director, assures us that the equipment will be repaired and running by Wednesday's matinee, and Wednesday is a double feature, *The Best Exotic Marigold Hotel* and then the classic *Driving Miss Daisy.*

"I've seen *Driving Miss Daisy,*" Ruthie says, unhappy with the news.

"But you haven't seen *The Best Exotic Marigold Hotel.*" We

walk slowly away from the Activities Desk, arm in arm. I don't want Ruth to fall. She might be ten years younger than me but her dementia has aged her. She's leaning on me, which is fine. But I have to concentrate so I don't trip us up. It wouldn't do to hurt her. The nurses aren't happy that I lead Ruth around. They say we're an accident waiting to happen but I say fiddlesticks. Ruthie relies on me. She needs someone to take care of her, and unlike the nurses and aides, I'm not paid to care for her. I care for her because I do.

"I think I have," she says.

"I haven't seen it yet, so I don't think you have. It's new. It was out in the last year or two and it's supposed to be very good—"

"I don't think so."

"How do you know?"

"I've seen it."

"You haven't seen it. This is the first time they've shown it here."

"I'm sure I've seen it and it's terrible."

"It's highly rated."

"Rubbish."

"Well then, since you've seen it, what is it about?"

"Flowers. Marigolds."

Ruthie can be so exasperating at times. She's more and more like a young child, and I've never been fond of young children. "No, dear, it's not."

"You just said it was."

"That's the name of the hotel—"

"I don't care. I don't want to see it. It sounds stupid."

Ruth and I sit down on one of the benches lining the wide hallway. We often sit here and people watch. On weekends there are always people coming and going as adult children and grand-children come for their weekly visits.

Ruth is silent now and I'm fine with it. It's better to sit in silence than have her argue with me about nothing.

Lately it seems as if everyone and everything irritates me. I've never been known for my patience, but my patience is at an all new low.

Maybe it's because I have a birthday coming at the end of summer. I'll be ninety-five in September. Imagine that.

One hundred years old soon. And what do I have to show for it? No family. No kids. No grandkids.

Just Ruthie.

I smile at her now. She smiles back. It's a sweet smile. But she's not here. She's not here very much anymore. Maybe it's better this way. She doesn't know she's aging. Isn't aware that there isn't much time left.

Ruth was one of those who lost everyone in the Holocaust. Parents, sisters, brothers, grandparents, cousins. Nearly all died at Auschwitz. Ruth rarely talked about it, but she did say once, she didn't know why she survived. And yet here she is, with adult sons and daughters with grandchildren of their own. I've met many of them. One of her sons and one of her daughters came with their children and grandchildren during Passover last month. It was nice to see them all together, but it distressed the daughter that Ruth kept getting their names wrong.

I never had children. But I was a teacher, a language teacher, and I had enough young people at school. I told myself I didn't need them at home.

Here at Napa Estates, you can't escape young people. At least, not on weekends. Sundays are the worst. That's when everybody comes, after church, after brunch, or for brunch. I try to avoid eating in the dining room on Sundays between ten and two. That's when there are the most visitors and the kitchen staff sets up buffet stations and carving stations as if we're the Ritz. I detest the buffets. I don't understand a carving station. Just put the meat on a plate and be done with it. And the last thing I want to do is walk around a crowded room carrying my plate. Yes, there are staff to carry one's plate or tray for you. We are old people after all. But still, it's pretentious. Many of us here have lived through one, if not two, World Wars. Our parents lost everything during the Great Depression. We spent decades expecting the Soviet Union to send some nuclear missile our way. We don't need carving stations or heat lamps above a hock of ham.

Ruthie slides a hand into mine. "Everything okay, Edie?"

I look at her and she's back. I pat her hand. "Yes, dear."

"Lots of kids today."

It's true. We have a lot of visitors today. Tomorrow will be even more crowded for the Sunday brunch. I wouldn't mind the visitors if the children just stayed seated during the meals. They don't. The younger ones are usually completely out of control. Even the elementary-school-age kids can't sit still, not without one of those gadget thingeys where they play games. Children today are raised with too much freedom. It's as if parents are afraid to enforce rules. Or teach manners. Today, kids can do whatever they want, whenever they want.

It's distracting. And it's not fair to the child. It's better that people learn young that life isn't fair and requires tremendous discipline and sacrifice.

Ruth and I spend the next hour sitting on our bench, letting the sun warm our backs as people come and go. The hallway is lined with benches and nearly every bench is filled with residents. I'm reminded of old Berlin and Paris where people crowded the sidewalk cafes, sipping coffees, watching the world go by.

We, too, watch the world go by, even though our world is smaller and wrinkled and gray.

A boy and girl race past our bench. A harried mother trots after. More slowly comes the father, pushing a wheelchair. It's Eunice Whitman. I'd heard her family was coming—she always has someone coming—and she calls out to me and lifts a hand in greeting.

I nod briskly and look away, not particularly interested in making conversation. Eunice feels differently as the man pushing her slows, and then stops with Eunice directly in front of us.

"Hello, Ruth. Hello, Edie," Eunice says.

Eunice used to be considered a great beauty. I know because she reminds us all the time. She even won a couple of beauty pageants and could have signed with a talent agency and gone to Hollywood to be a star. She didn't. Marriage and motherhood called.

I've come close to telling her that I've attended some of the best music schools in the world, including the Hoch Conservatory in Germany and the Imperial Academy of Music and the Arts in Vienna, studying with some of the greatest musicians, conductors, and composers of this century, but I can't imagine saying the words out loud. Even though every bit of it is true. "Hello, Eunice."

"What are you girls doing?" she asks.

What does she think we're doing? My smile is tight. "Enjoying the afternoon."

"No guests today?"

"No, it's just us."

She gestures up to the man behind her, and then the woman who has gone after the two children. "This is my youngest daughter's husband, Chase Reeder. Chase and Jennifer live in Ohio."

I focus on her son-in-law. He looks to be in his mid-forties. Maybe a little older. He's tall, but very thin and weathered. Perhaps he has cancer. Or maybe he's one of those distance runners. Marathoners. Never understood how someone would want to run that much just for fun. But then he does live in Ohio. "Where in Ohio?" I ask him, not all that curious but it's better than talking to Eunice.

"Dayton."

"Do you like it?"

"It's a nice place."

"You're a native?"

"He's a doctor," Eunice answers for him. "A podiatrist—"

"A psychiatrist," Chase corrects.

Eunice frowns and peers up to look at him. "I thought you were a foot doctor."

He smiles at me and then down at her. His face is so very wrinkled and he's not even fifty yet. "Close. A head doctor," he says.

She hesitates, working this through. "That's not close at all."

He grimaces. "Sorry. Bad joke."

She's no longer smiling. She looks cross while I'm wildly entertained. Eunice thought that her son-in-law was a podiatrist. Very funny. Very, very funny.

Eunice is done socializing. She crooks a finger, gestures for him to continue.

Ruth watches them roll down the wide sunlit hall. "Who was that?"

"Her son-in-law."

"In the wheelchair?"

"No. That was Eunice."

"Who?"

"Eunice Whitman."

"I don't know her."

No, I don't suppose she does anymore.

FIVE

Ali

I have a text message from Diana Martin, the florist I met on the flight, who has an extra ticket for an event at one of the wineries tonight. It's the annual Concert in the Cellar, so there's music and dinner and some kind of an auction, but I don't have to go glitzy. Even though it's a fund-raiser, it's not black tie. Apparently no one in Napa likes to dress up in formal wear because then the men couldn't wear their jeans and boots.

I go home and shower and change, and Diana picks me up at six. During the drive she fills me in on tonight's event. The Concert in the Cellar benefits the National Children's Leukemia Foundation and is hosted by a different winery every year, and this year it's at Dark Horse Winery. The tickets, she adds, sold out within a day of them going on sale.

"Is that unusual?" I ask, holding up my hand to shield my eyes from the slant of late-afternoon light. Soon the sun will drop behind the hills but it hasn't yet and the visor doesn't cut the glare.

"The event always sells out, but not within a day." Her brow creases. "You're not familiar with Dark Horse Winery?"

I shake my head. "Should I? Is it a new winery?"

"They've been around almost ten years, but they're definitely high profile, as Napa wineries go. The winery is owned by Craig and Chad Hallahan and was the basis for a Food Network reality show a couple years ago."

"Really?"

"The show only lasted two years, and tended to focus more on the handsome bachelor brothers then the winery itself." Diana shoots me an amused glance. "Craig and Chad are in their late thirties and gorgeous, wealthy, and still very much single."

"So that's why the tickets sold so quickly. They're popular with the ladies."

"Very popular," Diana agreed, turning off the highway to drive beneath a tall wrought iron and stone arch announcing the entrance to Dark Horse Winery.

The dusky sunlight gilded over the tight neat rows of grapes coloring the hills copper and gold, making the hills gleam. It had been a beautiful warm day and I roll my window down, letting my fingers open and catch the air. You can smell the soil, earthy and fragrant.

My mother, the gardener, would love the smell.

As we approach the winery, we brake to join the queue of cars ahead of us, all waiting for the valet attendants.

Diana had said people didn't dress up for the event, but the women stepping from cars are all in cocktail attire and heels.

I wish I'd worn something more elegant. My red knit dress is cute but it's not very sophisticated.

The winery is built of stone with a great weathered trellis off to one side. Miniature white lights glimmer in the dusk. The setting looks more Tuscan than Californian, but maybe I don't know what California style is. My parents might both be natives, but I was born and raised in Washington. I miss Washington's big mountains and lakes and evergreens in moments like these.

Diana and I are handed glasses of red wine as we join others drinking and eating on the flagstone terrace.

"I did the flowers for a wedding here a couple weeks ago," Diana says, sipping her wine. "The couple married in the chapel, and then had their reception here on the patio. It was a stunning wedding. They spent over one hundred thousand dollars on the flowers alone."

I think of the wedding I'd planned with Andrew. My throat squeezes tight. It's hard to breathe.

I look away and study a server carrying a silver tray of canapés. Salmon and cream cheese with a bit of dill on something. And I suddenly know why I feel out of sorts in my red knit dress in this swanky Northern California setting.

Andrew should be my date tonight.

Andrew should be partnering me through life.

I did everything with him for years and this is the first social event I've gone to without him.

I take a quick sip from my wine and another, masking the ache in my chest with the warmth from the wine.

I shouldn't have come tonight. Why did I accept the invitation? But on the other hand, it had sounded fun. I'd been excited to go out, do something, and Diana offered me the ticket, not someone else. I can't let her down. I can't be bad company.

I force myself to pay attention to Diana, even though she is now talking about yet another wedding and weddings aren't my favorite subject. But I smile and nod and ask questions when appropriate and then finally we're called to dinner.

I will get through the evening. Even if it means I'm going to have to drink a lot of Merlot tonight.

• • •

I do drink a lot of Merlot. I drink so much that I oversleep the next morning and am late arriving at Napa Estates to have Sunday brunch with Dad.

As we wait for the hostess to seat us, Dad asks me about last night's event. I tell him the music was excellent. It was a concerto for guitar and strings and the setting couldn't have been more lovely. "The only bad thing is that I might have had a little too much red wine."

"Headache?" he guesses.

I nod. "Food should help. Water, too."

"Have you taken anything for it, yet?"

"I will, as soon as we eat." Although honestly, food sounds horrendous right now. I'd like to be back in bed, in a dark room, sleeping the afternoon away.

"So you didn't enjoy your girl time," Dad says as we're seated at a table for ten.

I gaze longingly at the small tables, the ones set for two and four. I'd like to sit at one of those today. I'd like to just hide in Dad's apartment but that's not going to happen. Dad has become a very social senior.

"I did. It was fun," I answer, sitting down in one of the empty chairs next to his.

"Your friend. She's not married?"

"No. She's single." And Diana was funny when she talked about her love life and her dates and how horrible her last date was in bed. According to Diana, that's why she sleeps with them early on, to weed out the lousy lovers before she's emotionally invested. "She was sharing her dating adventures with me last night. They're pretty comical."

He leans on the table. "So when are you going to date again?"

I draw back, offended and caught off guard. "I don't know. When are you?"

"Hmph. Maybe sooner than you think." And then before I can even begin to process this, he gestures for some of his eighty- and ninety-year-old cronies to come sit with us.

The Extra Strength Tylenol begins to kick in halfway through brunch. Gradually I can eat a little more and focus a little better on the conversation at the table.

With the seventieth anniversary of D-day just a few weeks away, the invasion at Normandy and World War II is very much on everyone's mind, particularly as so many of these men served in the war, seeing action if not in Europe, then in the Pacific.

Dad chases his eggs around his plate with toast. "Just like people always remember where they were when they heard that Kennedy had been shot, I'm sure everyone here remembers where they were when they learned about the attack on Pearl Harbor." He finally gets his eggs and toast together and he looks up at the others, encouraging them to talk since he's twenty years younger than many and he enjoys the stories of the war.

"It happened Saturday," George says, needing little prompting. "But most of us didn't find out until Sunday, hearing it on the shortwave radio station broadcasting from Hawaii."

Harold nods. "Heard it Sunday morning, too. I was fifteen and had been out delivering newspapers and it'd been a quiet morning. Nobody was out and about. It wasn't until I returned home that I found out why. Everybody was inside, listening to the radio because hell broke loose."

"War," George says.

"War," Floyd echoes. "And I wasn't delivering papers that morning. I was collecting eggs. That was my job every morning and I came in all pleased that the hens were laying, and I was sure my mother would be happy with the number of eggs, because she sold the extra in town every day, but nobody wanted to hear about the eggs."

"Not that you could hear the radio well," he adds after a moment. "Damn static-y. I couldn't really hear what was going on and when I asked what the fuss was, Ma told me to hush because the Japanese had just bombed Pearl Harbor."

Graham adds milk to his coffee, spoon clinking loudly against the cup. "After that broadcast, my dad went out and bought a rifle and a map of the Sierra Nevadas, just in case we needed to head up to the mountains."

"We did, too. Stocked up on supplies and ammunition."

"But why?" I ask, unable to stay silent.

All heads turn in my direction, expressions incredulous.

"In case the Japanese landed," Graham answers. "If the Japanese were going to bomb Pearl Harbor, what was to stop them from coming here?"

"That's what folks were saying." Floyd shakes his head. "So I went and enlisted. I had to protect my family. My mother cried her eyes out, but it was the right thing to do."

I look at the lined faces of the men seated around me. "Did everyone really think the Japanese would land on the West Coast?"

"Oh yes." Graham's jaw is set. "Folks were told to have evacuation plans. They should be prepared to leave everything and head to the mountains."

For a moment there is just silence and I try to imagine what it'd feel like, thinking that enemies were about to attack any moment. Fearing you'd have an invasion on your own soil. I've never lived through a world war, but I do remember the terror following September 11, 2001. No one saw that coming and yet everyone was so very afraid.

Angered, and afraid.

I was just starting my junior year of high school and was about to turn seventeen. So many of the seniors who'd graduated in June rushed to enlist then, too.

"Seems like a long time ago," George says now.

"The whole thing was bad business, start to finish. The Axis powers were insane."

"Power-hungry bastards."

While they continue their conversation, I'm remembering the horrific September morning when Mom shouted for me to come. She'd just received a call from another teacher and she'd turned on the TV at home. Standing next to her, I watched the second plane crash into the second tower.

I watched as the towers fell.

It was one of the worst days of my life.

Until Andrew.

I'm suddenly nauseous and I reach for my ice water, sipping it, trying to shake away all memories. I force myself to focus on the moment, this dining room, and the people gathered here.

I've begun to recognize faces and families. There are the regulars and then the special guests. Across the dining room I spot Edie and Ruth, lunching together, but they're not alone today. There's a man sitting with them, a tall man. Not old from the size of his back and the width of his shoulders. He has dark blond hair that could use a cut.

I look from him to Edie, who is facing me. Edie doesn't smile but she's practically beaming today. "Look at Edie," I murmur to Dad, needing the distraction and the interaction. "She looks happy, doesn't she?"

Dad follows my gaze. "That's her great-nephew. Her sister's grandson. She dotes on him."

"Apparently."

"She says he's popular with the ladies, but I've found him to be a nice guy. I've played bridge with him a couple times. Not a bad bridge player, either."

"And that's what matters, right?" I tease.

"You're trying to get a rise out of me."

I laugh. "Maybe."

"He's a winery guy. Craig Hallahan—"

"From Dark Horse Winery?"

"Yes." Dad looks at me. "You know him?"

"I was at Dark Horse Winery last night for the Concert in the Cellar."

"So you met him?"

"No. It was pretty crowded and the focus was on the fundraiser, and then later his brother did the talking when they asked for donations for the foundation."

"Chad," Dad says.

I look at Dad, amazed. "How do you know all this?"

"Everybody knows. They were on a TV reality show a couple years ago. Or the winery was part of a food show I forget the details but Craig's the older brother, and Chad's the home wrecker."

I lift a brow. "The home wrecker?"

"He had an affair with his marketing gal, who was married, and the husband got wind of it and kicked her out and then punched out Chad on one of the episodes."

"And you know this how?"

"Everybody knows. It was part of the first season."

"I had no idea you watched reality TV."

"Well, I didn't. Your mother saw a little bit and I'd watch with her, and then after I moved here, Edie told me some things. She was not a fan of the show. She thought it was pretty disgusting."

"The show? Or Chad's affair?"

"Both. Edie thought Chad should have married the girl." Dad reaches for his cane and struggles to stand. "You want to go meet Craig?"

"*No.*"

"He's not the home wrecker."

"Dad, no. Sit down. Please." I wait for him to take his chair before leaning towards him to whisper, "What are you doing?"

"What do you mean?"

"Why would you drag me across the dining room to meet some man who's been on reality TV?"

"He's a vintner, and Edie's great-nephew. I thought you might like him."

"Like him for what?" I stare at Dad baffled by the changes in him, and his disconnect from my reality. Andrew has only been gone fourteen months. I am still in my own black hole of grief. Why would I want to meet a man now? And why would Dad think this Hallahan guy would be a good one for me?

"You need friends. You need to move on."

"Move on?" My voice rises and I lean closer to him to keep others from hearing. "What about you? Maybe you'd like to move on, too."

"I am moving on. I'm making friends here—"

"What about the house, Dad?"

"What about it? It's my house. I own it. Why do I have to do anything with it?"

"But *you* live *here.*"

"So? It's my investment property."

"You're paying someone to manage it. You're paying monthly utilities—"

"It's not a lot. I can afford it." He stares at me from beneath his bushy eyebrows. "Is this about money? Are you hurting for money?"

I owe thousands of dollars in loans, but this isn't about money.

I've never used Mom and Dad's money. Didn't want it then and still don't want it now. "I just think it's a lot for you to worry about—"

"I have nothing to worry about," he interrupts. "I have nothing to do but watch TV and play cards and wonder what's on the menu for dinner."

"Then maybe you should come live with me and—"

"That's not going to happen."

His sharpness silences me. I look away, hold my breath, hurt. I don't want to be hurt but I don't understand.

I don't understand how he'd rather sit here and stare at a TV screen and take his meals with dozens of strangers than live in my home with me.

"I'm trying very hard not to take this personally, Dad," I say, lightly, crisply, to hide the pain. It's the voice I use every day at work. "But I can't help thinking that if I were a dog, you'd want to live with me."

"But you're not a dog."

I should have been.

The corner of my mouth lifts even as a curl of hurt curves inside my chest. A hot painful question mark. Why doesn't he love me?

Why can't I be a dog?

A brown and white Spaniel named Freckles because then he'd touch me all the time.

And just like that, my eyes burn and I'm fighting so much emotion that I think it could take my legs out, lay me flat. The feeling. The grieving. How does one get from here to there? How does one get through life unscathed?

You don't.

Suddenly I need to get up, move. Murmuring an excuse, something about the bathroom, I rise, walk out, my striped sundress swishing, low kitten heels clicking on the dining room floor.

Heads lift, faces turn, eyes watching me. Leaving the dining room I use the ladies' room and wash my hands, studying my face briefly in the mirror. My tan is fading. My freckles are pale on the bridge of my nose. My mouth is too wide. It always has been. I smile at myself. My mouth is huge, all those teeth. But they're very straight and not that fake white advertised in the back of complimentary airplane magazines.

Leaving the bathroom I'm not ready to return to the dining room of the old and infirm. Instead I walk down the hall and slip out one of the French doors in the Reading Room to the wide, flat terrace overlooking the rolling hills covered with row after tidy row of grapes. What a view. Oak trees that give way to vineyards. Could Dad have found a better view anywhere?

Maybe Mom and Dad knew what they were doing choosing this as their final stop.

"You're Bill's daughter, Alison," a deep male voice says behind me.

I glance over my shoulder, towards the French doors. It's the Hallahan guy. The vintner. I recognize the blue shirt and the dark blond hair, shaggy at the back.

Incidentally, his broad shoulders have nothing on his face.

He's tan, which makes his eyes intensely blue. A man in his late thirties, mature, and ruggedly handsome. Like the Robert Redford my mom used to love in *All the President's Men*.

My mom would love him.

I feel my mom suddenly, with me, a prickle of my skin, little goose bumps covering my arms, a tingle at the back of my neck. *Hello, Mom.*

And the tingle is stronger.

I rub my forearm. "Yes. You're Edie's great-nephew."

"People have been talking," he replies. "But then, when you're my great-aunt Edie's age, I don't suppose there is a lot else to do."

I smile faintly. "No. I don't suppose there is." And then I don't know what else to say to him, aware that he is Craig Hallahan, the nice, older Hallahan, but nonetheless a most eligible bachelor and chased by all the ladies.

Uncomfortable, I turn back to the rolling hills. He doesn't take the hint, although I suppose it's not much of a hint, and joins me outside on the patio.

I don't know what to do now. I don't really want to talk but I don't know how to just stand here in silence, either. "It's a beautiful view," I say at length.

He glances down at me. "I don't see a view anymore. Just grapes." His mouth quirks. "A friend that once surfed professionally says he never sees the ocean, just the waves."

"Would you prefer the view?"

"I'd like to be able to see what others see." He looks at me, lashes lowered, lips pressed. "I'm no longer detached."

"Is that a bad thing?"

"Good question." He hesitates a moment. "When you look at people and they smile, do you see the smile, or the teeth?"

"Touché." My face grows hot as I admit, "I see the teeth."

The corner of his mouth lifts higher. "My aunt said you're a dentist. I think she worries about you."

"Because I'm a dentist?"

"Because you prefer Phoenix to Napa."

"I don't prefer—" I break off, frown, aware that Dad must have said something to her about me wanting him to move. Or me not wanting to move here. "My dental practice is in Arizona. And I love Arizona. The desert is beautiful. Camelback Mountain is beautiful—" I turn and look at him, brow furrowing. "Your aunt has a lot of opinions."

"She does. And she can deliver them in a very cutting tone."

"So it's not just me?"

He laughs softly, sympathetically. "No, that's just dear Aunt Edie."

"Why is she so rough?"

"She's old and she's lived a challenging life."

"Doesn't everyone?"

"You should hear her story. It's interesting."

"Hmm."

"But she does like your dad. Has quite a soft spot for him. Apparently he's a very good bridge player."

"And that's all that's required to earn her affection?"

"Not affection, but respect. I think his dog stories earned her affection. She's a big animal lover."

"I knew I should have been a dog."

He lifts a brow. He's amused. "Is there a particular breed you fancy?"

"A beloved lap dog. A Scottie or a spaniel. Or maybe something that could fit in one's purse and go everywhere."

"And you'd be happy in a purse?"

"Depends on the purse."

He studies me a long moment, a glint in his eyes. "I suppose it would."

I laugh out loud.

He cracks the smallest of smiles, and yet his storm blue eyes are full of light.

I've never met this man. I know nothing about him other than what my father has told me and this is the strangest conversation with a stranger. I like it. I feel free somehow. Nothing matters. Everything matters. Andrew would enjoy this moment. He was good with new and novelty. He enjoyed change.

The warmth inside me recedes.

I reach up to tuck a strand of hair behind my ear. "I was at your winery last night, for the Concert in the Cellar."

"Yes, I know." He's still smiling but his expression is different, less playful. "You wore red."

I just look at him, unable to think of anything to say.

"You were with Diana Martin, the florist," he adds. "I asked about you, but no one knew your name."

I snap my mouth closed. My cheeks burn. "I should get back to my dad. He must be worrying about me."

"Can't have that," he agrees.

SIX

Edie

I'm walking Ruth to the ladies' room when I glance into the Reading Room and see my great-nephew talking with Alison, the dentist, out on the terrace.

He's interested in her. I'm not entirely surprised. He likes smart girls, academic girls. He's always been more serious than Chad, more interested in the arts, too. As a boy I'd take him to the symphony in the city. I don't know if he liked the music, but he was always polite, and he'd dress up for the concert, even if it was a matinee, putting on a dress shirt, blazer, and tie.

He'd take my arm as we crossed the street, and would caution me to watch for traffic, as cars don't always slow down for people, and then when we reached the other side and we'd step up onto the curb, he'd give my elbow a little squeeze as if letting me know I'd done well. We'd made it.

Craig is the thoughtful one, but both boys have good manners. Ellie was very strict with Elizabeth when she was a child, stressing the importance of manners. Manners aren't just about good breeding, they are an essential courtesy and an expression of respect, values drummed into me and Ellie as the daughters of a man who made his career in the Foreign Service.

I help Ruth into the bathroom stall and step out to give her privacy. Earlier in the week, the management here forbid me from helping Ruth. They say it's dangerous, and a liability. I'm to get an aide when Ruth must use the lavatory. But where am I to find an aide, and how is Ruth expected to hold it? Yes, they've put her in diapers but if she's aware she has to go, why piddle in her pants?

And what is the worst that can happen if Ruth falls, and pulls me down with her?

I break an arm or a leg?

I get pneumonia?

I die?

It wouldn't be the end of the world if it happened. I have to go someday. I might as well go doing a good deed.

I told them that, too. But they thought I was being a smart aleck. I wasn't.

I was serious.

But of course they don't know that because they don't know me.

SEVEN

Ali

Over the past week, Dad and I settled into something of a routine. I run in the morning and putter around the house before getting a coffee in town and heading to Napa Estates to meet Dad for lunch.

I haven't given up trying to get him to leave the retirement home for lunch and try one of the picturesque restaurants downtown, but so far, he prefers the ease and comfort of meals in the home's dining room.

But Tuesday Dad calls me early, and announces he has plans for me, and I'm needed at his retirement home at eleven as the couple Dad and Edie usually play bridge with aren't well and so they need to find warm bodies for the game. I'm to be one of the warm bodies. Jerry, the widower from Detroit, is the other.

I've just been in the yard, weeding, and am still sweaty, with dirt-encrusted nails—a fact I forget until I clap a hand to my forehead and feel grit fall into my eyes. "Dad. Seriously?"

"I thought you liked spending time with me."

"I'm *not* a bridge player."

"You are. You're just not a good one."

"Even more reason why I shouldn't play!"

"But Edie's partner isn't, either. You'll be fine. It's Edie and I that will be challenged by our partners' lack of skill."

"I'm really not in the mood. Let's do something different—"

"Like what? Watch TV? Listen to a ballgame? What will we do?"

"We could pick up lunch from one of the cute Napa cafes and come here to the house for a picnic. I've been weeding the beds and getting ready to plant some flowers."

"Why? Are you staying in Napa?"

"You said you wanted to keep the house. You said it was your investment property. I'm making sure it's a good investment."

"Well, don't do too much. You don't want to get attached. You love the desert, remember?"

"Why should I come play bridge with you when you never do anything I want to do? Hmm?"

"Are you being serious, or a smart ass?"

I hesitate. "Both."

He hesitates, too. "Fine. Be here by eleven for the game, and then later this week, or before you leave, we'll go out to eat. Or go to the house. Or whatever it is you're dying to do."

"Promise?"

He sighs. "I promise."

I roll my eyes at his exasperated sigh—he sounds so put-upon—but at least I know he means it. Dad might not tell you what you want to hear, but he doesn't break promises.

I arrive at Napa Estates for the card game thinking that maybe, just maybe, Jerry isn't the fourth but Craig Hallahan will be. I don't know why I think it's going to be Craig, but I get to the center and head to the Reading Room where Edie likes to play cards because it's quiet.

It's quiet because it's a *Reading* Room. But that means nothing to Edie, not even the posted sign on the wall inside the door asking residents and guests to take their card games and conversations elsewhere. But rules don't apply to Edie. Others have to follow them, but not her. Apparently when you're almost one hundred, it's okay to say outrageous things and make demands and do what you want.

Thirty minutes into the game, we're in between hands, shuffling cards and sipping our iced drinks (which you're not allowed to have in the Reading Room but that's another rule that's ignored) when she asks me why I chose to become a dentist.

But before I can answer, she tells me I don't look like a dentist.

I'm not sure what to make of that. Do dentists come in certain packages? We can't be petite and blonde, with a wide mouth and a freckled nose?

"I'm good with my hands," I say, reaching up to rub the bridge of my nose, feeling the bump near the bridge that I got when I took a softball to the face in eighth grade.

According to Andrew one of my nostrils is also a hair wider than the other. He's right. But only a perfectionist would notice. Or care. He didn't care. I've never cared.

I've never gotten that hung up on looks. But I do like teeth. Straight white teeth. A great smile.

That's what I noticed about Andrew first. His smile.

"And I make decent money," I add, because it's true.

"You're not one of those altruistic people who choose medicine because they like helping people?"

I hear the bite of sarcasm in her voice. I get the feeling that Edie isn't particularly fond of me. And that's fine. I don't need her approval, or her friendship.

"No," I answer, smiling, but it's to hide my irritation. Edie seems to enjoy taking jabs at me, or maybe she just feels entitled to take jabs at everybody. Either way, I'm tired of it. I'm tired, period. This "vacation" to Napa has been rather grueling. Going back to work would be easier. "I wanted to make a good living. And I wanted to do something that not just anyone could do, and dentistry is challenging. Both in dental school, and in practice."

"So you've a mercenary streak."

"I have an independent streak. My mother worked, her mother worked, and I wanted to work. And if you're going to work, why not make money?"

"But you are a good dentist," she says.

"I think so." I can see from her expression that wasn't the answer she was looking for. "And my patients seem to think so, too."

"Have you killed anyone yet?"

"I'm a dentist, Edie."

She sniffs and reaches for her cards. "It can happen."

During the game Diana texts me that she'd love to go get a drink after work and would I like to meet her?

After hours of bridge at Napa Estates, I need a drink, as well as the company of someone a little closer to my age.

I meet Diana at the restaurant she suggested. Angele overlooks the river and we're seated outside on the patio. It's a comfortable evening and I sigh with pleasure as I settle into my chair.

"I am so glad you texted. I needed this badly."

"Are you still spending every day with your dad at his retirement home?"

"Not all day, but I usually meet him for lunch . . . and sometimes stay until dinner."

She wrinkles her nose. "How's the food?"

"Not bad. Could use more salt, so now I keep my own salt shaker in my purse."

"Do you really?"

Grinning, I reach into my purse and pull out the cardboard salt and pepper shakers I bought at the grocery store. "It makes a difference."

The waiter returns to take our appetizer and salad order. Diana also selects a bottle of wine. It's not until we're on our second glass of wine that she confides she's had a really shitty week. She lost two of her staff within a day of each other, and this weekend she has a huge wedding and she's panicking about being able to get all the bouquets and the centerpieces done.

"I don't know how I'm going to get it done." Her brown gaze meets mine, expression unhappy. "I even considered flying my mom and sister up from Phoenix, but that's stupid. I need to hire someone now. Someone from around here."

"Have you posted a want ad?"

"I've got an ad on Craigslist and I've taped a discreet sign in the window of the shop, but nothing yet."

"It'll happen."

"Hopefully sooner than later."

I see the stress in her face, her lips are pinched tight, and I feel bad for her. I know what it's like when you feel it's all resting on you. "Is there anything I can do? I'm not a designer but I can stick flowers in a vase. Show me a picture or give me a sample arrangement, and I can try to copy it." I lift my hands, wiggle my fingers. "I've got good hands. Or so my professors used to say."

"Stop it."

"I'm serious."

"Don't tease me like that."

But she's smiling a little and I smile back. "I have nothing else to do, Diana, and God knows, I cannot take another afternoon of bridge or keep up with this running. I'm getting shin splints. You'd be doing me, and my shins, a favor."

"You're good," Diana says, stabbing her salad with her fork. "I'm also tempted to take you up on your offer."

"You should. You'd be giving me a sense of purpose and providing me with some um . . . youthful . . . company."

She laughs. "As long as you don't mind working for minimum wage."

"Sounds perfect."

"You're out of your mind, but hey, I'm not complaining."

Although Diana won't be making up the wedding party bouquets and boutonnieres, and the twenty-five centerpieces for the reception until Friday, she could use help tomorrow taking and fulfilling orders, and possibly delivering a few arrangements if her driver is a no-show.

I promise to show up the next morning after I check on Dad, and I do, entering Bloom, the charming florist shop that looks more like a cottage than a store, with a quick step.

I breathe in the scent of lilies and roses, freesias and hyacinths, so different from the smell of chemicals in my office in Scottsdale, and find Diana at one of the large pine tables in the work area behind the counter, putting together an all pink arrangement with sixteen pink roses. "For a sweet sixteen birthday," she says.

I watch her work, noting the structure of the arrangement, and how she creates a triangle and then fills in, creating a pattern that gives the arrangement fullness and balance.

"That's pretty," I say.

"It's easy when you use one color," she answers, drying her damp hands and standing back to check her work. "Some of my favorite bouquets are all shades of pink or violets and purples."

She grabs a French blue pottery pitcher and sets it on the table. "But for this next arrangement, I need something different. It's for a seventh wedding anniversary and the husband said his wife loves jewel tones, and because she's an artist and eclectic he said she would prefer something fresh that isn't too staged. So I'm going to go for colors that contrast, to give it a bit of edge."

I watch Diana reach into the refrigerator for a bucket of dark red dahlias. "I start building my arrangements in my hand," she says, showing me how she then wraps the stems lightly with a flexible twig. "You can also use twine, you just need to secure them so there is a shape when you put them in the vase. Once in the vase, you start filling in with smaller flowers, contrasting flowers, dark blues and purples, paying attention to the shape and height. For the height I'm using white snapdragons and some of the blue larkspur, and then rim the base with greenery—ivy and hosta in this case would both be nice."

She's done in short order and it's a striking and rather bohemian arrangement, reminding me of gypsies or the kind of flowers you might find at a Parisian flea market.

"Very nice," I compliment. "But you make it look very easy. I know it's not that easy."

"I'll show you one more, that's our signature arrangement. You can do it in all colors and throughout the year if you have big, lush flowers. My favorite flowers to work with for this bouquet are hydrangeas, lilies, lisianthus, peonies, and roses. You need seven to nine flowers and then some height in the back—snapdragons for spring and summer, and pine or holly is always fun during the Christmas holidays. These lush flowers look extravagant, and they really do impress. They're all terribly romantic, which is what Bloom is all about."

Diana gets me to work on one of these lush arrangements now. I'm to use a low silver bowl that she has bought at a local antique mall. She's always on the hunt, scouring antique stores, thrift stores, and garage sales looking for unique and interesting vases, as the vase is as important as the arrangement at Bloom.

I'm working with blue hydrangeas, dark purple hyacinths, and violet tulips, and Diana sets me loose to work. I do as she did, form a base with my largest flowers, in this case the hydrangeas, tie them loosely, and start adding the tulips and hyacinths in small clusters, but it looks drab to me. I glance uncertainly at Diana who is working with stalks of gladiolas, flowers I always associate with funerals so I'm glad she's doing that one and not me.

"Something isn't right," I tell her. "It looks flat."

She takes one glance at the flowers and nods. "You want the brightest flowers in the center. It'll draw your eye to the middle, creating a pleasing focal point. Then keep the tulips in a cluster, all five together, and the two shades of hyacinths. You're bunching the flowers in this bouquet and then going to finish off with some height at the back. The dark bearded purple iris would look wonderful. Or you could experiment with some snapdragons, too."

She's right on all accounts. The bunched flowers make more impact, and the dark purple irises are stunning at the rear.

"You're good," I tell her, finishing adding in the dark green veined hosta leaves here and there at the base.

"I love what I do. I get to work with my hands and make people happy. I can't imagine a better way to pay my bills!"

It's a hectic few days at the flower shop, but the time passes quickly and I'm having fun. By the end of the day my legs are tired from being on my feet all day but I don't mind. Diana is fun and she's training a new girl who is young and sweet but not learning very quickly. Every night Diana thanks me for playing backup, and every night I go home feeling as if I've done something good.

By late Saturday afternoon I'm exhausted, though. We finish all the bridal bouquets and I deliver those to the church while Diana puts the finishing touches to the reception centerpieces. I return to the shop to help load up the truck she's rented for the occasion. Together we head to the winery, and place each arrangement on the twenty-five rounds, and the lush pink, cream, and coral arrangements look stunning against the cream and gold embroidered tablecloths.

It's going to be a beautiful wedding.

I return home to the house on Poppy Lane, and I'm exhausted but also very wound up. Too wound up to relax.

I was going to be an April bride. It was to be such a beautiful wedding with the reception at the Phoenician. A black-tie wedding with a big band for dancing. The Morrises had invited everybody from Arizona's high society. It was important to them that everyone got an invitation for their only son's wedding. They wanted everyone to celebrate how handsome and successful and happy Andrew was.

And yet, as it turned out, Andrew wasn't successful and happy. He wasn't happy at all.

I suddenly feel trapped in the house. I feel trapped with my thoughts. I can't handle the emptiness and anger and pain.

I change into shorts, a T-shirt, and running shoes and go out for a late-afternoon run now, heading down Poppy Lane. I know that eventually the road dead-ends, but there's a dirt path that cuts behind one of the old farmhouses and leads to an old orchard with gnarled and dying fruit trees, and then past a farm with a handful of horses with swishing tails, before the flat farmland rises up turning into a hill of grapes.

I found the dirt path by accident and I love the soft thud of my feet and the poofs and clouds of dirt. The ground feels good as my feet pound it and I don't even need music. I just need my feet slapping the dirt and my heart pounding in my ears and the sweat burning my eyes so no one knows I cry.

I want my life back.

I want my life back.

Dear God, give me my life.

I charge to the top of the hill, running fast, faster until I'm at the top, doubled over, gasping for air.

I do this every time—run so hard that at the end, as I crest the hill, I've run myself ragged, run myself to drain the pain and longing out.

When there are no more tears left, I jog down and the white horse that always looks at me, lifts his head and I look back at him.

My jog turns to a walk as I reach Poppy Lane. I walk even more slowly as I pass my favorite farmhouse, the one with the white picket fence. The fence is bordered with early blooming pink climbing roses that tumble in wild abandon across the white pickets. Dark blue, almost purple salvia has been planted between the rosebushes with low mounds of golden creeping Jenny for ground cover. I can bend forward and smell one of the elegant pink blossoms, wondering if this climber rose is an heirloom rose, since it is unabashedly fragrant. Once I would have asked my mother. Now I make a note to ask Diana.

It's Sunday morning brunch with Dad. And eight of his closest friends.

When I first arrived here, I didn't understand why Dad would prefer to live at Napa Estates rather than moving to Scottsdale to be with me, but I'm beginning to understand.

Dad has friends here. They joke, they talk, they argue, they laugh.

Dad laughs. And even with the splint on his wrist, he looks healthy.

Happy.

Mom would be happy for him, too. This is what she'd want. This is why they chose this place.

So if Dad is happy, and Mom would be happy for Dad, then I just need to be happy for him, too.

I need to let go of the idea of needing him . . . even though he is all I have left.

Conversation is easy until someone says something about "today's kids" that sets the men off. Before I know it, everyone has something negative to say about the younger generation and I glance at Dad, wishing he'd defend my generation, or at the very least, defend me, but he doesn't. He just lets them talk, and criticize.

"Kids nowadays, they don't know," Walter says grimly. "They have no idea what life is really like. They're entitled. They think they deserve it all. They think they know it all. But truthfully, they know nothing—"

"Now that's a little bit harsh," George interrupts.

"But true," Walter retorts. "They've never lived through war. Not a real war. Not like us."

"But did the war make you a better person?" Jerry asks quietly. "I'm not sure it made me a better person."

"Taught me to work hard," Walter said. "Taught me the value of a buck."

"That's true." Harold sighed. "It teaches a war ethic, an ethic kids today don't have. Kids today don't think they should have to work. They think it should all be handed to them, *just because.* My grandson, for example. He got an offer last year after graduating from college. He didn't like the offer. He said it wasn't good enough. That he deserved better. So what did he do? Turned it down and has spent the past year living at home, living off his parents. Easier to sponge off your folks then stand on your own two feet."

Walter pounds his fist onto the table. "Exactly. But why do they deserve a red carpet? What makes them so special? What makes them deserve more than we did?"

"That's what I'm talking about," Harold says, looking around the table. "Can you imagine any of us saying to our parents during the war, I shouldn't have to go, I'm better than this? I shouldn't have to work, so you go do it for me?"

Harold's gaze locks with mine. "Alison, explain your generation to me. What makes a twenty-two-year-old feel entitled to stay home while his mother and father work forty-, fifty-hour weeks? How can a twenty-two-year-old man justify allowing his mother to do his laundry and clean his room while he lays around playing video games and reading Japanese comics?"

All eyes are now on me and I don't have an answer. I'm not the twenty-two-year-old doing that. I've been making my own school lunch since sixth grade and doing my own laundry since my freshman year of high school when I needed a clean PE uniform and Mom had back-to-school night and couldn't do it.

I started helping grocery shop as soon as I got my driver's license and I'd even make dinners once or twice a week if Mom worked late, so Dad wouldn't go hungry.

I'm not the lazy boy or the entitled girl. My friends aren't, either. In fact, I don't really know those young adults he's talking about. Maybe there is something else wrong. Maybe his grandson has a mood disorder or a learning quirk. Maybe there is more to the story. But right now everyone is waiting for me to say something and I just know I can't throw his grandson—who I've never met, nor will probably ever meet—under the bus.

"I don't know," I say. "But if your daughter, his mother, doesn't have a problem with it, maybe it's okay?"

"It's never okay to shirk one's duty," Harold says fiercely.

George gestures broadly. "We understood duty. We understood

responsibility, because we all went through it. We all lost someone. We all struggled. We went hungry. We're different, and we know we're different."

The men nod and murmur agreement. The tension dissipates, the anger, too, leaving them quiet and reflective.

A few return to their meals, others begin to rise and walk away. Dad and I remain even after the others are gone. Dad is still silent, though, and I'm silent, waiting for him to say something. But he doesn't.

"You all right?" I ask him as seconds stretch into minutes.

"Just brings back a lot of memories," he says.

"But you didn't serve in that war."

"No, but I was a kid during the war and I remember how hard it was on my mom and brothers. Dad was away, you know, serving in the navy. Mom had to raise us three kids on her own."

"Grandpa was in the navy?"

"I've told you that."

"I didn't remember."

"Your grandfather never talked about it, but then, most men came home from the war and never said a word about what they saw or did. Dad didn't want to know how Mom got by. It was better to not ask questions. Better to not hear the details. Now my older brothers, they talked about the war. They were teenagers during the war and they both had to get jobs in addition to going to school. Johnny worked in orchards, picking fruit and strawberries, and my older brother Ed did construction work for a local company, since there was a huge housing shortage. Johnny would come home, and then Mom would leave for work. From the time I was a year old, she worked nights at the Southern California Telephone Company. Do I remember that? No. But do I remember my mother always carefully counting her change, and cutting coupons the rest of her life."

"That's why Grandma always used coupons."

"She'd lived through the Great Depression. She'd lived with rations. She'd raised children with rations. Instead of being embarrassed that she used coupons, you should have been proud of her. Those coupons allowed her to support her family."

"I was young," I say. "I didn't know better."

"But Harold and Walter are right when they say your generation has different expectations. You were raised comfortably. Your mom and I took pride in being able to provide you with a certain quality of life. If we wanted to take a vacation, we took it. If you wanted to go to dance or cheer camp, we could send you. There is a comfort and affluence now that didn't exist in the thirties and forties. Being forced to do without is unpleasant, but it won't kill you—"

He breaks off as Kathleen Burdick, the Estate's activities director stops at our table.

"How are we doing today?" she asks, smiling at Dad and me.

"Good," Dad answers, before introducing me.

"We've met," Kathleen replies. "And she's actually the reason I'm here now. We're in a bit of a bind, and I'm hoping she can fill in as our guest speaker this afternoon. The speaker we had booked, a photographer who has just returned from a trip to the Middle East, has cancelled at the last minute, and Edie suggested that perhaps Dr. McAdams would like to speak on dentistry today."

"Dentistry?" I repeat, wondering why Edie would suggest me, and the topic, when I know she's not particularly fond of me.

"We were thinking perhaps you could prepare a short program on dentistry for seniors . . . something useful, educational, that they could relate to."

The last thing I want to do is stand in front of a room and talk about dental hygiene for seniors, but Kathleen, the epitome of a pretty and cheerful camp counselor, is very persuasive and I can't tell her no.

I agree to speak for twenty to twenty-five minutes and then

take questions for another fifteen to twenty minutes, or as long as there is sufficient interest.

I don't have any handouts or a computer for a PowerPoint. I've no visuals or even dental models. Nothing to show. It's just me, at the front of the room, with a microphone (necessary when half the room is hard of hearing) talking for the next thirty-something minutes.

I hope no one comes. And then I can scoot out at two, if no one is here by then.

My hopes are dashed moments later when the first ladies enter the room. There are three of them, and they take seats in the middle of the theater, reminding me how empty the room is.

They face me expectantly, their gazes following every little thing I do from scribbling fresh notes, to organizing my index cards.

If they are the only three, then I could invite them to come to the front row, or I could even stand in the row in front of them—

Two ladies arrive, both with walkers. They slowly find seats on the outside aisles.

And then a woman is pushed through the doors. She's in a wheelchair and she has an attendant with her. The attendant parks the chair in the back row, the designated wheelchair section, and then grabs a folding chair from the back to sit down beside her. They, too, look at me, anticipating.

Seven. There is no getting out of the dental care for seniors speech now.

I skim my opening. *I'm Dr. Alison McAdams and I'm here to talk to you about your teeth.*

Boring. Yawn.

I scratch out the opening and scribble a new one. *Good afternoon, everyone. I'm Dr. Alison McAdams and I'm curious. When was the last time you saw your dentist?*

Another couple has come in. An older man and woman, arm in arm. I recognize them from my first day here. Dad was playing bridge with them.

The woman—Rose?—lifts a hand, waves to me. I wave back. They're the first to come sit in the front row. That's nine.

I feel a wave of anxiety. I don't understand why I'm nervous. What do I think is going to happen? This is a no-brainer. I'm talking about basic dental hygiene. Brushing, flossing, scheduling regular checkups.

I fold the notecard and write a new opening. *Good afternoon, everyone. My name is Dr. Alison McAdams. I'm a dentist in Scottsdale, Arizona, and the daughter of Bill McAdams—*

I lift my pen, reread the words, unsure of myself all over again.

Voices echo from the doorway. A group of women have just arrived, talking loudly. And behind the group comes three more: two ladies and a young man.

The ladies hold each other up, tiny and tall, dark and fair, one so frail and delicate, the other thin and slightly hunchbacked.

Ruth and Edie, accompanied by Craig.

I exhale with a sharp rush.

I wish he weren't here.

He's handsome. He is. The kind of face and frame that reality TV loves. I'm not surprised the Food Network made a show centered around the Hallahan brothers, but I'm already nervous about speaking this afternoon and I'm even more unsettled now with Craig Hallahan in the audience.

I try to focus on my notecards but the words blur.

I don't see words. I see Scottsdale. Dr. Morris. Andrew.

Andrew wasn't classically handsome. He was tall and lean, with a lean face and laughing eyes. His eyes were hazel green and they crinkled at the corners when he looked at me. I remember seeing him for the first time in dental school, his mask on, hiding his mouth and smile but his eyes were so alive in his face, so bright and full of good humor.

Everyone that met him wanted to know him. They wanted to be part of his circle. His *friend*. So did I.

And now, with him gone, I don't know what it means.

Does it take away from who he was? Does it negate everything he thought, felt, dreamed, believed?

Sometimes at night I lie on my side and hold the pillow against my chest and I pretend Andrew's behind me, holding me, and I talk to him about my day—not out loud, of course—but in my head, I tell him about the patients I saw, the work I did. I tell him about going to his parents for dinner and how different it is without him. His parents have his sisters but his sisters can't fill the hole he left.

I want him to know that we're not able to move on, not with the way things were left.

Not without understanding.

He should have talked to us. Had a conversation. That would have been the right thing to do, the fair thing, because you don't come into the world without help. You don't just belong to yourself. You have others. You have ties. Family. Community—

"Dr. McAdams."

I jerk my head up. It takes me a moment to focus. It's Craig Hallahan. "Hi. Hello."

"My aunt asked me to bring you a water. She thought you might need it during your presentation." He hands me a plastic tumbler of water. "There's a table with pitchers at the back."

"Thank you."

He exhales slowly, and it sounds suspiciously like a sigh.

I look up at him, frowning faintly. He's not my type. He's far too handsome. He's almost ten years older than me, as well as wealthy and adored by women everywhere.

Not my type.

No, my type is quirky and creative, like my Andrew.

"My aunt requests the pleasure of your company," Craig says with a hint of amusement, and maybe even pain, in his voice. "But not for her. For Ruth. It seems that Ruth thinks you are her . . . granddaughter."

"Her *granddaughter*?"

"Mmm."

"Did someone tell her I'm not?"

"Yes."

"And she still thinks I am?"

"Yes."

I glance over to Edie and Ruth where they sit in the folding chairs, and Edie is staring at me intently. It's not a friendly look. She has a piercing stare. "Draconian" might be the word.

"So what am I to do?" I ask Craig. "Go tell Ruth I'm not her granddaughter?"

He grimaces. "I'm not sure. My aunt sent me to you. I wasn't in the mood to argue."

I understand. Seniors have spent their lives perfecting tenacity. Which is just one reason why I don't want to go over. And then there's the fact that I'm nervous about speaking and would really like to review my notes.

But she's still staring at me. She fully expects to be obeyed. Dammit.

I shoot Craig a dark look and head towards her, walking briskly, summoning authority as I form my thoughts. I will be professional, polite, brief—

Ruth's hand darts out, wraps around my wrist. "Sit down," she says, tugging me towards her. "Come sit down with Grandma Ruthie."

I stiffen and pull back. "Ruth, I'm Alison. Alison McAdams—"

"Come sit, and tell me about your day. How was your day?" She gives another tug on my wrist, drawing me even closer.

Her fingers are wrapped tightly around my wrist and she has a surprisingly firm grip. I could break free but I don't want to hurt her. There's no reason to hurt her. "Ruth, it's Alison. Alison McAdams. I'm the daughter of Bill McAdams who lives here, and I'm a dentist—"

"Why don't you sit down? I want you to sit down."

"There's nowhere to sit."

"Sit on my lap. Come on. There's a good girl."

"Ruth—" I break off as she jerks me onto her lap. I practically crash into her, and I cringe, feeling huge and heavy, but her arms are around me, hugging me, holding me. "My pretty girl," she croons, rocking me. "I've missed you. Your parents don't bring you to see me enough."

And suddenly the fight leaves me.

My tension and resistance deflate and I feel foolish and exposed, but I give Ruth a hug. I hug her carefully, gently. She's tiny. She feels lost in my arms but I feel her relax. She sighs, happy.

My eyes burn and I'm able to extricate myself so that I'm now standing.

Edie looks at me, one of her brows lifting.

I don't know what the look means. I just know that I feel raw and tender on the inside.

Bereft.

None of us are immortal, and only those that die young, stay young.

B ack at the podium, I end up going with my first introduction, the one I'd scribbled while still at the breakfast table, and then ad lib, mentioning my father and how he's been here about a year now and what a wonderful place Napa Estates is.

From there it's an easy segue into discussing dental care.

"Brushing and flossing daily is essential. You want to keep your own teeth, especially if you've kept them this long." I look up, smile brightly, the confident professional smile bestowed on my patients in the office. "And the best way to do that is by using a fluoride based toothpaste. Kids aren't the only ones who need fluoride. Seniors do, too. The brushing and flossing will help fight plaque, which if left untreated, leads to tooth decay and gum disease."

The plaintive voice from the audience drowns me out. I am pretty sure it is Ruth. "What is she saying? Why is she talking?"

Someone—I think it's Edie—hushes her.

"But when is the movie going to start?"

I glance up from my notes, forehead furrowing, distracted, but also sympathetic. Poor Ruth.

I don't want to develop dementia.

I don't want Alzheimer's.

I don't want to lose my memory, or my mind. I love my brain. It's a good brain. It's served me well so far. I was always good in school. Always academic. And I knew early that I wanted to go into some field of medicine. But it wasn't until I was thirteen that I realized dentistry was the direction I should go. My parents have no idea that I chose dentistry because of my orthodontist, Dr. Clevenger.

I had such a crush on him.

He was young, early thirties, and single. He drove the coolest red convertible. I still don't know what year the car was, or if it was a Fiat or a Triumph, but it had cream leather seats and a cream dash and with his dark glossy curls and aviator glasses he looked like the ultimate of cool and sexy as he drove into work. I know, because I always had an early-morning appointment before school and I was the first patient he saw those days and Mom inevitably had me there before Dr. Clevenger arrived.

I loved him. (He didn't know it.) I loved his style, his confidence, his success, his personality. He had energy. And he had his own office.

He was the man who had everything and I was going to marry him.

My best friend, Kelly, set me straight, helping me with the math.

"You're thirteen, Ali, and he's thirty-two. By the time you're out of college, you'll be twenty or twenty-one, and he's going to be . . . oh God, *ancient*."

I didn't mind ancient. Not if he had dimples and blue eyes. And drove me around in his gleaming red convertible.

He got married when I was a freshman. I was so glad when my braces came off at the end of the year. I vowed then to never become an orthodontist. I'd be a dentist instead.

I'm suddenly aware of the faces in front of me. Everyone is waiting for my next words of wisdom. I stand taller and force myself to concentrate. "Be sure to continue seeing your dental professional once a year—"

"When is she going to stop talking?" Ruth's voice is even louder now. "I want to see the movie."

Edie is trying hard to quiet her, but Ruth doesn't want to be shushed.

"This is the movie theater." Ruth jabs her finger at the rows of empty chairs. "We're supposed to be watching a movie."

I pause, and wait. There is no point going on. No one can hear me, not at the moment anyway.

"Not today, Ruthie. Today we have a program. A guest speaker."

"What is she talking about?"

"Teeth," Edie says, patiently.

"But why teeth? She doesn't know anything about teeth."

"She's a dentist."

"My granddaughter is a dentist?"

Edie gives up. "Yes."

Ruth looks at me, puzzled, and then disappointed. "Ew."

Ew.

I go cold all over. It's not the first time I've heard that about my calling, and I know it won't be the last, but I freeze as my gaze drops to my notes, and the list of issues seniors face—tooth loss, thrush, root decay, stomatitis, darkened teeth, gum disease . . .

Do they want to know that their dry mouth is caused by reduced saliva flow, which is normal with aging, but that it could also be a side effect from cancer treatments?

Do I need to explain that their darkened teeth are due to natural changes in dentin, the tissue beneath one's tooth enamel?

That stomatitis is usually caused from bad oral hygiene, bad fitting dentures, or the buildup of candida?

Ew, is right.

For a moment I want to be anybody but Dr. Alison McAdams, but then I look up and out, and my gaze meets Edie's and she gives me a quick nod, as if to say, *Continue.*

And then I see Craig Hallahan next to her and he's smiling. At least his eyes are smiling and I feel some of the ice inside my chest ease.

I gulp a breath, and exhale.

It's okay. It's going to be okay.

I give my cards a little tap, and with another breath, I dive back in.

"There will be questions about the date of the last exam and why the patient is being seen now. The dentist will ask if you've noticed any recent changes, like sensitive teeth, loose teeth, or pain anywhere. The dentist will want to know if the patient is experiencing difficulty chewing, tasting, or swallowing."

Ruth continues to talk throughout the rest of my presentation but it no longer rattles me. Of course she doesn't understand why there is no movie. This is the movie theater, after all, and no, she doesn't understand why I'm talking about teeth. I am, in her mind, her granddaughter so that's how things stand.

Fortunately, the interruptions don't seem to surprise anyone. Everyone in the audience but Craig is a senior and they all know Ruth, and if they don't know Ruth, they've encountered memory issues before now.

I finish my speech and take questions. There are lots of questions. Well, comments and conversation. Everyone seems to have a story to share. The abscessed tooth. Adventures with dentures. Problematic bridges.

But I'm amused, and enjoying myself. And it's not because Craig Hallahan is in the audience, smiling that faint, warm, somewhat crooked smile at me.

But I suppose that faint, warm, somewhat crooked smile doesn't hurt.

EIGHT

Edie

After Alison's presentation, a nurse's aide helps Ruth into a wheelchair so she can swiftly push Ruth back to Memory Care. Ruth looks so small as she's wheeled away.

I hate it when they take her, but I can't keep her with me. I know my limits. I'm exhausted as it is. After the weekends I am always tired and spend most of Mondays in my room, recuperating.

Craig offers me his arm. I take it gratefully.

"You have an hour before dinner in the dining room," he says. "Would you like me to walk you to your room so you can rest?"

"Yes, please."

We slowly make our way down the corridor to the elevators. I'm on the second floor, in the middle of the hall. It's not that far, but suddenly I'm not sure I have the energy.

Craig squeezes my hand. "You doing okay, Aunt Edie?"

"Just a little out of breath."

"Want to rest?"

"No. I'll rest when I'm dead."

His hand squeezes mine again. "No talk like that. I'm planning a big party for you on your centennial."

"I don't think I have six more years."

"Good, because you don't even need five and a half."

I laugh shortly, shake my head. Everyone thinks Chad is the charmer but I have a soft spot for Craig. He's a dear, sweet boy, and I don't have a favorite great-nephew. They are as different as night and day, but I do enjoy them both. I don't see Chad as often. He's the social one, and always on the go, attending wine conferences and events, which is where he is now.

Craig likes traveling but he's not as fond of all the conferences. He's an introvert, and introspective. He likes his alone time. He makes the business decisions for the winery and Chad is the face of Dark Horse. People gravitate to Chad. But then, they always have.

I've always wondered why the boys chose wine making. It's not as if it runs in the family. Farming and ranching does, not on their mother's side, but their father's. They turned their father's ranch land into grapes and have done quite well for themselves.

Chad lives in the original farmhouse on the property. He fixed it up, a couple of years back, spending a small fortune on the remodel, but that's where he entertains, so it needs to be nice.

Craig also has an old house, but his is on a separate property, a couple of miles from the winery. It's an old house, a big Queen Anne with an equally large porch. It was falling down when he bought it. Everyone thought it should come down. But Craig had to restore it, and we're not talking a fashionable remodel like Chad did on his farmhouse, but a serious restoration, making it period authentic.

It's what he does on weekends. It's how he fills his free time. Every now and then he takes me there to show me what he's accomplished since my last visit. Victorian inspired wallpaper, brass kick plates and fixtures, and dark stain paneling and refinished wood trim.

In many ways the house reminds me of the home my parents bought in New Rochelle after we returned from Morocco. High ceilings, big windows, handsome proportions.

I waited years for him to marry a girl and bring her home and fill the upstairs bedrooms with babies. But he never found the right girl. And I'm worried now he might think that the McAdams girl is the one for him.

She isn't.

I tell him, too, once we're in my room. I'm not as tactful as I once was. I don't know why I should mince words when there is so little time left.

"What do you think of that McAdams girl, the dentist?" I ask him once I'm settled in my favorite armchair in the living room.

He leans against the wall, arms crossed over his chest. "She's quite pretty, and intelligent, and I think she did a really good job today."

"She doesn't strike me as a very warm person."

"I wouldn't say that. She's certainly not cold. And given her profession, I imagine she's probably very analytical."

"She's been through a bad breakup, you know. It left her quite scarred."

"And you're telling me this because . . . ?"

"I know you like brainy girls."

"Yes, I do."

"Which is why I wanted to speak to you about her. She's not the girl for you. She's got . . . issues. And you certainly don't need that, not if you're serious about settling down."

He lifts a brow. "Who said I was serious about settling down?"

"You have that big house and all those bedrooms—"

"I didn't restore the house to fill it with babies, Aunt Edie. I bought the house because it was close to the winery, dirt cheap, and had historical value."

"You're almost forty."

"This is true, but as men can father children into their sixties, I feel absolutely no sense of urgency on that front." He pushed off the wall and approached her. "Besides, you've said many a time you are not fond of babies. Have you changed your mind? Are you suddenly longing to have a great-great-grandniece or nephew to shower with affection?"

"No," I answer crossly, glaring up at him. "And I'm glad you don't feel any urgency with starting a family because I don't think Alison is the girl you've been waiting for. Especially as she doesn't even live in the area."

The corners of his mouth tug into a smile. "Especially."

NINE

Ali

I'm really busy Monday, but I sneak away from Bloom to take lunch to Dad, thinking we can have a quick bite together and catch up, but he's racing off to meet friends for cards.

"You don't usually play until later," I tell him. "It's only noon. Don't we have an hour?"

"The game's at one, but we're meeting up for lunch today."

"But you told me we'd have lunch today."

"I forgot to call and cancel. I should have remembered—"

"I picked up sandwiches for us. Your favorite. Hot pastrami and Swiss—"

"Throw it in my fridge. I'll eat it later."

I'm frustrated. Annoyed. And maybe a little bit hurt. He doesn't seem to realize how hard I try to be close to him, or how much I need to be close to him.

He sees my expression and stops short. "What? You're mad?"

"Not mad. Disappointed. You and I had a lunch date."

"I don't think it was a formal lunch date—"

"Fine. No worries. I'll put it in the fridge." I lean forward, kiss him, not wanting to quibble as it'll just frustrate me more. "I probably won't be back tonight though—"

"So you are mad."

"No. Diana just has a lot of orders today and the delivery guy is having car troubles so it's crazy in the shop."

"Well, call me later if things change."

"I will."

Back at Bloom, Diana hands me a half-dozen new orders that have come in during the past hour and while we make the arrangements we discuss the week ahead. It's going to be another stressful week, with not one wedding, but two, on Saturday. Both weddings are smaller than last Saturday's wedding, but they're also more involved in terms of the flowers, as one has requested flower garlands for the church, along with bouquets and centerpieces, and the other wants the reception tent's chandeliers decorated with floral wreaths and the tent's support poles covered in flowers as well.

Later in the afternoon, while Diana remains at the store to fulfill new orders and put together a shopping list for the flower market, I head out to deliver orders, since the delivery guy's van isn't going to run before the end of the day.

My phone's GPS makes the deliveries relatively easy and it was nice driving around the valley. The rolling hills and oak trees, interspersed with patches of farmland and old barns is certainly picturesque.

I can see why people like to visit. There is a great deal of rural charm. But I must have spent too many years growing up close to Seattle because I can't imagine living in such a quiet little place.

One of my stops is a little town nine miles north of Napa named Yountville. You can't miss it, it's on Highway 29. I'm taking flowers to a woman for her eighty-eighth birthday and I carry them into the entrance, proud of the arrangement I made. I filled in the card, too, as the order was called in this morning. It's from the woman's grandchildren. She'll be so happy to get the flowers, I think.

The sliding glass doors open and I enter a stark white lobby. The front desk is set back from the sliding doors and elderly men and women line the entrance, sitting in wooden chairs and wheel chairs, most still in pajamas and hospital-looking dressing gowns.

I suddenly feel like a little girl going to sing Christmas carols with my Girl Scout troop.

It smells here, just as it did back then, the scent of sweat and age and urine clinging to the air.

I wait at the front desk for the woman to get off the phone. I'm eager to hand the flowers over and go. And all the while I'm standing, waiting for the woman's attention, I keep thinking, Napa Estates doesn't smell.

And no, it shouldn't. It's not just a boardinghouse for the aged and infirm. It's relatively affluent and either the seniors are financially secure or someone in the family is—but here, this, this is exactly the kind of place I don't want to end up in when I'm old. This is the kind of place that haunts children when they're small.

Every year as a Brownie and Cadette, we'd go to the local convalescent homes during the holidays and sing carols to earn our merit badges, and I've never forgotten standing in doorway after doorway of rooms where gaunt old women with unseeing eyes lay in hospital beds, mouths open, smelling of old pee.

"Can I help you?" the woman asks from behind the counter.

"A delivery for Florence Steadman." I smile to hide how much

I dislike this place. I am so very glad Dad doesn't have to be here. "Birthday flowers."

The woman doesn't smile back. She sighs, irritated, as if I've brought her a set of problems she's not equipped to handle. "Just put them down."

I think about the call from her granddaughter this morning, a woman who'd phoned from Charleston and was most adamant that we send her nanna not just any flowers but really beautiful ones, and the flowers are beautiful. Dark pink roses, delicate pink peonies, and tufts of fragrant white freesias. "Would you like me to take the flowers to her room?" I offer, angry at all of this. This aging and life-and-death stuff.

The woman shrugs. "Fine. Great. She's down the hall, on the right, near the end. Her name is on the door."

I carry the flowers down, passing a dozen rooms with the doors all open, and just like when I was a little girl, the hospital beds are filled with gaunt-looking men and women, and I don't know if it's because I've been spending more time with Dad lately, or if it's just because I'm thirty and not nine, but today I feel like they watch me curiously, hopefully, wondering if something good and interesting might happen.

I reach Florence Steadman's room, and yes, her name is on the door. I knock lightly and step in. A tiny lady in a pale aqua bed jacket sits propped up in bed, her long white hair hanging over her shoulder. Her eyes are closed. Her mouth is slightly open. I can hear her snoring faintly.

I don't want to wake her. Quietly I go to the side of her bed, and even more quietly roll her hospital table close to her side and put the flowers there, next to her water container with the straw, so she'll see them when she wakes up.

This is Lindsey's nanna. Lindsey used to love Saturday after-noons at her nanna's. They'd bake together, cookies and cakes, and Nanna would also make Lindsey special matching dresses for her and her favorite doll.

I take a moment to look around the room. A balloon bouquet with a miniature teddy bear is on the windowsill. There's another floral arrangement, too, by the balloons, a small cluster of yellow and white daisies in a yellow teacup with a happy face.

The flowers are so far away I don't know how Florence is supposed to see them.

I'm turning to leave when Florence's eyes open. She looks at me. I'm suddenly not sure what to do, or say. "Hello."

She looks at me carefully. "Are you an aide?"

"No, I'm from Bloom Florist. I'm delivering flowers from your granddaughter Lindsey."

"Oh, that's nice." The woman looks at the flowers. "Those are very pretty."

"Are you having a nice birthday?"

"I am. Thank you."

"I'm glad."

And then I'm leaving, hurrying out to walk quickly back down the long sterile white hall and through the sliding glass doors to the parking lot.

Life is hard, I think.

And then it's over.

I go see Dad immediately after. He's in his room, having had an early dinner, and he's got his feet up in his favorite recliner.

He's surprised to see me. "I didn't think you were coming by again today."

"I wondered how your game went this afternoon."

"We won."

"Which should make you happy."

"It does."

I lean over and kiss him. "Mom hated that chair," I say, flopping down on the couch.

"I don't know why, as she bought it for me."

"It's such a guy chair. Men love their La-Z-Boys."

"Your mother secretly wanted one, too, but she wouldn't ever admit it."

"How do you know she wanted one?"

"Because every time I came home, I'd find her in mine."

I smile, because I can picture her in his chair, reading and doing paperwork. She did spend a lot of time in that chair, now that I think about it.

As if aware of my thoughts, Dad says, "I talk to her all the time."

My heart falls. "Do you?"

He nods, his gaze still glued to the TV.

"So how is she?" I ask, trying to be funny, but failing. I miss her, and Andrew. I miss how life used to be. I'd once felt so stable and confident. I knew where I was going and what I was supposed to do.

Now I'm just lucky if I can put one foot in front of the other.

"It makes me feel close to her, talking to her."

"I'm glad you talk to her."

"Do you?" he asks, after a moment. "Talk to her?"

My gut churns. I feel guilty. I talk to her a little bit, probably about the same amount I talk to Andrew.

Not that I always talk to Andrew. Sometimes I yell at him.

Or ignore him.

I'm still so mad at him. He had no right leaving the way he did.

You don't just get to quit. You don't get to opt out. Life isn't a survey.

My eyes burn and I tilt my head back, press a hand to my eyes, covering them. Not going to cry. It won't help to cry. "Do you think she can hear you?" I ask, my voice suddenly husky.

"Yes."

"Good." I wait, fighting tears, fighting hard. "Then will you tell her I love her?"

I arrive back home to 33 Poppy Lane just after sunset, the house swallowed in lavender shadows. Twilight is bittersweet. Neither here nor there.

I sit in the car and just look at it, knowing it's just a matter of time before Dad does sell it. There is no point in him hanging on to it. California real estate has bounced back following the recession. Dad should put it on the market while he can make a nice return on his investment.

Should he sell it, he'll want to spruce up the entrance . . . add flowers to the plain green hedges, pretty colorful perennials to add some curb appeal.

During Dad and Mom's first year here, Mom planted dozens of dahlia bulbs with zinnias and gerbera daisies in the front. Her summer garden was spectacular. Her only regret was that it was such a quiet street, no one would ever see the summer color show.

One day I'll plant a garden like that. A garden full of orange, red, and purple flowers.

Diana wasn't exaggerating. It is a busy, stressful week, and now on Thursday she's driven to San Francisco's flower market to purchase all the flowers for this weekend's weddings, since she can get a much better deal there than in Napa.

She's left me in charge of Bloom for the day. I told her I didn't think it was a great idea. She said it was me or close the shop since the other part-time girl she hired is flakey and can't be trusted to open, take money, or close. So here I am at Bloom, making sure

the part-time girl is making up the right arrangement while I schedule the deliveries with the driver and his unreliable vehicle.

Diana is back by four and she begs me to run a box of candles,
glass hurricane vases, and a huge urn filled with freshly cut
branches of blooming lilacs out to Dark Horse Winery, to the
caterer who has just placed a desperate call for flowers because
the other florist failed to deliver.

"I'd go myself," Diana says, "but my car is filled with thousands
of dollars of flowers for Saturday's weddings and I've got to get
them into fresh water in the refrigerator."

I call Dad to tell him I'll be late for dinner and he says not to
worry, he'll just see me tomorrow but I should know that Edie is
looking for me. Ruth has a dentist appointment tomorrow and
Edie would like me to take Ruth to it.

"I can't, Dad. Diana's desperately short on help and we're going
to be working late as it is tomorrow, getting everything ready for
the two weddings on Saturday."

"Ruth's scared," Dad answers. "Edie thinks she'd be calmer if
you accompanied her. Ruth likes you."

"I would if it were another day, but tomorrow is impossible."

"Would you at least come by in the morning and tell Edie? She
never asks for anything, Alison, and maybe if you talk to her, she
can reschedule?"

"I promise I'll come by early and talk to Edie."

I arrive at Dark Horse Winery and am met by a frazzled-looking
caterer. "Thank God," she says, wiping her hands on her white
apron. "We had no centerpieces, no flowers, nothing."

"Where do you want everything?"

"Three hurricanes with candles on the main buffet table,

another one on each of the small rounds. If there are any extras, I'll find a home for them."

"And the flowers?"

"I'm going to leave them as they are, in that silver urn, and put it on the table at the entrance for wow factor."

She rushes off, back to her food prep, and I'm putting the candles where she wanted them when I spot Craig Hallahan heading my way.

"When did you become the deliveryman?" he asks.

"When the deliveryman couldn't deliver." I smile. "How are you?"

"Good. Need a hand?"

"I've got an enormous urn of lilacs in the back of my car. If you want to put them on that table at the entrance to the patio, that would be great."

He does, and then helps me carry the empty cardboard boxes back to the car. "Have a lot more deliveries?" he asks.

"Nope. You're it." I bury my hands in my jean pockets. I feel a little sweaty and grimy after the long day. But it's a good feeling. It's so much better than sitting around Dad's room watching golf with him in the afternoon.

"What's next? Going to see your dad?"

I shake my head. "I'll probably grab something to eat on the way home, or just go home and run."

"You run a lot?"

"Just enough to keep me from going crazy."

He smiles, and his blue eyes are warm. "Never underestimate the power of crazy."

I laugh. "That's funny."

His teeth flash white as he fishes into his pocket and retrieves car keys. "If you're not expected anywhere, come join me for dinner."

"I couldn't."

"Why not?"

I glance down at my T-shirt, stained orange in spots from my attempt to remove the lily stamens earlier. Diana had done it without mishap yesterday. I clearly hadn't paid enough attention to her lesson. "I really can't go out like this."

"I was going to cook. Super simple. Shrimp scampi and a glass of wine."

I hesitate. I'm not sure I'm ready for this.

"We'd be eating in less than thirty minutes and you can be on your way right after," he says.

I'm tempted, but I don't want romance. I can't imagine replacing Andrew, but at the same time, I'd like a friend. Someone kind, someone interesting. "Thirty minutes?"

"It takes ten minutes to prep, ten minutes to cook, and I live just five minutes away."

"You've given yourself a five minute cushion."

"I'll have to give Bruiser some love. He's very demanding when I first come home, but as soon as I've pet him, he'll crash again on the couch, and go right back to sleep."

"Bruiser?"

"My bulldog."

I love bulldogs. They look scary but they have the sweetest personalities. "How's his overbite?"

"Huge."

"Does he drool?"

"And farts."

I laugh. "I have to meet him."

I follow Craig in his work truck back down Highway 29 about two miles before he takes a right down a nondescript lane.

Grapes line both sides of the narrow road and I don't know what I expected Craig's house to look like, but I certainly wasn't anticipating a huge brick Queen Anne house with gables, angled bay windows, a widow's walk and tower.

I climb out of my car and tip my head back to take it all in. Craig slams his truck door and comes towards me, boots crunching in the gravel driveway.

"This is your place?" I say.

He nods and glances at the house. The sun has dropped behind the hill, outlining the curve in silver and gold. The glow of gold on the horizon makes the house look dark in comparison.

"Let me turn on the porch lights."

I follow him up the front steps. There are five, and on the top stair I see that the front porch wraps all the way around the side.

"Do you live here by yourself?" I ask, as he unlocks the front door.

"No." He smiles at me, and holds the door open. "Bruiser's here, too."

And yes, there's Bruiser, a huge, muscular male bulldog with dark brown spots on a white body and a big brown patch over his left eye, dancing in the doorway, greeting Craig with absolute joy.

He does his welcome home dance for about sixty seconds, and then with his tongue hanging out, he collapses on the floor.

Craig steps over him and leads me through the paneled central hall, down a narrow corridor, to the kitchen in the back. "What did I say?" he asks, flipping on lights as we go. "Unbridled enthusiasm and then nothing."

"It was a very good happy dance."

"He's a great dog. Loves sleeping, eating, and car rides."

"You can't ask for more than that."

Craig washes up at the sink and then opens his refrigerator and draws out a bottle of white wine. He shows me the bottle. "White okay?"

I nod, but it's not a Dark Horse label. "You don't make white wines?"

"We do, but I'm always trying different wines, and I was just in Italy and came home with a few new favorites. This Pinot Grigio is really crisp and light and cuts nicely through the butter and garlic of scampi. But I also have a great Sardinia white, which is a medium to full body wine and can handle the sauce."

I listen, rather dazed and enchanted because I don't know wine at all. I'm not a foodie and it's almost as if he's speaking a foreign language. But I like it. "Whatever you want. Might as well let you know now, but I'm not very sophisticated when it comes to wine. I usually drink light beer or those fruity flavored wines they sell in six packs at the grocery store."

"I will not hold it against you," he promises, uncorking the bottle and pouring us two glasses.

He gives me my glass, directs me to a chair at the big farm table and tells me to relax.

I sit down and sip my wine and watch him. From the doorway Bruiser snores loudly. Craig glances at me as he puts a pot of water on for pasta, and then while the water comes to a boil, he swiftly deveins the fresh shrimp, pats them dry on a paper towel and gives them a good shake of salt and pepper.

He adds the pasta to the boiling water, gives the noodles a stir. Soon butter is making little crackling noises in a medium sauté pan and Craig adds the shrimp, and then a minute later, the freshly minced garlic.

The shrimp comes off, into a bowl, and then he scrapes the browned bits off the bottom of the pan, adds vermouth and lemon juice to the bits of butter and garlic, and sets that aside to drain the pasta.

And then it's time to eat.

We carry our plates and glasses of wine outside to his garden right off the kitchen. Globe-stringed lights stretch across the walled garden. There's a little fountain trickling water on one brick wall. We sit down at a small wrought iron table and Bruiser pushes open the back door, and staggers down the steps to flop down at Craig's feet.

He reaches down to scratch Bruiser's ear. Bruiser sighs with pleasure, before emitting an ungentlemanly fart.

"He has no sense of decorum," Craig says, grinning.

"Bruiser likes keeping it real."

Craig lifts his wine glass. "To you, Alison McAdams."

"Why to me?" I ask.

His blue gaze meets mine and holds. He's still smiling, a half smile, but his expression is strangely serious. "Why not?" he answers.

I don't know what to say to that.

I have nothing to say to that.

I drink my wine and we eat, and as we eat, I feel like I'm somewhere far away. This could be Charleston, or a garden in the French Quarter of New Orleans, or even in Provence.

"This is lovely," I say.

Craig has refilled our glasses and the meal is over and I feel like Bruiser, lazy and content.

"I'm glad you enjoyed it." Craig stretches and settles back into his chair. "I'm glad you came. It's nice to have some company. Usually it's just Bruiser and me."

"Have you ever been married?" I ask. I hate the question but I'm curious. He's good-looking, and successful. He owns a winery. He's a great cook. He has this incredible house and a wonderful dog. Why is there no woman right now?

"No. You?"

I shake my head, slightly disappointed that in answering so quickly he turned the focus from him to me. But I'm still curious. I want to know more about him. "Was this a family house?"

"No. It had been abandoned years ago and it sat here, empty, falling into ruin. Kids would come and graffiti the outside, or break off the boards covering the windows and vandalize the inside. I couldn't stand it. I thought she deserved better. So I bought her and have been fixing her up ever since. It's definitely a labor of love. I do most of the work myself."

"How long ago did you buy it?"

"Just before I got Bruiser. So it's been a little over five years."

"You must love this place a lot."

"I do, and I enjoy carpentry and everything else that's gone into restoring the house. If I hadn't become a vintner, I would have been a contractor. I like using my hands. I like making things, creating things. It's good for the soul." He sips his wine, swallows, and waits a moment before asking, "Why did you choose to become a dentist?"

I slouch lower in my chair, and cross my feet at the ankles so I can see the tips of my shoes. "I made the decision in junior high."

"Really?"

"I had a crush on my orthodontist. He was young and sexy. He had swagger."

I grin, embarrassed even as I laugh at myself. "I liked everything about him. He had a really cool office and he drove this amazing car and everyone in his practice hurried around doing the hard work and the boring work while he'd make all the decisions."

I bite my lip, my cheeks hot. "I loved the idea that I could have my own office and a team that'd execute my decisions. I wanted to play rock and alternative music while I worked and take long lunches when I could go play tennis and then come back to the office refreshed. It would be a great life . . . I'd be the boss and happy and people would want to be me . . ." My voice fades. My face burns. I'm uncomfortable with my innocent fantasies.

And no, I don't have that life.

I work for an old-fashioned dentist who doesn't believe in anything cool, progressive, or new. He's a good man but not open to change. It's his way or the highway. It's not the practice I ever wanted for myself. It's not the life I would have picked.

I pause, and draw a slow, painful breath.

Maybe it wasn't the life Andrew wanted, either.

"So you became a dentist because you had a crush on your orthodontist," Craig repeats, his tone teasing.

"Pretty much."

"And from what I understand, you've just been through a pretty bad breakup."

"Is that what your great-aunt told you?"

"More or less."

I exhale and set my wine down. My eyes are hot and gritty and there's a lump in my throat now, too. "I guess you could say it was a pretty bad breakup. He, uh, died six weeks before our wedding."

Craig winces. "I'm sorry."

"Yeah. Me, too." I study my wine, where the line of liquid hits the glass. I keep my gaze fixed to keep from looking at Craig, not wanting to see whatever it is that might be in his face. And then for reasons I don't understand I blurt, "He killed himself. Hung himself at home, from the chandelier in our entry hall."

Craig says nothing.

I exhale, my chest tight, my throat squeezing closed. I fight for air. My eyes burn, but it's not sadness. It's rage. Rage at what Andrew put me through.

To find him like that.

To walk in with a paper bag of ice cream and . . . and . . .

"I will never forget what I saw." I cross my arms over my chest, my hands beneath my armpits, nails digging into my ribs. "I'll be your great-aunt Edie's age and it'll still be there, burned into my mind." I finally look at Craig from across the table. "You're a man. Tell me. How could he do that to me? If he loved me—" I break off, hating myself for saying anything at all. It was the wine that loosened my tongue. The wine that made me speak. I jump to my feet. Bruiser lifts his head, looks at me.

I'm not going to cry here. I'm going to get in my car and drive home and go to bed without shedding a single damn tear.

"It's late," I say roughly. "I should go."

He gets to his feet, sets his wine glass next to mine. I think he's going to walk me to my car but instead he hugs me. A warm, hard silent hug that takes me completely by surprise.

And then he walks me to my car.

"Are you okay to drive?" he asks as I open the car door.

"I didn't even drink two full glasses of wine."

"Maybe I should rephrase that." He hesitates a moment, brow furrowed. "Are you okay?"

I hesitate even longer. "Not yet," I say finally. "But I will be. One day." I look up, meet his eyes. "Right?"

B ack at the house on Poppy Lane I drag a lounge chair from the patio out onto the lawn and lie there in the garden, hands behind my head, staring up at the stars.

I look for the Milky Way. And then the Big Dipper. The Little Dipper. Orion's Belt.

Hello, Andrew. Hello my love, my heart.

Do you know how angry I am with you?

Do you have any idea how upset I am?

Do you have any idea how much I miss you?

Do you know how many things I'd like to say to you? How many things I'd like to ask you? But mostly, *why*?

And is it better now? Is it what you thought it'd be?

Is it the peace you needed?

The quiet you wanted?

The stars glow and glimmer. Countless pricks of pure white light. And that moon, waxing and waning and tonight luminous, a stunning geisha flawless even without her makeup.

I am sure Andrew is happier.

But what about his parents? What about his sisters? What about the nieces and nephews he left behind? How are they to ever be totally happy again?

And me . . . I don't want another man. Andrew can't be replaced and won't be. But it's not because Andrew was so perfect—he wasn't—it's because I can't do this again. Can't feel. Can't love. Can't care.

Love is too capricious.

It's selfish and it wounds. It bites. It cuts. It's too full of suffering and strife.

Andrew.

Look what you did to me. Look what you did . . . you took the best of me and threw it away, like trash rotting in a Dumpster.

Or a dead animal on the side of a road.

And then I think of Bruiser, with his sturdy body and ridiculous overbite and I wish I could wrap my arms around his stocky neck and give him a hug, and hold him, and hold him until some of the ice inside me thaws.

I wake up cold.

I'm still on the lounge chair. It's still dark but there is moisture in the air. Shivering, I swing my legs over the side of the chaise and put them down in the damp grass. Dawn must be close.

I've survived another night.

I'm still here.

In the house I climb into bed and feel Mom. She's with me. She believes in me. All that potential, she used to say, brushing my hair back from my face. So much potential . . .

TEN

Ali

Edie is downstairs in the Napa Estates lobby when I arrive the next morning with warm buttery croissants for Dad. Dad doesn't have much of a sweet tooth, but he does like croissants.

She rises from her chair, and comes towards me. "You're early," she says, with a glance at the clock on the wall.

"Early?" I repeat puzzled, noting that she's in a skirt and blouse, the white blouse tucked into the waistband of her pleated gray skirt. Her hair is neatly combed and drawn into a knot and she's even wearing a string of pearls. She's dressed and ready to go and I suddenly remember my conversation with Dad yesterday about accompanying Edie and Ruth to the dentist.

My heart falls. I'd forgotten all about it, and yet, from the way Edie's expression brightens when she sees me, she believes I'm going with them.

"She's not ready yet," Edie says, hands smoothing the sides of her skirt. "The aides are still getting her dressed. She really should have breakfast first, too, since she might not want to eat, after—"

"Edie, I am so sorry, but I can't take Ruth today." I have to interrupt. I can't let her continue. "I've promised a friend, my friend Diana, that I'd help her today—"

"But Ruth needs you."

"She doesn't need me—"

"But she does. And we were planning on you going with us. I spoke with your father about it—"

"I know, and I forgot. I'm so sorry."

"So you're not here to go with us?"

"No, I'm just here dropping off croissants for Dad." I jiggle the bag. "I'm sorry."

"You're sorry?"

"Yes."

"Well, if you're sorry, you'll drop off those croissants and come. We're planning on it. And we need you."

"Edie, Ruth doesn't need me, she needs her dentist, the one that's going to take care of her pain. There's a special van that will take you, and the driver will help Ruth and you inside."

"But your father said you'd do it. He said you'd help us."

I hold my breath, determined not to let her rattle me. She's very strong willed, and she can be quite intimidating but surely even Edie realizes I can't be in two places at one time. "He shouldn't have committed me. He should have remembered I've been working at a local florist, helping a friend out who is very short staffed, and today we have to do all the flowers for two weddings tomorrow."

"But Ruth won't go to the dentist if you don't go. And she needs to go. She's in terrific pain. Her tooth aches."

"I'm sure one of the aides could go with you today."

"She won't go without you. For whatever reason, Ruth trusts you—"

"Because she thinks I'm her granddaughter."

"Yes. Sometimes she does, but if it means you can get her to go . . . ?"

"I'm not going to pretend to be her granddaughter. That's terrible."

"How is it so terrible? You're making her happy—"

"Because her idea of happy and mine are two different things."

Edie stares me down. "Is this because she made you sit on her lap in the theater?"

"It was not comfortable, Edie."

"Ruth craves affection."

"But not from me."

"You don't like affection?"

"It's uncomfortable being hugged and kissed by a stranger." I draw a quick, sharp breath. "What about you? Would you like strangers hugging and kissing you? Sitting on your lap?"

"It's different. I don't have memory issues."

"Well, neither do I." I glance at my watch. It's nine. Diana will already be in the shop. I should be there, too. I start towards the exit. "I'm sorry I can't help—"

"It wouldn't kill you to do something for someone else," Edie interrupts.

I freeze in the doorway, my entire body stiffening until I feel hard and cold from the inside out.

I blink, taken aback. "That was mean and uncalled for, and I am helping someone in need. Diana is in a jam—"

"*Flowers?*" She snorts derisively, her blue eyes fierce, bright. "You're telling me you can't help Ruth because you have to muck about with flowers?"

I should walk away now.

I should.

I should remember that Edie is ninety-four and counting.

I should remember that my father is fond of her and she's Craig's great-aunt.

I should remember she's upset because she's protective of Ruth and she thinks I've refused to help Ruth.

But I don't remember any of that because I'm so tired of trying to keep it together so that no one worries about me, or is troubled by my grief.

And so I come swinging right back at Edie.

"Maybe more people would help Ruth," I say tightly, "if they didn't have to deal with *you*."

And then I leave, walking quickly to my car. But I don't feel better.

I've just hit below the belt, and worse, I've hit a ninety-four-year-old lady.

ELEVEN

Edie

I can't sleep tonight. That McAdams girl has upset me. I shouldn't let her upset me. She's what? Twenty-eight? Twenty-nine? What does she know of the world? What does she know of life?

It's not easy, living. But it is what it is.

It is what it is.

For a long time I sit, and stare at the small framed etching of Rothenburg by Ernst Geissendörfer. I bought it in Germany on the trip with Ellie back in the late seventies. It was to replace the beautiful black-and-white etchings that Franz and I had bought for our home, following our honeymoon in Bavaria.

Ernst's original etchings were all black-and-white. This one is colored and quite pretty but it's not as valuable, having been produced after the war.

Looking at it, I think more of Ellie than Franz. I wish I'd been a better sister to Ellie. Perhaps if I'd been the younger sister I would have been a good sister. Perhaps I would have admired Ellie the way she always admired me.

Or how she admired me until I married Franz. No one understood that. I'm still not sure anyone does. That's why Ellie wanted me to publish my journals. She thought people should see. She thought people should know.

But I've gone through them, the early journals and the later ones, from the last two years I kept during the war, and I don't think they say anything that explains what was really happening. How could they? I was just a girl and couldn't understand what was happening.

Slowly I rise, and make my way to the small spare bedroom, turning on the light to look into the room I think of as my office. There's a narrow twin bed against the wall, with an upholstered spread and bolsters, a simple oak desk that once belonged to Father, and a large closet filled with filing cabinets and stacked cardboard boxes that I have Chad and Craig vacuum for me once a month to keep from collecting dust.

The boys are good like that, always happy to help me. Sometimes when they visit, we pull out photos and letters. We are a shell of a family. Ellie only ever had one child, and Elizabeth had just the two boys.

They—Ellie and Elizabeth and the boys—were the reason I moved to California after the war. Well, Ellie was the reason. The others didn't come along for years. But Ellie was working for the *San Francisco Chronicle* as a reporter and hoping to become a feature writer. She thought if she could write enough bylines she could maybe find work in New York, and then get into publishing.

I couldn't imagine returning to New York after the war. I couldn't be anywhere that people might know me. I feared what they might say . . . both behind my back and to my face. I needed to be invisible. Anonymous.

In California I could be.

Almost right away I found work doing translation, and I did that for several years before earning a teaching credential and becoming a language teacher in Northern California schools.

I liked teaching, even though I know the students weren't always very fond of me. I know they complained that I assigned too much work, and had terribly high standards. I was also very strict and lacked a sense of humor. But I was there to teach, to help them succeed so they could get jobs and go to college and have a life that mattered. A life of meaning.

Sliding open the louvered doors on the closet, I take in the stacked boxes with the neat ivory labels, each label typed, carefully identifying the contents.

Baby Albums & Keepsakes 1920-1925
Father's Foreign Service 1925-1934
Music Studies 1934-1939
Berlin 1940-1944
San Francisco 1944-1949
Teaching I 1950-1964
Teaching II 1965-1980
Germany 1978

There are more recent files, but those are all in the filing cabinet. Labeled, of course. Once I retired from teaching in 1981, I did a little bit of tutoring and some freelance translation work here and there, but I didn't really want to work anymore. I had had enough teaching and translating. I was ready to return to my music. It was, after all, my first passion, and next to Franz, my one true love.

Each box has letters and papers, photos and souvenirs from the time period. I am not a hoarder but I have compulsively collected cards and letters, along with playbills, ticket stubs, and even the paper slips from Chinese fortune cookies.

I don't know why I've kept everything. Maybe it's because I don't have children, who would be a living legacy. Instead, everything is organized here, preserved for . . . what?

Perhaps it's time to edit some of these items. Consolidate. These old envelope boxes I use for storage could be crushed and recycled. There's no point in saving items no one will ever want to look at.

Studying the labeled boxes I know which ones I could easily discard. The boxes from the teaching years. The box of translation work. Even the trip in 1978—although maybe my grandnephews might want a few of the photos since I went with their grandmother—could go.

It would be harder for me to throw out the boxes from the war. In fact, I know I couldn't, not unless I saved the journals as they are all I have of Franz.

I reach for the box labeled Music Studies, and carry it to the oak desk. I sit down and lift the lid, and draw out the leather diary hidden beneath the bundles of letters, each stack tied with string.

I don't look at this diary often. I was so young when I started it. A seventeen-year-old girl who'd only just graduated from high school.

Flipping through the first twenty pages, I skip most of the entries about my boyfriend Patrick, the Harvard Law student who proposed Valentine's Day 1937. My parents were upset—I was far too young to think of marriage—and would only give their blessing if I promised to follow through with my music studies in Germany at the Hoch, where I'd been accepted for a certificate in music and composition.

Initially Patrick didn't have an issue with me spending a year abroad, but his attitude changed as my departure approached.

I stop turning pages and read.

June 6, 1937

Patrick and I quarreled terribly last night. I cried all night. He and I have had disagreements before but never like this. He doesn't think I should go abroad to study music next year. He doesn't think it's essential, especially in light of the growing tensions in Europe.

June 7, 1937

Mother keeps asking if everything is fine. Apparently I'm not myself. I tell her everything is wonderful and then spend the next hour at the piano playing the most melancholic music imaginable.

June 8, 1937

Spent so long at the piano that Father finally asked me to cease and desist with the funeral hymns. I told him they weren't funeral hymns but requiems.

June 9, 1937

Mother wonders when Patrick will call or come by. I promptly burst into tears as I am wondering the same thing.

June 10, 1937

Patrick showed up this afternoon. At first he was so very stern and grave that I was certain he'd come to break off the engagement. He asked to see my hand and I was shaking, thinking he was about to take the ring back. Instead he lifted my hand to his lips, kissing it most tenderly. He said he loves me very much and believes in his heart that we are meant to be together, but he feels my parents have given me too much freedom and independence. If our marriage is to work, then we must learn to yield and compromise. I was so happy to sit with him on the couch, to feel his arm around me and be showered with kisses that he could have said anything . . . but now I can't help worrying that when he says we must learn to yield and compromise that he actually means me.

June 13, 1937

Patrick and I went for a walk this evening once it'd cooled down, and everything was pleasant until he remarked that his father says I am obviously attractive and intelligent, but he's concerned I might be "overeducated." (!!) He said his father found me a bit too lively. I'm aghast. I fully expected Patrick to defend me but he agrees with his father that I have not been given enough discipline and direction. (!!!) I couldn't respond. I was close to tears the entire walk home and didn't trust myself to speak, lest I broke down.

June 14, 1937

Father and I had a long talk this morning about Patrick and Mr. McDougal. Father doesn't seem particularly surprised by Mr. McDougal's opinions, and has said for me not to judge him too severely, as Mr. McDougal hasn't had the luxury of travel and higher education, and might not place the same value on music and the arts, either.

This gave me much to think about.

I could give up books and the theater but I couldn't ever give up my music.

June 15, 1937

Father, Mother, and I have been trying to decide the best date for sailing, and we've decided that we should try to book a one-way passage for me for late July or early August. If Father comes with me, we'd probably sail on the Washington *on July 27th so he could see his friends in Vienna at the embassy. If Mother accompanies me, we'd leave early August so she could see Ellie settled into her summer camp. Ellie doesn't want to go to summer camp but Mother isn't about to leave her to her own devices for all of August. Ellie has become a terrible flirt. Everyone comments on her beauty and she hasn't even yet turned fifteen.*

June 16, 1937

Patrick came over this afternoon while Mother was on the phone with the travel agent, inquiring about availability on one of the USL ships. She'd been on the phone quite a long time, as it seems we've put off booking our passage until rather late in the season. But Mother is very good at dealing with travel agents and such, after all the years overseas, married to a member of the Foreign Service, and of course there are options, just not the options Mother wanted.

Patrick is there with me as Mother jots down fares and sailing dates for the Washington *and* Manhattan. *The* Roosevelt *and* Harding *have nothing but Third Class, which we wouldn't take. Father isn't particularly fussy but he does like to be comfortable when traveling, particularly crossing the Atlantic.*

It's not until Mother leaves to the kitchen to go consult with Father about the options that I realize Patrick is in a state.

He'd thought I'd given up the idea of studying abroad. He thought we were in agreement about the future. I told him we are—we've agreed to marry next year, after he finishes law school. Yes, he answered, but that plan doesn't include me going away.

He left after giving me an ultimatum. It's him, or Hamburg. I can't have both.

June 19, 1937

I cried all night. Mother says to give Patrick time. He just needs to calm down. Father says that I should listen to Mother. She is Mother and knows. But then later he pulls me aside and tells me that regardless of what happens, it's better to have this happen now, than later. The whole point of a long engagement is for people to discover if they are truly compatible before they marry.

Father means well but I feel worse.

June 20, 1937

Patrick came over tonight. He was cool, almost aloof in the beginning, so I swallowed my pride and told Patrick I was sorry for the fight and hoped we could put it behind us. He visibly thawed and kissed me, saying I'd given him a great deal to think about but he was relieved that I'd "come round," saying that it was important to him that I respect him and could yield to his leadership, as a horse can't have two heads, and a car can't have two drivers, and so on.

That's when I realized he thought I'd given up on going to study abroad.

He looked so happy and had become so affectionate that I dreaded telling him the truth because I knew the moment I did, it would ruin everything.

I don't even remember how I told him. I just did. Very fast.

He held his hand out for the ring and he left. I don't think he even said good-bye. This time I know he won't be back. Not unless I abandon my studies and go crawling back to him to beg forgiveness.

And I won't do that.

June 21, 1937

Ellie was the one who first noticed that I'm no longer wearing my ring. She was pestering me with questions that I wouldn't answer. Mother finally told her to leave me alone.

June 23, 1937

I'd always thought Mother liked Patrick a great deal, but the fact that Patrick would demand I give up my music infuriates her. "But you gave up your music for Father," I remind her.
  "But he never asked me to," she answered.

June 27, 1937

Father is glad the engagement has ended. He says I'm far too young to marry, and even if I were ten years older, Patrick wouldn't be the right one.
  Father also said that he'd vowed to not interfere in Patrick's and my relationship since his parents had interfered in his (Had they? That was news to me!), but since Patrick and I aren't together anymore he feels at liberty to say that educated women are far more interesting than uneducated women and he would view his life as a failure if Ellie and I should turn out to be dependent, weak-minded young women.
  I burst into tears. I have the best father in the world.

July 1, 1937

We've booked the last Cabin Class room on the Manhattan's July 13th sailing.

It's finally been decided that it's Mother accompanying me, not Father. I can't say anything to them, but I'm secretly disappointed. I have far more fun with Father. And he doesn't get migraines.

July 3, 1937

The radio news broadcast tonight said that Amelia Earhart is missing. It's been twenty-four hours since anyone has heard from her. She was supposed to have landed for refueling. Instead she's disappeared over the Pacific. So sad.

July 4, 1937

The search is underway to locate Amelia and her plane. There is still a good chance she could be alive . . . or at least, that's what Mother and I were saying before Father said he thought it most unlikely, considering the location of the island and the wide expanse of sea.

Tonight the entire family attended a picnic and outdoor concert at Iona in honor of the nation's birthday. Patrick McDougal was there. He pretended I wasn't there.

It's after two now and I can't sleep but I refuse to cry. He's not worth it. He's not.

July 12, 1937

We leave tomorrow. Can't wait. I am so ready to leave all of this behind.

Patrick dropped by tonight to say good-bye. I was shocked to see him here and everyone quickly found other things to do so he and I could be alone. He didn't stay long and he was oddly formal and aloof while here, but just before he left, he kissed my cheek and told me to be careful. Perhaps I'm imagining it, or only wanting to imagine it, but as he leaned in to kiss me, I thought he looked quite sad.

July 13, 1937

On the ship and settled into our room. The luggage was here when we arrived and our butler introduced himself. I think he's Greek. Mother thinks he might be Turkish or Croatian. Both of us agree that he's quite handsome, as well as most out of bounds. Mother doesn't need to worry about me falling for a handsome foreigner. I've had enough of men. I'm ready to focus on my music studies.

July 14, 1937

Being at sea makes me think of Amelia Earhart. There has still been no sign of her plane, but now that we are in the middle of the ocean with just water, water everywhere, I can't imagine how one would ever find her plane. It's so morbid but I find myself wondering if she was even aware she was in trouble . . . did she know she was going to crash? Did she try to save herself at all . . . ?

I don't like these thoughts. They are not cheerful at all, but I don't feel cheerful when I think about poor Amelia and selfish Patrick and how very disappointing life can be.

July 15, 1937

Mother and I spent the day reading in deck chairs and then came in to dress for dinner. It was a lovely dinner, too, and Mother was in such good spirits. She seems so gay on this trip, as if she's just a girl and not a forty-year-old mother of two.

July 16, 1937

Can't write much, far too seasick. We were woken in the night by the groaning and rocking of the ship. Even this morning it continues to list. Our cabin steward said it is quite normal and Mother puts on a brave face, but I think even she is a little afraid.

July 17, 1937

Thank goodness it's just a six-day crossing. The weather is terrible and the ship is rocking so much that if the furniture weren't fastened to the floor, everything would be flying across the room.

Mother and I spent most of yesterday in bed, but because our cabin is in the middle of the ship, we are mostly queasy but not as violently ill as some.

This afternoon the ocean was a little calmer and Mother and I roused ourselves and went outside to sit on the promenade deck and get some fresh air. While sitting there, she'd commented that she wishes we had splurged and taken the Queen Mary over, certain we would have been more comfortable. One of the gentlemen seated on the deck near us overheard and corrected Mother, saying it's not the ship's fault, it's the sea's. Mother was most irritated, murmuring to me that men always thought they knew everything and yet isn't it ironic that women bring life forth.

July 21, 1937

We've reached Southampton but we don't disembark here. We have another few days before we'll reach Hamburg. We are both ready to get off the ship!

July 24, 1937

Have checked into a hotel in Hamburg. Mother has one of her headaches and is in bed resting. I'm eager to go explore but don't feel right leaving Mother alone.

August 9, 1937

We can't possibly attend everything at the Salzburg Music Festival, but Mother and I are certainly going to try! We were poring over the program and we've missed quite a few things, but there is still so much in the final three weeks of the festival. Don Giovanni, Faust, Elektra . . . 9 concerts, 4 recitals, 7 serenades and so much more I can't list now, as I'm very sleepy but also very relaxed. Lovely, lovely Salzburg. So glad now that Mother insisted on bringing me!

August 17, 1937

Mother says the revival of Falstaff was the best she's ever seen. She is enjoying herself enormously. We attend every concert and then when we leave, Mother hums the music for the rest of the evening.

August 21, 1937

Saw the most gorgeous production tonight of Die Zauberflöte. Eight more days before our little holiday together ends.

August 23, 1937

Mother was crying tonight during the concert. At intermission I tried to get her to tell me what's wrong. She said this has been the happiest she's been in a long time. I didn't know what to say. I had always thought she was so very happy with Father.

August 27, 1937

Today is our last day in Salzburg. The porter has taken our luggage already to the train station so we are off to buy a few souvenirs for Mother to take home with her.

On the train in our car. While shopping earlier, Mother confided that as much as she loves Father, she wishes she had continued her music, and would have if I hadn't come along (!!). No wonder she is so excited that I am enrolled at Hoch.

September 3, 1937

Settled into my little apartment in Frankfurt. Mother takes the train tomorrow to Hamburg and then sails home soon. We had a silly argument today about jazz music, of all things. Mother commented that she didn't like swing and jazz and found it grating to the ear. I told her that America loves big band and jazz and swing, just look at the popularity of Tommy and Jimmy Dorsey but she dismissed Tommy as merely a trombonist, not a true musician.

I don't mind if she doesn't like new music, but she doesn't have to be such a snob.

September 9, 1937

Mother has been gone for six days now and I'm settling in. Food is simple but tasty. The Germans like to eat. And drink.

September 14, 1937

I can see why Father spoke well of Frankfurt am Main. It's a large city and well located with an excellent train station for travel. He, of course, would appreciate the convenience. I've enjoyed discovering the city on the weekends, and would find it easier to fall in love with Frankfurt if one wasn't subjected to all the politics. In the US, no one expected Hitler to find any real support, but he is still here, and seemingly more influential than ever.

September 28, 1937

Much discussion this afternoon among the students during tea about the legitimacy of women conductors and composers. According to Walther there have been very few truly gifted female musicians. Renate retorted that she supposed Clara Schumann was no one?

Everyone laughed (except for Walther) as Clara was one of the most famous of all Hoch's faculty, and helped the conservatory achieve international acclaim. Renate and I boldly replied there have been a number of great women musicians to have studied, or graduated, from Hoch like Ethel Leginska, and Ruth Schönthal, but Walther crushingly shot back that Schönthal attended the Stern in Berlin, not Hoch, and from all the crowing of the boys, Walther had apparently won that round.

I dislike Walther more and more. And yet he is a brilliant composer.

October 6, 1937

One of Father's friends, Henry Rich, who once worked with Father in Cairo, but now works at the American embassy in Hungary was in Frankfurt and he took me to dinner last night as Father asked him to check on me. We had a very nice dinner, even if I did have a little too much wine and woke up with a headache.

Mr. Rich gave me his number at the chancery and made me promise to call should I need anything.

I told him thank you, but I didn't expect to have any problems. He gave me a long look and said quite flatly, "Things are going to get much worse here, before they get better."

October 18, 1937

It's my 18th birthday today. Several of my classmates surprised me with an impromptu birthday concert this morning. Herr Volk disapproved but at the same time, he didn't stop the brief concert. After class ended, a number of us went for coffee and cakes. One of the girls presented me with a small gift from everyone—a locket wrapped in a lace handkerchief, and the locket is lovely with intricate locks and silverwork. It looks quite old, too, and the girls tell me they got it for an excellent price at the flea market last weekend as the seller was desperate. She was trying to buy a ticket on one of the steamer ships for her son, so he could *go to Chicago to join her brother there. She wanted to send all her children but she could only afford to send the one.*

I do love the locket but the story behind it is quite sad. I am quite sure the mother desperate to sell the locket is a Jew, but I say nothing to the girls. They were trying very hard to do something nice for me.

October 21, 1937

Had a very unpleasant exchange with Walther who thinks any music that is not German should no longer be taught in Germany, and holds Wagner and Bruckner up as the greatest composers of the 19th century. I personally don't respond to all the Teutonic heaviness but then again, as Walther mentioned, I'm not German.

October 30, 1937

It is Walther's life ambition to write a symphony for "der Führer." I shouldn't be surprised. He is a rabid nationalist.

Sieg Heil! Sieg Heil! Sieg Heil!

Sigh.

I should probably care more about politics but I'm uncomfortable with the zealots surrounding me.

November 15, 1937

Not sure why I thought Hoch would be the best music program for me. There is no freedom, and certainly no freedom of expression. Creativity is unheard of here. One can't do something new. One must only copy the "German masters." Yes, it's the thing to study music here in Europe, particularly in Germany, and all the important American composers continue to come here to study the dead "Bs" (Bach, Beethoven, and Brahms), but I'm not a dead German man and I don't even know if I want to compose music anymore. But if I do, this isn't where I want to study.

November 25, 1937

I wrote a long letter today to Mother and Father about my studies here in Frankfurt. I don't want to leave Europe, but I don't think the Hoch is the right place for me with its emphasis on Wagner. I so much prefer German romanticism and am hopeful the Stern Conservatory in Berlin might have room for me.

I am writing to Herr Kittel, the Stern's director today, and am enclosing some of the pieces I have composed, along with some of my papers from Hoch.

December 8, 1937

Received a reply from Director Kittel. If I am serious, I must go to Berlin and audition.

December 10, 1937

Mother replied to my letter regarding the Stern. She said "absolutely not."

December 14, 1937

I wrote Herr Kittel asking when I could come audition. I mentioned that I was free for three weeks over the Christmas holidays. I then wrote to Mother and Father about my studies at the Hoch. I laid out a most intelligent but passionate argument as to why I must change schools.

December 21, 1937

I will be spending Christmas in Berlin!

December 23, 1937

Letter from Mother today. She said no. No, no, no, no. And Father supports Mother.

> *I'm going to Berlin anyway. I have to audition.*

January 2, 1938

Had the most wonderful holiday in Berlin. I absolutely love the city. The theater scene is still very vibrant despite all. Can't imagine what Mother would say if she knew I not only auditioned for Herr Kittel, but attended a New Year's Eve party at the Adlon.

January 6, 1938

Not happy back at school. It's beyond dull. Want to be back in Berlin.

January 8, 1938

I didn't get in. I'm so disappointed.

January 11, 1938

I really don't want to be here anymore. I want to be in Berlin. Have written privately to Father expressing my desire to do something else but haven't had a response yet.

January 20, 1938

Still not happy but at least this semester I have an instructor that studied with Schoenberg in Vienna as part of the Zweite Wiener Schule, *and he is introducing us to totally chromatic expression, as well as Schoenberg's serial twelve-tone technique. I'm not sure I'm comfortable composing without firm tonal center, but I'm fascinated by Schoenberg's creativity.*

February 13, 1938

German troops have been entering Austria since yesterday. Germans aren't concerned, as both Germans and Austrians (including those belonging to the Nazi party and those who don't) have being calling for a Heim ins Reich, *for years. Many view this as the natural order for things, and as Walther reminds everyone constantly, if Hitler can accomplish so much in Germany in such a short period of time, just imagine what he can do for Austria?*

March 13, 1938

Anschluss *dominates the headlines in today's paper. Austria has formally been annexed to Germany today. Reports say that ninety-some percent of Austrians voted in favor of the annexation. I wonder if that's true . . .*

May 15, 1938

Yesterday England's football team defeated Germany's, 6-3 and the Germans are protesting, crying foul.

Apparently Germans are supposed to win everything.

Perhaps England didn't know?

June 18, 1938

The world is full of news of hate and aggression. Jews are being attacked and their property in Poland confiscated. The Nazis can confiscate art from "degenerates." Japan has declared war on China. It's better not to listen to the news. I get terrible knots in my stomach and feel sick all day.

August 16, 1938

Attending the Salzburg Festival with Frieda, Katrina, and Boris from Hoch, but the atmosphere is remarkably different from last year's. Hitler's soldiers are everywhere, creating an over- whelming, and oppressive presence. Worse, Jedermann—which has been part of the festival since the beginning—has been banned, along with my favorite, Faust. The music festival has come under the jurisdiction of the Nazi party so anything asso- ciated with a Jewish musician or composer is forbidden. Of course there are new productions of Wagner and Mozart to take the place of the banned productions.

And of course Hitler would idolize Wagner. Wagner himself was anti-Semitic. Thank goodness I am American and not German.

August 30, 1938

Met two brothers from San Antonio, Texas who have grown up spending most of their summers in Bavaria with their grand- parents, and always attend the festival with them before re- turning to Texas, but don't expect to return next year, due to politics.

They were quite shocked that I am here, on my own. I explained that I am not on a grand European tour but studying music at the

Hoch. They still found it shocking, and I don't know if they thought it indulgent (in view of American citizens being warned that they should not travel in war zones) or simply too dangerous.

I was annoyed at the time, but now I wonder if they know something I do not.

I don't feel in jeopardy here. But then again, I am not an undesirable.

September 2, 1938

Tonight's radio broadcasts announce that Mussolini has declared that Jews in Italy have no rights.

So he, too, is now targeting the Jews.

I think back on my education and my first music teachers in Mexico were Jewish emigrants. And again, in Chile and Cairo, there were teachers and musicians who helped my studies.

How can people fear them?

And yet, I dare not say anything here, because I am clearly in the minority. But what is happening in the world? And when will it end?

September 10, 1938

Walther has not returned to Hoch. He has joined Hitler's SS.

I am surprised. He loved his music but I suppose he loves der Führer more. At the same time, it will be a relief not to have to listen to him lecture us girls on our proper place and responsibility (that women should be wives and mothers . . . producing the next generation . . . filling the Reich's nurseries with blond-haired, blue-eyed infants . . .).

Maybe I should go home. But if I go home, I will not know what happens here.

October 1, 1938

The German radio announced tonight that it has annexed the Sudetenland to the Reich, as all ethnic Germans belong to Germany.

October 30, 1938

Spirited debate tonight over tea regarding the American Archbishop Beckman from nowhere Iowa, declaring swing music the "music of the devil." Apparently all those who listen, or dance to it, are going to hell.

I am constantly amazed, and disappointed, by the ignorance of people.

Must write to Mother. I know she's not a fan of swing, but I think she'll be amused, if not dismayed, by Beckman's condemnation.

November 9, 1938

Violence throughout Germany and Austria today as Jews were beaten, arrested, and murdered in retaliation for the assassination of the German diplomat, vom Rath, in Paris by a young Jew. I don't know how many were killed, but by all accounts, it was close to one hundred.

November 10, 1938

I walked out of my theory class when Berthold said that the only bad thing about Kristallnacht was that more Jews weren't murdered.

November 15, 1938

Goering announced earlier in the week that he thinks all Jews should go to Madagascar. That Madagascar should be their homeland. I laughed when I first heard the statement—does Goering even know where Madagascar is? And then I realized but of course he does. And I nearly cried.

Things are becoming very bad and no one is doing anything.

Tragically, I think Hitler understands far too well that "might is right."

TWELVE

Ali

I take Ruth to the dentist late Monday morning. Edie comes with us but she and I don't speak. I hold Ruth's hand as we leave the car and walk to the office. And then once I've signed her in and filled out the paperwork, I again hold her hand until they call her name. I carefully walk her back to the chair, and make sure she's comfortable. Later when she's relaxed, I return to the waiting room. Edie is staring at the TV screen; the sound is muted so she's just watching the images.

I reach for a magazine and flip through it.

At the moment we are the only two people in the waiting room but we don't talk. We haven't said a word directly to each other since the other day. It's not a comfortable silence now and part of me would like to apologize but another part is still angry.

An hour later, Ruth's procedure finished, I walk her to the car, keeping a close eye on Edie who clearly doesn't want any help from me.

"Thank you, Sophie dear," Ruth says, patting my hand as I assist her buckling her seat belt once inside the car.

"You're welcome, Ruth."

Driving, I glance into the rearview mirror, checking on Ruth and Edie who are in the backseat together. Ruth is looking out the window while Edie stares straight ahead.

"Are you feeling okay, Ruth?" I ask.

"Yes, dear."

"Nothing hurts?"

"No."

"Good." I focus on the road, and we travel a mile along the same street, eventually slowing for a red light.

As we sit at the intersection I hear Ruth sigh with pleasure. "Look at all those beautiful flowers," she says, focusing on the flower stand. "Aren't they lovely?"

"They are," I agree.

"You like flowers, don't you, Ruth?" Edie says.

"I do."

I glance again into the rearview mirror. "Do you want to stop and have a closer look?"

Ruth nods. "Oh, yes, please."

I signal and pull into the gravel parking lot. Ruth is eager to get out of the car but Edie doesn't move. I think she's going to stay behind but at the last moment she unclicks her seat belt and swings her door open and carefully climbs out.

"Do you need an arm?" I ask Edie.

"No. Just pay attention to Ruthie."

I give Edie a tight smile, refusing to let a crabby old lady get me down, and escort Ruth to the stand, aware of Edie following slowly behind us.

The woman inside the flower stand greets us. I tell her we've stopped to admire her beautiful flowers. She tells us to take our time.

Ruth pauses to examine the long-stemmed red roses. "My mother always had the most beautiful rose garden," she says. "Red and white roses."

"My mother loved roses, too," I tell her.

She looks at me. "My mother was a dancer. A ballerina."

"My mother was a teacher."

Ruth leans over to smell the red roses, inhaling deeply, but when she straightens she's no longer smiling. "They don't smell like anything."

I lean over and take a sniff. The red roses aren't without fragrance, but it's admittedly very light, almost an afterthought. "That's disappointing."

"Yes."

We walk slowly along the stand, Ruth's hand tucked into the crook of my arm, as we examine the flowers in each silver bucket, with Ruth smelling each.

Ruth talks about her mother the dancer, and from my peripheral vision I track Edie, aware that I'll have hell to pay should anything happen to her.

We reach the end of the stand and we're turning away when I hear Edie tsk-tsking. Glancing back, I discover her bent over a bucket of summer dahlias, a mix of spiky pinks and oranges with dinner-plate red and purple, and she's beaming as if she's just bumped into long lost friends.

Edie catches my eye, and straightens abruptly. "Dahlias are such show-offs," she says with a snort.

But I'm not fooled. And I smile.

Back at Napa Estates, an aide takes Ruth in a wheelchair back to her room. Edie stalks off without a word to me.

I stand in the lobby entrance and am frustrated and hurt and confused.

I don't know how to make this right. I am trying so hard, too.

Abruptly Edie stops walking and turns to face me. "Well?" she demands. "What are you waiting for? Come with me."

THIRTEEN

Edie

In my little apartment kitchen I show Alison where I keep the teacups and the canister of tea. I tell her to plug the kettle in and get everything ready.

I sit at the small kitchen table watching and giving direction as need be.

I have to apologize to her, and I don't know how. I am not very good with apologies.

I was going to talk to her once we had our tea, but I find it difficult to sit in silence, while we wait for the water to boil.

I fuss with the red pom-pom fringe on my white tablecloth. I've had this round cloth with the red cherry embroidery for years. I remember once how one of Chad's girlfriends admired my "vintage" linens.

The kettle whistles just as I'm about to speak. Alison pours the water, filling the cups, floating the tea bags.

She carries both cup and saucers to the table.

"If you like sugar, there's a spoon in the top drawer and the sugar bowl is already on the table," I tell her.

"I don't need any," she answers. "Would you like sugar?"

I shake my head and she sits across from me. We sit stiffly, and yet so politely. I should have apologized the moment we reached my apartment and gotten it over with. I don't know what to say now. I've lost my nerve and my energy.

I can be a sour old woman and I know it. I am not kind to most people anymore, not tactful, either.

Finally I can't bear it any longer. "I'm sorry," I say quickly, my voice not entirely steady. "I am sorry for what I said Friday. It was mean-spirited and I displayed poor manners." I take a quick breath. "I would also like to say thank you for taking Ruth today. Not just to the dentist, but to see the flowers. That was very kind of you and appreciated by me."

The girl's been staring down into her teacup this entire time but now she lifts her head and looks up at me. "I wasn't very nice, either. And I'm sorry, too."

"Your father said you had a broken engagement."

She dunks her tea bag once, twice. "He died last year. Six weeks before our wedding." She looks back down, into the tea. "He killed himself . . . and I was the one who found him."

Her father hadn't told me this. I frown, at a loss for words. Quiet stretches.

"We met in dental school," she adds, as if compelled to fill the uneasy silence. "We studied together, lived together. He was my best friend."

I take the tea bag out and place it in the saucer next to the cup. "You thought you were going to be a bride and a wife, but then he was gone."

"Yes."

"You feel cheated."

"And confused. How could someone I love so much, just . . . go?"

"Without a good-bye," I add softly.

She looks up into my eyes. "Yes. Exactly. There was no good-bye. No warning. He was there with me, and then he was gone."

I rub my knuckles, kneading the ache in my hands. "I loved someone once, like that. And I didn't get to say good-bye to him, either."

FOURTEEN

Ali

I leave Edie's and go up a floor to see Dad. He's napping in his recliner chair, the TV on, the sound muted. I stretch out on the small couch next to him and watch the TV without the sound.

It's a program on the Battle of Normandy on the History Channel. With the seventieth anniversary of D-day rapidly approaching, everyone is remembering Normandy.

I don't know my dad's awake until he speaks. "Everything go okay with Edie?"

I turn my head and look at him. "You mean, Ruthie?"

"Wasn't Edie the one upset with you?"

"Yes. And we talked. I think we're okay."

"Good. I'd hate to lose a great bridge partner."

I smile and for a moment we're both silent, watching the old black-and-white film footage of boats filled with young American GIs surging towards the French beaches. Some of the young soldiers look grim. A few smile at the camera.

They had no idea what was to come, did they?

He turns the volume on the program up, and we listen until

the commercial break. He mutes the sound again and asks if I'm still planning on working at that downtown florist this week.

"I've agreed to help her for the rest of the week but have warned her I might not be available after that. I've got to get back to Scottsdale soon."

"I've been expecting it."

I sit forward on the couch. "I'm quite sure I know what you're going to say, but I have to ask anyway. Are you sure you don't want—"

"*Yes.*"

"Why won't you even consider it?"

"Because it's hot. Too damn hot. And Phoenix is ugly. I hate the sprawl—"

"I'm not in Phoenix. I live in Scottsdale—"

"Same thing."

"It's not. But regardless, *I'm* there."

He lowers the footrest, and sits up. "And I like seeing you, Alison, I do. But I can see you here."

"But it means I won't see you often."

"I understand. You've got your career, and bills . . . all those bills from dental school. Now's the time you focus on work. That's what you do in your twenties and thirties."

My chest tightened, so much pressure inside. "You're not a spring chicken. I won't have forever with you."

"But we don't have forever with anyone, which is why you need someone your age. As much as I love you, I'm not your future."

I stand up and kiss him good-bye. He reaches out to catch my hand. "You're the one unhappy in Scottsdale. Why stay there? Why stay in that house—"

"It's all I have of him, Dad."

"Then at least get a dog. You need a dog."

"I'm not home enough to have a pet."

"Then take the dog to work. Everybody does it these days."

It's Tuesday and Dad and Edie play bridge on Tuesday mornings, so I know where I'll find them when I show up at Napa Estates.

The game hasn't started yet. They are waiting for the other couple to show. Dad uses the time to go to the rest room, leaving Edie and me alone in the Reading Room.

"Edie, yesterday you told me you didn't get to say good-bye, either. Why not? What happened?"

"War happened."

"Had he enlisted, or been drafted?"

She shuffles the cards carefully, once, twice. "He wasn't American. He was German." She taps the cards into a tidy deck. "I met him in Germany, in Berlin, when I was working at the American embassy."

I struggle to make sense of this. "He worked at the embassy, too?"

"Not exactly." She taps the cards on the table, glances at the doorway, anticipating the arrival of the others. "When I first met him, he worked at the German Foreign Office, and then later, for the Ministry of Propaganda. During the twenty months I worked at the American embassy, our paths crossed many times, formally and informally. It was a clandestine affair. It shouldn't have happened."

"Because he was a . . . Nazi?"

"After a certain point, virtually everyone was required to be a member of the Nationalist Socialist German Workers' Party. Once Hitler had consolidated his power, there wasn't a choice."

"So he was."

"It's not that simple." She set the deck of cards in front of her. "I know countless Germans who were sent to concentration camps for making a flippant remark, and they were reported." She folds her hands on the table. "You don't know what happened, so you are in no position to judge."

"I'm not judging."

"Not all Germans were bad."

"But the Nazis were."

She leans towards me, eyes sharp and bright. "Germans weren't the only ones with propaganda ministries. The Allied forces had their own agenda, and the US entered the war too late. And when they did enter, they were more interested in winning the 'battle' than saving lives. Millions died in those camps who didn't need to die—" She breaks off, shakes her head, and reaches for the cards again.

She shuffles them once more. "I am happy to discuss the Germans and the Nazis and the war with you. But you should have your facts correct before you make assumptions."

I woke up sympathetic and curious about Edie's life this morning and stopped by Napa Estates to speak with her, but when I leave the retirement home for Bloom, I'm annoyed. Agitated.

Edie is a hard woman to like.

She's imperious and cold, critical and acerbic. I don't know why I've tried to bond with her. She's too difficult. She's not someone I want or need to know.

I arrive at Bloom eager to get to work. I don't enjoy being in a bad mood and I am hoping that the beauty of the flowers will distract me and help my mood improve.

Diana has a lot of orders waiting for me and I quickly get lost in the flower arranging. This morning it's a variety of bouquets, too. There are orders for birthdays, anniversaries, new babies, and high school graduations.

I'm lucky that Diana likes my work and gives me a lot of freedom. Once I have selected a vase and have a vision in mind, I can lose myself in the physical task of arranging the stems and creating order. It's nice to be able to have busy hands and free thoughts.

As a dentist I have to be very focused. The work is all about precision. My freshman year in dental school was the most stressful year of my life. I hadn't anticipated the pressure to be perfect . . . it is the only acceptable result . . . and it doesn't end, not in this profession. I remember back in school the angst we all felt as we learned new skills: making wax teeth, drawing teeth, drilling teeth, and how you couldn't pass if you didn't have great hands. Not good hands. Great hands.

And great judgment.

That was another eye-opener. You were constantly being judged on your judgment, just as everyone around you was being judged, too.

Dental school was relentless and it is such an enormous high—and relief—when you finish school and pass the WRED. There is new pressure, of course, as you must now find patients and fill out a schedule and figure out how to address your debt. Some of us left school a quarter million dollars in debt. And you don't make much in the beginning. You're lucky to earn a hundred thousand a year and that's before taxes and expenses.

You can see why it takes a long time to whittle the debt down.

It's a relief to not have to be as intensely focused now. I can work on the arrangements and hum along to music, or daydream, or think about things.

Like Edie telling me that the love of her life was a Nazi.

I hadn't seen that one coming.

And Edie was so prickly and defensive about Germany and the Nazi party that I can't help wondering if she hadn't been a Nazi, too . . .

I'm just finishing up my second high school graduation arrangement when the Bloom's front door opens and Craig Hallahan walks in, carrying a box filled with the glass hurricanes from the event at the winery last Thursday night.

I feel a quick bright surge of emotion, a happy emotion, and I smile at him. "Good afternoon."

"Good afternoon," he answers, smiling back as he sets the box on the counter. "I thought Diana would like these back."

I peek into the box; the hurricanes are sparkling clean. Considerate man. "She's just run to the bank, but I'm sure she'll be very happy to have them back," I answer, surprised by the pleasure I felt when he walked in. I haven't felt anything like that in a long time. It's probably a good thing I'm leaving Napa soon. Down the road when I do decide to date again, whoever it is won't be related to Edie Stephens.

"Have you had lunch yet?"

"No, but I don't usually take lunch here. There's too much to do to leave."

"Diana said you were dedicated."

"I enjoy the work. No one is scared to see me, and I don't cause anyone pain."

"I've never been scared to see the dentist," he answers. "But my brother is one of those nervous patients. Never understood why."

"Some people have to have more work done than others, and there are those who are more sensitive or don't numb up as well. Fortunately, I usually only get one patient a day who's nervous, so that's not too bad, but I've had days where there are a few really terrified patients, and when they are back to back, it's discouraging."

"So you enjoy your work."

"I do. It feels good to know I help people."

"So you're not going to stay up here and be a florist?"

"No. I need to get back to my real life."

"Diana will miss you."

There is something very quiet and real in his voice and I look up into his face and search his eyes. His expression is as steady as his voice, and I feel a stab of regret that I'm leaving.

It was good for me, being here.

It was good to get away from the Scottsdale office with its chilly air conditioner and whir of drills and wash of chemicals. I can see now that I felt frozen there, surrounded by Andrew's work and family. Here in Napa I've begun to warm up. Wake up. I can see that there might be light—and life—at the end of the tunnel. "It's been fun, helping Diana out. I feel like a kid at camp, getting to participate in all the craft activities."

He grins, and creases fan at his eyes and bracket his mouth. He's tan—sun kissed—and I swear he exudes a mix of earthy soil and pungent wine. "You went to camp?" he asks.

I nod. "Girl Scout camp at St. Albans every summer. Loved it. It was a traditional overnight camp . . . hiking, horseback riding, archery, canoeing, crafts, campfires, all of it."

"A Girl Scout, huh?"

"From kindergarten until my junior year of high school. Brownie, Junior, Cadette, Senior."

"You really liked Girl Scouts."

"I did. And I earned every badge you could." I bite the inside of my lip as he laughs, but it's a good laugh, deep and husky and it makes me feel warm, even a little giddy. "Scouting isn't just cookies and camp. It's about building skills and leadership."

"That does fit into your profile."

"You didn't do Boy Scouts?"

He shakes his head. "Chad and I played both sports—football, basketball, baseball—and participated in 4-H and FFA, along with our work on the ranch."

"FFA?"

"Future Farmers of America."

"Ah." He's all about the outdoors and growing things and building things and he's a bit like summer camp . . . wholesome adventure. Healthy activity. Fresh and fun.

I smile at him. I can't help it.

"I love your smile," he says, lips curving, but his voice is low. Quiet. He's not flirting. He means it.

I'm flattered, but flustered. "I have good teeth."

"The teeth have nothing to do with the dimples, or the way your eyes crinkle. You smile with your whole face. It's beautiful."

Andrew said the same thing, which is why he loved to tease me, to make me smile, and suddenly I feel the old lump back in my throat, the one that makes my chest feel tight and heavy. "You sound like Andrew," I whisper, struggling to keep smiling but my eyes burn and the ache inside me grows, wider, larger. I miss him so much still. I miss my best friend. He was such a good friend. He knew everything about me. He understood my jokes, my anxiety, my need to please as well as accomplish great things. "He'd say the most outrageous things just to make me laugh. I loved how he could make me laugh."

"Sounds like a good man."

He was.

I almost break down and have to turn away, facing the back wall and running my fingers beneath my eyes to stop the tears before they fall.

I haven't felt like crying in days. I'm caught off guard by all the emotion now.

"I should probably get back to work," I say, when I'm able to turn around, smiling stiffly. I feel stoic. Martyr-like. I hate it.

"I should get back to the winery, too. It's busy in the tasting room. Make sure I'm not needed." He turns to leave but hesitates. "Oh, and Ali, I don't really know what happened earlier this morning with you and my aunt Edie, but she's got herself worked up over whatever was said—" He breaks off and drags a hand through his shaggy blonde hair, pushing it back off his face. "Don't know if you could go by tonight, on your way home, and talk to her . . . maybe smooth things over?"

I look at him, uncomfortable. "Your aunt can be quite sharp."

"Yes, I know. She's not an easy person."

"She shared with me about her past." I wait for him to jump in, say something but he doesn't. "About when she worked at the American embassy in Berlin. During the war."

"Did she? That's interesting. She rarely talks about those years."

"It made me uneasy."

"Those were difficult years."

"Yes, but . . . she was American. And she married a German."

"Yes."

"A Nazi."

"Yes, I guess he was."

"Was *she* a Nazi?"

Craig's brow creases. "No! Why would you think that?"

"Because of who he was—"

"I don't think she's told you enough. Franz was a German officer, and a member of the Nazi party, but he was also part of the German Resistance, and he paid for it with his life."

FIFTEEN

Edie

I sit in my room in the deepening shadows. It will be dark outside soon. I should turn on lights. But I like the shadows of twilight. It is now, when day turns to night, that I feel the ghosts of the past.

It is here, now, when I can feel Franz best.

In September, it will be seventy years since he died. In July, it will be seventy years since he kissed me good-bye.

I didn't know when he put me on that train to Ascona that I would never see him again. If I'd known, I wouldn't have gone. I am sure that's why he didn't tell me. He knew I couldn't leave him. That's why we married in the first place.

The shadows deepen and my room is blue black. If I don't turn on a lamp soon, I could trip over something and fall.

Reluctantly I rise and make my way to the wall, and flip the switches for the overhead light. I blink and move to the kitchen, and turn on the light there.

I don't think I will go down to dinner tonight. I think I shall heat up a can of soup and have some crackers. Some saltines. If they are not too stale. Chad says I keep my crackers and biscuits too long, but I don't understand throwing out a perfectly good cracker just because it is not as crisp as it used to be.

Opening a can of minestrone, I pour it into a small saucepan and place the pan on the stove.

As I stand over the pan and wait for the soup to boil I keep thinking about my conversation with Alison this morning, and her expression when I mentioned Franz, and how we met.

This is why I do not talk about my life. This is why I've learned to remain silent. There are things you don't say. Things you can't say. Who will listen? Who wants to hear the truth, because the truth is never simple? The truth is complex and dark and sometimes very dirty.

War is sordid business.

War requires a victor and that means someone must win and someone must lose and then there are the consequences . . . winners, and losers . . .

Reparations.

I cannot talk about what I know and what I've seen. Who wants to think about what was done?

The Germans weren't all bad. There were many who were very good. Many who tried to do the right thing.

When I first returned to America, I was told not to make excuses for them. And then again, later, when I tried to share how it was, I was criticized and condemned. Even Ellie told me it was better to be silent than share what I know. *It is just to protect you,* she'd say.

I agree that those in power had to be punished, but not all Germans were aggressors. There were plenty who didn't agree with the government, thousands involved in the Resistance.

I stir the soup as it starts to boil but my spoon is short and the side of the pan burns my hand. I yank my hand back, dropping my spoon with a clatter, and go to the sink to run cool water on my skin.

I'm running the water when a knock sounds at my door.

I tense, and glare in the direction of the door. I'm pretty sure I know who it is and I'm not feeling conversational.

The soup boils over as I return to the kitchen with Alison trailing after me, talking at my back about misunderstanding me or something along those lines.

I wasn't happy when I answered the door and am even less congenial now that my soup is bubbling and splashing all over my stove. With a wrench on the dial, I turn the heat off and shove the pan off the burner. I've burned the bottom of the pan. I can smell the scorched odor.

"Let me help," Alison says, grabbing my dishrag from the sink and coming towards the stove.

"Leave it alone," I snap, taking the cloth from her and wiping away the mess. "It's my kitchen. My dinner."

She falls back a step and watches me, her expression reproachful.

Or maybe I'm just feeling ashamed for being so crotchety. I look at her as I wipe the last of the soup. "Have you eaten? Are you hungry? Would you like a bowl?"

She manages a weak smile. "From the pan, or your dishcloth?"

My lips flatten and press, and then relent. I smile faintly, amused. "Craig would have my head if I gave you dishrag soup."

"Then I probably shouldn't tell him."

"I've told him you're not right for him."

"I agree with you. I'm not right for him. He's far too lovely for someone like me."

I shoot her a suspicious glance, wondering if she's being a smarty-pants, but she meets my gaze directly. "So what is wrong with you?"

"I'm just not interested in a relationship, so you don't have to worry. Craig is safe."

"You don't like him?"

"I don't like anyone—"

"Because you're grieving."

"Yes."

"Well, everyone's heart gets broken at least once or twice. That's just a fact of life. And don't think you're going to meet a man who hasn't had his share of grief. Craig lost his first love to leukemia. He was just a freshman in college when she died, but they'd been together since junior high and he adored her." I reach into the cupboard for two small cups. "Last chance. Soup?"

She shakes her head. "I'm meeting Dad for dinner."

I take down just one cup. "Eventually you'll feel differently."

"I don't know. I can't imagine ever wanting to go through this again."

I get a spoon, and my crackers from the pantry, and carry my cup to the table. The soup is still very hot. I can feel the burn on my hand, the skin tender.

"Wait here," I say to Alison, and instead of sitting down, I go into my guest bedroom and retrieve the box with the papers and letters and dark brown leather journal. I carry it back to the kitchen where Alison watches as I sort through the various papers to find a large manila envelope that has yellowed with age.

I take out the envelope, my fingers running lightly beneath the flap. "This is all I have left from my courtship with Franz. I've always kept a diary, and had kept a detailed diary from the day I moved to Berlin, until the night Pearl Harbor was bombed, but we had to burn everything at the embassy on December eighth. Anything that could be used against the US government or our allies had to go, and as I'd written a great deal about embassy life,

I had to destroy everything from the past two years so that we could close the embassy down."

"That must have been absolutely chaotic," she says.

"Leland Morris and George Kennan were responsible for overseeing the transfer of American interests in Germany to our Swiss representatives. Bank accounts had to be closed. Foreign staff terminated. US citizens protected." I set the envelope on the table and sit down, careful not to slosh my soup. "Because of my language skills, back in June, I was one of those involved in the closure of the remaining American consulates in Germany, and so I was integral to the closure of the embassy in Berlin."

Alison sits down across from me. "Were you afraid?"

"Worried, more than afraid. I grew up overseas, my father attached to several consulates during periods of turmoil and war, so I felt physically safe, just deeply troubled by the fact that the US was now at war with Germany."

"How old were you?"

"In 1941?" I frown, trying to remember. It's been so long. A lifetime ago. "Early twenties, I think. Let me see. I was born in 1920, so I would have been . . . twenty-one."

"And your parents weren't worried?"

"Oh, I wouldn't say that. My father and mother were both quite anxious to get me home. They'd wanted me to return back in June, when I was assisting closing the consulates, but my language skills and translation services were needed too badly for me to return then. So I stayed. It was not an easy decision, and ultimately, I do think it placed too much stress on my father. He was already having health problems—" I break off, shake my head, and focus on stirring my soup. It's so hard going back, talking about a world that doesn't even exist anymore.

I set the spoon down and fold my hands together. "He died before the war ended. Ellie said it was not my fault, that his heart wasn't strong anymore, but it couldn't have been easy for him, knowing I was there, doing what I was doing."

Alison's brow creases. "I can't even imagine."

I nudge the envelope towards her. "There's not very much here. Just twenty or thirty pages that one of my girlfriends from the embassy took with her after we were released from the Grand at Bad Nauheim, promising to mail it to my family in New Rochelle once she arrived back in the United States."

"What was the Grand? And Bad Nauheim?"

"The Grand was the hotel in Bad Nauheim, a small resort town outside Frankfurt, where the embassy staff was interned after the declaration of war. We thought we'd be there for two weeks. We ended up at the Grand for nearly four and a half months."

I pat the edge of the envelope. "My sister Ellie thought I should have these pages published, but I couldn't. They were so very personal, and I don't really think they explain the war, or Franz, or his friends. But it's all I have of our courtship. All I have of those first few years together."

I fall silent, and the past weighs on me, as does the guilt.

Why didn't we do more?

Why didn't America take action sooner?

"You can read it, or not read it," I add shortly, dipping my spoon into my soup, ready to be alone. "It's up to you."

SIXTEEN

Ali

I've been dismissed again, but I'm not surprised. These conversations clearly tire her, and Dad's waiting in the dining room.

I take the envelope with me, tucking it into my purse and head downstairs. Dad is already seated at a round table with eight place settings. Half the chairs are filled. "Wasn't sure you were still going to join me," Dad says, as I take one of the empty chairs.

"I was upstairs, talking to Edie."

"Is she coming down?"

"Not tonight. She made herself some soup."

"Everything okay?"

"Yes." I hesitate, aware that the others at the table are listening, and I'm not sure how much Edie would want revealed. "She was telling me about how she worked at the American embassy in Berlin and was there in 1941, when Pearl Harbor was bombed and the US declared war on Japan."

"Which meant, Germany declared war on the US," he adds.

I nod. "She had a diary she'd kept during her embassy service, but she had to burn it, along with all the official confidential papers."

"Who are you talking about?" Floyd demands, looking up over his fork.

"Edie Stephens," Bill replies. "Right?"

"Edie worked at the American embassy? Doing what? Nagging?"

"She was a translator," I answer. "She speaks five languages."

"Huh." Floyd's not impressed.

"She was married to a German," George adds. "During the war."

All eyes are on George.

"Here, in the US?" Bill asks.

"No. Over there, during the war, and when she returned to the US after the war, she had to go to one of those camps for Germans for a while. Not sure how long she was there—"

"There was a camp for Germans?" I interrupt.

"Sure. Just like for the Japanese. I think there were six or seven camps, with half of them in Texas, but far fewer Germans were actually locked up. You couldn't put them all in internment . . . just too many in this country, and most of those interned were living on the coast. You couldn't leave them there, you see. You had to protect the borders. Had to make sure there were no spies. Which is why Edie was sent there. Government didn't know what to do with her, or if she could be trusted. I don't think she got out until the war was over."

Walter clears his throat. "The government must have thought she was a Nazi, if she'd married one."

Isn't that what I'd thought, too?

More than ever, I want to get home and read her diary.

• • •

An hour later I'm back at Poppy Lane, in my pajamas, climbing into bed with the envelope. I carefully draw the papers out. They are very thin, almost like tissue and the handwriting is quite delicate, almost spidery.

I lean over to turn on the lamp next to me, and begin reading.

December 11, 1941

Frantic day destroying files and burning all papers at the embassy. The sky was so black with smoke that the police complained that the ash was blanketing the streets and cars.

After work I met F. at the Adlon for drinks and dinner. We talk about the future and what we expect to happen. He tells me not to worry, everything will work out. Yet I worry anyway. I appreciate his calm and confidence but the situation is very different now.

December 12, 1941

F. stayed with me until quite late and then slipped away while still under the cover of darkness.

I didn't want him to leave.

I didn't want to return to the embassy this morning, but I'm here now and we wait in empty offices for our next orders. It sounds as if we are to be sent somewhere for a few weeks until our passage home can be arranged. I know the US is now formally at war with Germany but I do not want to go home.

Throughout the day, Leland Morris insists we stay inside, but as the hours wear on we become increasingly quarrelsome, anxious to go home and pack and make decisions regarding our furniture and possessions in preparation for our expulsion. Rumors continue to swirl about where we are to go, and what's to happen next. Some say we are to go to a villa in Potsdam. Others say Bavaria. I would much rather stay close to Berlin to remain near F.

Finally at 7 p.m., Morris released us and allowed us to go home with instructions not to gather with other Americans, speak English in public, or draw attention to ourselves in any way. We heard that many members of the American press corps are being arrested and questioned before being released and placed under house arrest.

It is a most uneasy night, tonight, as friends come and go to say good-bye and I give away everything I no longer need, from extra ration cards to my best coats and boots since it is so difficult for my German friends to get the food, soap, toread, and clothing they need.

And each time there is a knock at the door, I feel a little ripple of unease. The Gestapo prefer to make their arrests under the cover of darkness and I wonder if the knock will be a friend, or foe.

The Gestapo do not come. But then, neither does F. I fall asleep waiting for him to come by.

December 13, 1941

Everyone is tired and subdued this morning at the embassy. We'd been gathered for an hour or two before we were given firm travel plans. Tomorrow we leave Berlin. We may take all our personal belongings, and there is no limit on our luggage, provided we have it at the embassy in time for the 10 a.m. departure. Morris reminded us that there will be no taxis tomorrow, Sunday, so luggage must be at the embassy tonight.

We leave to go home and finish packing and say our final good-byes.

At home I can delay no longer as I must return with my trunks tonight. F. has a car but I do not know if he will be able to assist me so I pack my clothes, my books, and personal mementoes. I'm dragging my big trunks down the stairs from the third floor to the second when I hear voices at the bottom of the stairwell— the traditional *Heil Hitler* salute followed by the sharp click of boot heels on the steps.

I know that voice. I know that step. F. has arrived.

December 14, 1941

Difficult saying good-bye to F. He left very early in the morning while it was still dark. He says I am not to worry, that I might not know his whereabouts but he will always know mine and I will not leave Germany without seeing him again. He promised and I believe him.

But my bed was so empty after he left and I rolled into the spot where he had lain, trying to keep it warm, trying to pretend he was still with me.

We still have not made love. F says it is not responsible, that we cannot take such risks when there is so much uncertainty. I told him my feelings were not uncertain and he tapped my nose and said I was deliberately turning his words around.

"Then I wish you were not so old-fashioned," I complained.

"But you would not love me if I were not honorable," he answered.

How well he knows me, for I do love him. Dearly.

Ich liebe dich, mein Schatz.

Dawn is breaking now, and in the next hour I shall make my last cup of faux coffee and gather the last of my things, and put on my coat and hat and scarf and walk down Unter den Linden for the last time. I shall pass the great buildings and hotels, the Staat, the opera house I have so loved, bombed earlier in the year and already being rebuilt so it can reopen in the coming year. Germans need their art. I need my art. I remember the first opera I attended at the Staat when I was just a little girl, traveling through Europe with my family. It was such a different Europe than now. All the light is gone. Hope dimmed. If it were not for F., I would have no hope at all. But he believes that Germany can be saved, and reborn. But first the enemy within must be contained.

Walked to the embassy in the rain. I didn't mind the rain though, it hid my tears. Police and soldiers inside and outside the embassy check papers and cards. Kennan mentioned quickly and cryptically that attaché office's chief clerk, Herbert Burgman, would not be joining us as he'd chosen to remain in Berlin. Everyone knew what that meant. He was defecting.

Kennan's announcement didn't seem to disturb the fifteen or so American newsmen who have joined us this morning at the embassy. They are adventurous fellows, quick-witted and full of stories. Not everyone enjoys their jokes but I find it a relief after the tense past few days. Some of the embassy fellows aren't happy

to have the journalists with us, predicting trouble. I can't imag-
ine how they can cause any more trouble than the Germans
themselves! Several of the newsmen are quite handsome (although
none as handsome as my F.!) and have learned to survive on
coffee, cigarettes, liquor, and a devil-take-all attitude during
these past few years in Germany. I feel sorry for our embassy
men. The newsmen make our diplomatic corps appear quite dull.

It rained the entire way to the Potsdamer Platz train station where
we boarded our cars. The rain continues now as the luggage is
loaded. There is far more luggage than anyone (much less the
Germans) anticipated and the luggage is delaying our departure
now. With the newsmen joining us, I believe there are now 114
or 115 of us altogether. Oh! And there are birds traveling with
us, too. One of the press brought a birdcage . . . with birds!

No, the newsmen are nothing like the rest of us.

We finally set off some time after one o'clock.

And it is a Mr. Alex Small who brought the birds. They are
canaries.

We arrived last night at Bad Nauheim very late, around ten
o'clock, and were told it was too late to disembark. We were
going to have to sleep on the train. Much grumbling but every-
one relieved to know we will at least be staying in Bad Nauheim,
a well-known spa just north of Frankfurt. Of course I know it
from my time at Hoch. I came here once with some of the girls
for a weekend and they took great pains to tell me that this is
where the parents and family of American President Roosevelt

would holiday and that the young Roosevelt, before becoming President had even attended some German language classes in Bad Nauheim.

December 15, 1941

I woke up early this morning, freezing. I must have been cold all night for I found myself pressed against poor Frances Sievert, practically burrowing into her shoulder. She must have been cold, too, since she didn't complain or push me off. I did shift position as it wasn't fair to squeeze her, but couldn't fall back asleep as one of our corps—who shall go unnamed—snores like the heavy horn on a freight train, making it impossible to fall back asleep.

We were allowed off the train for brief walks. It was all very organized and the walks were supervised by guards, and, while not pleasant, it was far, far better than the train cars which reek from the lavatories.

I already miss Berlin. Despite the blackouts, despite the air raids, despite the bombings and the fear, there was something so extraordinary and alive about the city. It isn't like Vienna or Paris. It has its own intelligence and energy—vigor—much like F. himself. I shall miss both. More than I can say.

December 16, 1941

Still on the train. Conditions atrocious. Lavatories overflowing. There is food but the stench makes it impossible to eat

Last night Kennan had promised us that we would start moving into the Grand Hotel today but he's just returned from a visit to the Grand which hasn't been in use since late September 1939 when it was closed due to the onset of the war, and *the hotel's director had no idea we were coming until three days ago and has been working night and day to open the hotel for us.*

Kennan said that the first order is to get electricity, water, and plumbing restored, and now they are working on furniture, china, silver, etc. Everything had been wrapped and put in storage for the war, so it's an immense undertaking to find the staff (many local men are all on the front somewhere) and then to make the necessary preparations to move us in. Kennan said once windows have been blacked out and security established he can start sending small groups over so he has excused himself to come up with the room assignments (everyone must share since there remains a shortage of furniture, linens, etc.).

Twenty were moved to the Grand tonight, mostly women and those with children. I wasn't one moved, but then, I'm not nearly as old or fussy or demanding as those who were transferred tonight. I expect the rest of us women will go tomorrow and as much as I hate this train, I am certain to remember this experience the rest of my life. And perhaps, like the newsmen, I will soon be able to joke about it, too . . .

December 17, 1941

The first group moved to the hotel last night, returned to the train this morning for breakfast. Apparently Kennan wasn't exaggerating. The hotel wasn't at all prepared for guests and there are no towels or water for baths. No glasses to drink from or drapes at the windows, which creates tremendous anxiety regarding safety.

One of the girls who was moved over to the hotel last night said the German guards at the hotel had them all lined up in columns of three this morning and practically insisted on them marching, but the very handsome German Captain Patzak, whom we were introduced to yesterday, interceded and said that the ladies were not prisoners of war and they did not have to walk in columns or march.

The girls were grateful for his help and I wonder if F. and he might not know each other . . .

December 18, 1941

Am finally settled into my room at the Grand. It really once was a grand hotel, too, with luxurious public rooms, but it was designed to be a summer resort—always closed early each fall at the end of the season—and does not handle the freezing December temperatures well.

December 19, 1941

Feeling at loose ends. We can't make phone calls out, or send telegrams but Kennan and Morris said they are working to get permission for us to receive them. We can write, and receive letters, though. They will be censored (of course) but at least we are allowed to communicate.

I spent the morning writing to my family and my friends back in Berlin, including what was meant to be a brief cheerful note to F., but which grew considerably longer as I had time on my hands, as well as much to say. I thanked him and his sister Frieda for their friendship and all the wonderful times we spent together in Berlin. I asked him to give her my love *and gratitude. I wrote that we are all safe and comfortable at the Grand, and that our German hosts are treating us well (just in case someone opens the letter). I specifically mentioned Captain Patzak as he is just a few years older than F. and he, too, attended university in Berlin, after having been instrumental in Berlin's Hitler Youth Program, and then I wrote that I still cherish the memory of attending the Salzburg Music Festival this past August with him and his sister for the 150th anniversary of Mozart's death. I add that I will always be grateful for my good German friends who appreciate German music as much as I do. I was laying it on a bit thick but hoping to survive the censors!*

Passed the afternoon playing cards with some of the newsmen. We were playing gin and then one of them—Gordon? Glen?—wistfully mentioned bridge, and I mentioned I knew how to play. They found a fourth expecting to have to still teach me, "the girl," the game. Much hilarity when "the boys" realized "the girl" could play as well as them . . . if not better. We've agreed to play again tomorrow. At least I have something to look forward to!

December 20, 1941

Someone found an old piano and had it brought upstairs. I played in the late morning to exercise and occupy my hands, and then this afternoon I intend to write more letters and play cards if there are any interested in a game.

While I was at the piano, Dr. Herman, the former pastor

from the American Church in Berlin, asked me if I knew of any church hymns. He would like some music for the Sunday church service he is planning in the morning. I told him I would be happy to accompany him.

December 21, 1941

This morning's service was held in the lounge and we had over fifty people in attendance. Dr. Herman spoke from the front of the room and I was at the piano in the corner. His sermon was thoughtful, saying we should all contribute to the community here and that it is through service, etc., that we will be blessed. I suppose the words were meant to inspire but it feels wrong to sit here when I feel that I could do something else. Something to help others.

Something to help F.

December 23, 1941

A letter from F.

He received my letter and was very glad to hear from me and know that we had settled in well. He said Captain Patzak has an excellent and unblemished reputation and years of loyal service to the party. He is known to be a very honorable and fair man, as well as a good judge of character. F. promises to send my love to his sister and is quite sure she would want to send kisses and affection back.

I almost cried when I read that. I have so little of him here and I regret more than ever destroying my diary during that big paper burning and purge at the embassy following the declaration of war.

Destroying the diary was the right thing to do, but selfishly, I can't help wishing I'd been able to save it, either by sending it home or hiding it in the lining of one of my trunks. But should the Gestapo go through my trunks and discover it, there would be hell to pay. I couldn't take the risks, I couldn't. How could I jeopardize my friends?

I still shouldn't keep a diary, not until I'm out of Germany, but it's such a habit now. I don't know how not to make my daily entries, and tomorrow is Christmas Eve.

December 24, 1941

Some lovely enterprising gentlemen (no doubt the newsmen, as they were the same to help organize yesterday's calisthenics class) managed to purchase a Christmas tree. We spent the afternoon crafting ornaments, including plundering our jewelry boxes for anything appropriately sparkly.

Captain Patzak helped us with the purchase of wood so we could have a fire in the drawing room and so we had a gorgeous crackling fire tonight, and I played carols at the piano, while everyone decorated the tree. There was a great deal of merriment during the decorating, and even our German guards joined in locating ornaments for the tree and singing the carols they know, in particular, "O Tannenbaum."

Those that didn't know the German lyrics fell silent and so it was left to those of us who did speak German to carry the tune, and I could feel the emotion in the room during the stanza with the words—gibt Trost und Kraft zu jeder Zeit—give comfort and strength in this time.

Indeed, we all need comfort and strength in this time!

December 25, 1941

Dr. Herman conducted Christmas services. I again played the piano. Everyone once again was quite complimentary regarding my skill, and appreciative for my contribution to the service.

I wonder how Mother would respond to the praise. Would she be pleased that all my years of private lessons and schooling have come to this?

After our service, we had a most lovely Christmas meal—schweinebraten, rotkohl, und kartoffel—*a very traditional German meal of roast pork, red cabbage, and potatoes, and I don't think there was a scrap of potato or bit of cabbage left after.*

I wonder if F. went home for Christmas, or if he stayed in Berlin. I hope he wasn't alone. I would have liked to be with him . . .

December 27, 1941

No one has been allowed to walk for several days due to reprisals for the German diplomats in the US being locked inside their hotel. It's a silly game played by governments. Kennan is protesting most strenuously on the behalf of all.

December 29, 1941

Bitterly cold today. Played Mozart's Piano Sonata in B Flat this morning in mittens. In my music I can feel F. with me.

January 1, 1942

It is a new year and everything is new. And old. It is the same old war for Europe, but new for Americans here who have become the official enemy, too.

January 3, 1942

I looked up from playing today to discover I had an audience. Captain Patzak and a number of the German guards were in the doorway quietly listening.

The guards applauded when I finished. I hadn't even known they were there.

January 4, 1942

Captain Patzak asked me where I learned to play, and I told him that I had come to Germany in 1937 to study music at the Hoch. "Ah," he said, "Frau Schumann taught there, yes?"

"Yes," I answered.

He speaks perfect English. Kennan said it's because before the war he worked for an American business. He is very tall, even taller than F., and even though he is as handsome as any Hollywood film star, he is not as handsome as my F.

January 5, 1942

F. and I write frequently as the postal service between here and Berlin—indeed to all our German friends—is quite exceptional thanks to Captain Patzak's efforts.

Kennan isn't as pleased and suspects Captain Patzak's motives. However, I fully intend to continue taking advantage of the freedom and write to my friends in Berlin daily.

January 6, 1942

Captain Patzak surprised me today with a gift of sheet music. Clara Schumann's Piano Sonata in G Minor.

I am touched by the gesture.

For hundreds of years Germany loved its music and art and in the last fifty years it has been reduced to arrogance and war.

I play the Piano Sonata in G Minor this afternoon as an ode to the Germany of music, art, and culture, not to Hitler, a monster if ever there was one.

January 8, 1942

Every few days I discover new sheet music at the piano. Today it was Brahms Piano Sonata No. 3 in F Minor Op. 5. I know now when I play that the guards are not far off. They lurk outside the lounge to hear me play. Some of the embassy staff think I should not accept the sheet music or encourage them by playing, but I tell them that music is essential to preserving our humanity.

At least, it is to mine.

January 10, 1942

F. writes that he is to be away for a number of weeks for business.

It is a very brief and quiet letter that makes me uneasy. I sit down at the piano and play Schubert's Piano Sonata in A major, D. 959, lingering over the second movement, letting the notes say all I cannot say.

January 15, 1942

Sat down at the piano today, homesick. I miss my family and am so very torn by the world around me.

I played Beethoven's Sonata 14, closing my eyes, closing my mind and heart to everything but the music and my love for Mother and Father and how they always dreamed of more for me.

They wanted to give me the world. Indeed, they did. Am I not here in Germany? Did I not come for my music? So here I am, here I am . . .

I play for my mother who wanted to be a composer and conductor.

I play for my father who wanted to be more than a consular.

I play for my sister who is young and dreams of being a great writer.

I play for my F. who knows how much I love my music and yet music is not enough if one has no freedom, much less freedom of expression.

I play for all this caught in the chaos and war.

I play because it is all I can do.

And even though I was antagonistic and resistant to studying only the "old German boys" when I first arrived at Hoch, the music of the "old German boys" so beautifully expresses my soul!

January 16, 1942

We are to have our first dance tonight. Herr Zorn and Captain Patzak have found a record player but all the records are quite old. I've been asked if I could play some contemporary songs— the usual swing and jazz and big band that is apparently so popular in America these days—and I've agreed to try. It's better than sitting around, moping, and I've no wish to dance with anyone but F.

January 17, 1942

The dance was a surprising success. Everyone up late, drinking and dancing, so most everybody is sleeping in today, although the mothers with children are of course up. I don't envy them. It's hard to keep the young people busy and happy.

We'd all thought we'd be on the way to Portugal by now. Not sure when we will be put on the train—seems talk between the countries has broken down with the Germans being interned in North Carolina.

Fortunately, I think the dance did help revive flagging spirits. Kennan said this morning that Captain Patzak will allow us to hold a dance every Saturday night, provided everyone cooperates and follows the rules, etc.

January 19, 1942

A letter from F.

He is back in Berlin and reports that all is well in the "City of Light" but hints that he will be traveling again if he gets a new appointment, and it is an advancement he didn't seek and could mean that he would be away much longer this time, possibly months.

I have heard something of the German broadcasts (one of the newsmen has a radio hidden in his room) and Hitler has ordered offensives against the Czechs, from enslavement to extermination to teach "subservience and humility," so I do not know if F. would go there, or to Russia, or northern Africa where there have apparently been heavy casualties lately but the German news insists they are getting the upper hand.

January 20, 1942

They're starting a school of sorts here, offering classes and studies to help ease boredom and provide opportunities for furthering one's education. I was approached by Perry Laukhuf from the embassy about participating. I thought he was asking if I would be interested in taking one of the classes. Instead he was curious if I could teach either a language class (they are hoping to offer a full spectrum of language courses including German, Russian, French, and Spanish, and I am fluent in all but Russian, and somewhat proficient in that), or perhaps even something related to music? It seems that Laukhuf remembered I'd earned a music certificate from Hoch and thought I would be a good addition to the newly created "faculty." I've agreed to help out any way I can and look forward to having something else to do to pass the time.

January 26, 1942

We are to start our official classes next week. It will be something new.

    During cards today, the newsmen casually mentioned that the British "bombed the hell out of Bremen" last night but said no more. I wish we all had access to news, not just propaganda.

    I write to F. asking for an update on Frieda and his family. Are they all well, and safe? This is how we write, he and I, masking our interest with inquiries for others. What I really want to know is where will he be going when they send him off this next time . . .

January 29, 1942

Kennan found me at the piano this morning and wanted a word with me. He expressed concern that I remain very close with some of my friends in Berlin, in particular F., as he isn't just a member of the Nazi party, but an officer. I gently reminded Kennan that the US might be at war with Germany, but we are not at war with the people. My answer didn't sit well with Kennan and he gave me a long look before walking away.

I resumed playing but my hands were not as steady and I missed a few keys on one of the easier passages. I knew Kennan was aware I was "friendly" with F., but I hadn't realized he was paying that much attention to me . . . or my correspondence.

Which leads me to believe that Kennan isn't the only one aware of my correspondence, either.

February 4, 1942

While I worry endlessly about F., some of the "students" and "instructors" at our new "university" are not happy with Laukhuf, saying he is too rigid and demanding. I personally quite like him and do not mind his approach, but then, my music classes have always been rigorous so I am not disturbed by his expectations or desire for structure and discipline.

February 5, 1942

Haven't heard from F. in several days. Worried. Hope everything is fine. I hope his most recent letter hasn't been lost or detained as he is usually a very reliable correspondent.

February 7, 1942

"Badheim University" has a new president. Poor Perry stepped down today (although he was quite good-natured about his *dismissal) and Phillip Whitcomb is to take over. Phillip sought me out this afternoon to ask me to remain on as one of the instructors. He says he can't imagine a successful language and music program at the "University" without me.*

February 8, 1942

Have begun to get to know one of the American journalists, Ed Shanke, a younger newsman from Milwaukee. He was telling me during tea yesterday about the final press conference on December 10th where Paul Schmidt, Joachim von Ribbentrop's press spokesman, ordered all the American journalists from the press conference that day, which the reporters had half expected.

What was remarkable, though, was how the rest of the journalists in the room stood and formed a line to say good-bye to the Americans on the way out. Shanke said that unless one is a journalist it's hard to understand the bonds—and respect—shared by members of the press.

I admit to being rather envious of such a relationship. I don't have that with anyone here. I think the fact that F. and I continue to correspond so frequently has raised some eyebrows, with him being a German, and an officer.

February 13, 1942

Shanke asked me about F. today. He wondered if it was true that I was "in love with a Nazi." I didn't know how to answer. I think my inability to answer said more than words ever could.

It wasn't until I was in my room—alone—that I could think of an appropriate response. I'm not in love with a Nazi.

I'm in love with the most amazing man.

February 14, 1942

The newsmen have organized a newspaper. It is meant to be both amusing and informative, but no one knows if the stories in the paper are true or merely gossip.

February 18, 1942

Ash Wednesday. Dr. Herman conducted a non-denominational service. I accompanied for the hymns. Several of the German soldiers joined in. Complaints from a few but most aren't bothered. Missing F. terribly but he wouldn't enjoy the services like I do.

February 19, 1942

F. wrote today.

He asked if I'd been playing as much lately with all my new "teaching responsibilities" and wondered if I'd played anything by Wagner recently, which puzzled me to no end as he knows I dislike Wagner and would never play Wagner.

Then in the next line he wrote how Lohengrin was his favorite opera, but he supposed that was because of the "Bridal Chorus," surely one of the most lovely pieces of music ever written, and did I agree?

I had to stop reading. I put the letter down. I paced my room, my thoughts in a whirl.

Why did F. labor on so about the bridal march? He says nothing by chance. Everything is coded, everything means something.

He can't possibly be asking me my thoughts on marriage . . . can he?

February 20, 1942

Discovered new sheet music waiting for me at the piano today. Beethoven's Piano Sonata No. 1 in F Minor, Opus 2. The tension in the piece, the sense of agitation almost too perfectly reflects my mood, and yet I couldn't feel anything as I played, my thoughts racing ahead of my fingers. I finished the piece without even remembering touching the keys . . .

February 21, 1942

Another letter from F. He has not yet received my response but is leaving for his new assignment and doesn't expect to have received my letter before he goes this evening, flying out of Berlin to a location that promises to be much sunnier and drier.

He said that he hoped he hadn't surprised me with his passionate feelings for Wagner, but he is German after all and most devoted, and sincere, and he trusted that by now I knew that about him.

He did add that should my tastes run more to Mozart (which he suspected was true given my background and all), he liked Mozart, too, in particular the Overture from The Marriage of Figaro.

The bridal march.

The Marriage of Figaro.

For a moment I couldn't breathe. He is saying what I thought he was saying.

I finished reading the letter quickly at that point. His mail should be forwarded to him and he looks forward to hearing from me.

And Frieda sends her love and many many kisses.

I spend a long time holding his letter to my chest, cherishing the kisses and love, and aware that he is going to somewhere dangerous and sunny . . .

Benghazi, Gazala, Sicily, Malta . . .

But why? Why would an officer with the Reich's Ministry of Public Enlightenment and Propaganda be sent to a front line?

February 22, 1942

A letter today from my parents. It's been a long time since I heard from them. I almost cried when I went to my room to read the letter. I miss them. It seems like forever since I saw them. I suppose it has been forever, too.

Mother said Father is anxious for me to come home. She adds that he is not comfortable with Ellie's decision to go to California, either. This was news to me. Ellie has decided to follow in Jack London and Mark Twain's footsteps and be a journalist in San Francisco with hopes of later becoming a "real writer." Mother wrote that this isn't the time for Ellie to take risks but Ellie won't listen and Father suffers because of it.

And because of me.

He has regretted encouraging me to travel and study abroad and not insisting I return before the outbreak of war.

I immediately sit down and write a letter in response. I am well, and I am to be home soon, and Father isn't to worry. Ellie and I are intelligent young women, and yes, we are both ambitious and have a strong adventurous streak, but thankfully, we were not sheltered and so, wise to the world, we can at least attempt to protect ourselves. Father must take comfort in that.

February 25, 1942

Woke up in the middle of the night sweating even though the room was terribly cold.

I had a dream I was at the embassy and translating for a (German) Jewish father who was begging us to get his wife and his five young children out of the country. He had money in his hand and he kept shoving it in front of the clerk, Bill, saying, "Take it, take it, please take it, all of it and get my children out of here."

Bill shook his head. "It's not enough. It's too late. I am so terribly sorry, but there is nowhere to send them. There is no place for them to go."

The father was weeping.

I was weeping.

I woke up weeping and couldn't fall back asleep because I dreamed it, yes, but it wasn't a dream. It happened. Not just that one time, but over and over, every day for month after month. That dream was just a memory of an ordinary day at the embassy this last year.

If the Jews hadn't left by 1939, it was all but impossible to get them out. And tragically, so many waited to go, either because they didn't have the money, or they had ties too deep to leave, and so they'd hoped to wait the madness out.

February 26, 1942

I finish my music and language lessons but cannot play cards today, can't relax. Instead I sit at the piano and play to try to ease the intolerable ache in my chest, an ache that comes from knowing that we at the embassy did far too little, but our hands were tied by our government that didn't want to be involved. They didn't want to engage. They didn't want to change the immigration numbers and policies.

Living here, working at the embassy, surrounded at the Adlon by the press, I have heard what is happening in Poland, Czechoslovakia, Hungary, Romania. I have heard what the Germans and the fascists are doing as the soldiers and tanks roll through Lithuania and Latvia. All autumn we heard of the growing numbers sent to the concentration camps. We heard of the new camps being built. We heard of the relocation of Jews from their homes to ghettos, and from ghettos to camps. From the whispers that reach beyond the barbed wire camp walls we know what happens there . . . it is nothing short of murder. Massacres.

But that is not our affair, the government says. It is not for us to intercede.

If they were here, if they had sat in the embassy listening to the Jews beg for assistance and protection these past few years, perhaps they would have felt differently.

Perhaps the ordinary American citizen would have responded differently—the mothers and fathers—if they had heard how these mothers and fathers begged for the lives of their children.

Perhaps if America were here amidst the bombings and night raids, perhaps they would not have been so complacent these past few years.

The world may very well shout condemnation at Germany now, but the world shall have to look at itself and ask—did we do enough when we could have?

Did we care enough, when we should have?

February 27, 1942

A brief letter from F. He said Frieda misses me terribly.

I read and read the letter. It is so short that it worries me. I want to know where he is. I want to know what he is doing. I want to know when this horrible war will end.

March 1, 1942

Romance is everywhere these days. Everyone discusses the most obvious romances, as well as the supposedly secret relationships. With so much free time and yet so little space and freedom, there is intense interest and speculation about who is with whom, and doing what to whom, and how this particular coupling will go once we are all sent home.

I am part of the gossip. I am the beautiful, musical American that spends her time writing long anguished letters to her handsome Nazi.

I can't say anything, can't defend myself as they all knew F. They met him when I did. They knew him in the same official capacity as I.

But they can be smug and superior. They didn't develop a personal relationship. They knew better than to admire someone in the Propaganda Ministry.

March 6, 1942

I've been asked to play proper dance music—anything by Artie Shaw, Jimmy Dorsey Orchestra, the Andrew Sisters, Sammy Kaye, Glenn Miller—for tonight's dance. Thank God I don't need sheet music for most of the popular stuff and can pick up almost any tune after hearing it once or twice.

March 7, 1942

Last night's dance got a little out of hand. Too much drinking and singing and throwing of spittoons . . . the dance for next Saturday has been cancelled and no one is now allowed to drink in one's bedroom. I am fine with the punishment as I wasn't drinking, or throwing spittoons. In fact, I was in bed trying to sleep, and finding it impossible due to the wild drunken antics of my colleagues and newsmen friends.

March 9, 1942

Over ten days without a letter from F.

But the mail brought a letter from Robert Best today. Robert left for Berlin six days ago but now he's written to say he's not returning. He's choosing to go home, back to Vienna. Morris has forbidden us from communicating with Best, saying he is no longer stable, but I understand how pulled he is. Vienna has been his home for twenty-some years. He views himself as an Austrian now, not an American.

He is not the only one. There are others here with deep ties to "our enemy."

Elfriede has a German fiancé, Joachim has a pregnant German wife (who is back in Berlin, and having to fend for herself during the air raids).

And I have F.

March 10, 1942

Received a letter from Mother today. Father was hospitalized end of last month with congestive heart failure. He is home *again and Mother said Father thinks he will be on his feet very soon. She isn't so optimistic.*

I attempt to distract myself playing Schumann's Concerto for the Piano.

It doesn't help.

March 12, 1942

Haven't been able to eat or sleep since receiving Mother's letter.

I need to go home.

I think he will recover better once I'm home. I'll write Ellie, too. I'll write Ellie and we'll both go home.

March 13, 1942

I wrote F. today and told him I didn't like Wagner's bridal march or Mozart's Figaro. I thought perhaps there were better choices for both of us.

My heart is broken.

Das ist alles.

March 15, 1942

Haven't heard back from F. I don't know when he'll receive my letter, or if he has already received it.

Haven't heard from Mother since her last letter and am most anxious for an update on Father. Hoping Ellie will be home soon and can update me properly.

Played what I could remember of Bach's Piano Concerto in D Minor. I was surprised by how much I did remember and when I couldn't recall a passage perfectly I improvised, and yet I couldn't feel the music, not when every note conjured F. I could see us in Berlin, walking arm in arm beneath the big handsome lime trees on Unter den Linden. I could feel the warm light on our faces as we walked, the sunshine dappling the sidewalk. I could smell the air, sweet, fresh.

We won't ever have Berlin again. We won't have the future. I cry as I play, filled with despair.

I can see it all, remember it all, our trips to the country . . . the Sunday drives to Potsdam to stroll through the gardens at Sanssouci and then coffee and plum cake before returning home.

I can't play on. It's too much.

I feel too much.

Music today just causes more pain.

March 16, 1942

Herr Zorn found a box of sheet music in the basement and brought it to me. He thought perhaps I would like some new music, but suggested I avoid anything "controversial," which means I should focus on the Germans and Austrians.

Spent the hour before dinner playing Robert Schumann's Piano Sonata No. 2 in G Minor, Opus 22, and the first part is fast—schnell, noch schneller—and Doris complained at dinner that it gave her a headache as it was too loud, fast, and frantic, but it was good to play as quickly as my fingers could fly. Better to play than to pace or hide and cry.

March 19, 1942

Morris shared with all tonight at dinner that the Drottningholm departed New York for Lisbon two days ago. We should be sailing home soon.

March 23, 1942

A letter from Mother. Father died.

I am inconsolable. I should have been there.

The piano is the only place I can find comfort. I play Mozart's Requiem, tears falling, the keys wet.

I hope he knows how much I love him.

March 25, 1942

Ellie wrote to tell me she was at the house with Father when he died.

Mother is working on the funeral arrangements and has asked Ellie to select the readings so she can focus on the music selections. As expected, Mother is set on Handel's "I Know that My Redeemer Liveth," but hasn't decided on the rest.

March 26, 1942

More devastating news.

F. has been injured.

I received a letter from him today—but not written by him. He dictated it to a nurse who was kind enough to assist him.

He was injured a fortnight ago and is now at a hospital in Rome recovering. I am not to worry as he is receiving excellent care but he apologizes for not writing sooner.

He promises to write more soon but he doesn't want me to worry.

I worry.

He doesn't sound as if he's received my letter. I must write him back. I do not know how to tell him, not when he's injured.

Not when I don't know how seriously he's been wounded because whenever F. tells me "not to worry" it usually means the situation is very serious.

March 29, 1942

Not only is it Palm Sunday, but Morris shared with all today that yes, it is the Drottningholm that will take us back to New York. The ship is being prepared, and Herr Zorn and his staff will soon inspect the hotel rooms and shall begin invoicing us for damages and payment.

I don't know what to think, or feel.

March 30, 1942

Everyone remains very excited about the transfer home. Much speculation as to when this could be as Morris was advised by our Swiss contacts that it could be a while but that doesn't dampen the enthusiasm in the least. All is ready to go.

Received a letter from F. today, and it's still not his handwriting. His injury must be more serious than he lets on.

But his letter was to let me know that he has just received the packet of my letters, forwarded on to the hospital and he was very sorry to learn of my father's passing, and sends his condolences and sympathy to my mother and sister.

He asks my forgiveness with the shortness of this letter but he isn't able to hold a pen just yet and feels guilty taking the nurse's time when she is needed elsewhere. However, he wanted me to know that my letters did arrive and he is so sorry to get all *my news and while he disagrees with me, he is too much of a gentleman to criticize my taste in music.*

For a long time I just sit with his letter.

My heart aches.

It hurts to breathe.

April 3, 1942

Received a letter from Ellie. Ellie is trying to convince Mother to move to San Francisco with her.

I long for a letter from F. but nothing comes.

April 6, 1942

It is Easter Sunday. I played for the morning Easter service today but played with a heavy heart. I cannot find the words to express my sadness. At least I have music. It speaks for me.

April 9, 1942

Received a brief letter from F., written in his own shaky hand . . . written using his left hand!

He is being discharged from the hospital in Rome this afternoon and will be traveling back to Berlin to see a specialist as he shall require more surgery to make his right arm and hand more fully operational, and while recuperating he will return to work at one of the Reich's war offices.

April 13, 1942

Captain Patzak stopped by the lounge where I was playing to tell me that Herr Zorn had some questions about damages to my room and to please go examine the bill and make arrangements to settle the outstanding debt.

I arrived in Herr Zorn's office and his secretary walked me in, and then shut the door, leaving me in the office.

I turned to protest and F. was there.

I couldn't believe it. I didn't know what to do.

He was in uniform and didn't look hurt, at least not at first glance, but then I saw the cane and the gauze and bandages beneath the cuff of his jacket.

"What happened to you?" I asked, wanting to touch him, but afraid to move.

"In the wrong place, at the wrong time," he answered with a wink and a smile.

I cried then.

It was the same F. wink and smile.

I have missed him so very much.

I told him that, too.

"You kept me alive when I was wounded in Malta," he said quietly, not smiling anymore. His blue eyes are now so very serious. He looked so very serious. "I thought of you, and how much I love you, and how much it means to me that you believe in me. I realized there that I'm not afraid to live, but I'm also not afraid to die."

It was as if my throat was being squeezed. I couldn't swallow, or speak.

"I would very much like to marry you, and have a life with you, my darling," he added, "but if you feel you must return to your family, I will support that decision. But I couldn't let you leave without coming to see you. Without telling you that you give me courage and strength to do the right thing."

I went to him then, and lightly, gently touched his face. I

touched the corners of his eyes where there are those creases I love so very much. I touched his mouth with my fingertips. "I love you," I whispered. "I will always love you."

"You should be sailing for the US in a month's time. Arrangements are being made for the transfer of all internees to Lisbon by train—"

"What is the extent of your injuries?"

"That is neither here nor there, Liebchen."

"You need more surgeries."

"I'd like to get my hand back, if possible."

"Is it possible?"

"I hope."

He hopes.

My heart had begun to hammer harder.

I might have lost hope these past few weeks but he hasn't. He still hopes . . . believes . . .

Here is someone I can believe in.

Here is someone that needs me.

"I don't want to leave you," I tell him.

"Then don't."

"You make it sound so simple."

"It is, if you're my wife."

And so that settles that. We are to be married soon . . . immediately . . . before F. continues to Berlin. He has asked me to trust him, and leave all the details to him. And so I have.

April 14, 1942

Did not see F. today, nor did I hear anything from him, but I think Morris is suspicious. He kept me at his side all day translating documents that didn't need translation, and making odd comments on one's moral responsibility to one's country, particularly during a time of war.

April 15, 1942

New sheet music was on the piano today. Bach. The Art of Fugue. I sit down to play Part 1 and immediately lose myself.

F. has said to leave everything to him. He has said to trust him.

I do.

F. is to be in Berlin in two days' time. If we are going to do something, it must be soon.

April 17, 1942

We did it. Or F. did it and I'm not sure who helped him—Herr Zorn or Captain Patzak or one of the other guards—but yesterday F. was able to get me out, using a laundry cart and then a steamer trunk. In town, one of Franz's friends, a judge, married us in a civil ceremony. Franz had booked us a room at a small hotel for the night but we were only able to be there a few hours, but it was bliss to be alone, together, husband and wife.

Husband and wife.

Did I really write that?

And yet now, he is already gone. Off to Berlin and his appointment and we shall see what comes next.

But I know this, I won't be leaving Germany with everyone else.

April 20, 1942

Letter from F. They want to operate immediately. It's that or his hand will be amputated. His hand may need to be amputated anyway, possibly up to the elbow.

He will write more soon.

A nd that's it. That's the last line of the last thin, tissue-like page.

Jarred back to the present, I check the old worn envelope, but there are no more pages inside. I glance at the clock. It's almost one thirty in the morning, but I don't feel as if I've been reading for hours.

Why does the diary end so abruptly?

Is there a section missing? There must be a section missing, because I need to know what happens next.

SEVENTEEN

Edie

Ali returns in the morning with questions, knocking on my door before I've had a third cup of coffee.

I still make my coffee myself in a percolator I've had for over thirty years. Parts have needed to be replaced—the crystal knob in the top for example—but it still works just as well as when I bought it in 1967 and I see no reason to get one of those fancy coffee machines now.

"Where is the rest of the diary? Why does it end there? And what happened to Franz?" Alison asks, firing questions at me as she enters my apartment before I've even invited her in, clutching the envelope I gave her yesterday.

I close the door and head to the kitchen to refill my cup. "There were a few more pages, I'm not sure what happened to them, but when I left Bad Nauheim at the end of the month, I made arrangements for my diary to go home with one of the girls. She promised to send it to Ellie, once she arrived, since she was heading to California herself."

"But what happened to Franz?"

I take a sip of my coffee. "He lost his hand."

Alison's mouth opens and closes. Her brow furrows. "I don't understand."

"What don't you understand?" I'm cross. I didn't sleep well and she might be educated, but I'm not sure how smart she is.

She sits down at my kitchen table—again, uninvited—and faces me. "America was at war with Germany. You'd been held in an internment camp, Bad Nauheim, for four months. How could you not go to Portugal, Edie? Wasn't it mandatory?"

"Not if you revoke your American citizenship."

The girl stares at me, judging me. That's fine. They all judged me. They were all so angry, then. Not just the embassy staff, but their families, my friends, the journalists, even the German guards.

I married the enemy.

"It wasn't a comfortable situation," I say. "There was tremendous pressure for me to do what I was told. Franz was ill—his surgery didn't go well—and I was summoned to Berlin. So before we were all put on the train to Lisbon, I went to Berlin."

"How?"

"I showed the paper, my marriage certificate, proving that I'd secretly married Franz four weeks earlier, and as his wife, I could become a German citizen. So I demanded to be made a German citizen."

Alison just stares at me, eyes wide.

I'm silent, too.

Even now, the audacity of it shocks me. But I was just twenty-one at the time. What did I know of the world? What did I know of politics and government? I was in love and I believed love would save us. Protect us.

She glances at the envelope in her hands. "So eventually you were allowed to remain behind?"

"The embassy staff was beside itself. At first they refused

to accept that I would give up my American citizenship for a Nazi. And then they were angry. They accused me of being a traitor. They accused me of maybe working for Germany, of being a spy. I denied it. And I understood their anger, and their confusion. Germany was at war with the US, how could I become a German?"

I fuss with a dish towel and wipe up an imaginary spot, needing a moment to gather myself.

It's been seventy-some years and I can still see that day, still feel the terrible blistering rage and suspicion.

The Americans were livid, and I was conflicted, first "interviewed" by the Americans, and then interrogated by the Germans, and neither side trusted me.

No one in that moment wanted me.

It was up to Franz in the hospital, in Berlin, to convince his officers and the police that I would be loyal to the Party.

Yes, Franz was a registered member of the Nazi Party. But then, back then, everyone was a Nazi. It was the only party.

"But you did," Alison says, breaking the silence, focusing the conversation. "You became German."

I carry my coffee to the table and sit down opposite her. "I did, and I was told I'd never be welcome in the US again. I believed it. I was told I might have gained a husband, but I'd lost my friends, my family, and all respect. And I believed that, too."

"And that didn't worry you?"

"Of course it worried me! I remember the backlash and condemnation back in March when the reporter Robert Best left Bad Nauheim to return to Berlin. I knew people would speak of me in the same way. But I loved Franz and I wanted to stay with him. I wanted to help, although I didn't yet know how."

"And you couldn't tell the Americans, or your friends, that Franz was part of the German Resistance?"

"Absolutely not. I couldn't risk his safety, or the work he was doing. Telling anyone would have been a death sentence for him, and everyone he was associated with."

I reach out for the faded yellow envelope and she hands it to me. I'm glad to have the diary back. There are not many pages in the diary, and yet these few precious pages tell our story, and it's a testament to love.

Or foolishness.

It's hard sometimes now, as old as I am, and as cynical as I've become, to perceive a difference between the two.

EIGHTEEN

Ali

"I'm tired," Edie says abruptly, thin lips tightening as she lifts a hand, as if to shoo me away.

I take the hint, and stop for a coffee on my way to Bloom. I've a headache today from being up so late last night reading, but my day is just beginning. I don't want to be heading to the shop, though. I'd rather be hiding out in the Napa library reading everything I can get my hands on about the German Resistance.

I know a lot about many things, but I don't know enough about Edie's world, or her husband. In fact, despite reading pages and pages of her diary, I still know nothing about her husband.

While waiting for my coffee, I do a quick Internet search on my phone on the German Resistance and there are pages and pages of links and websites.

I type in *Franz German Resistance* and get an entire page of names.

Franz Jacob. Wilhelm Franz Canaris. Franz Halder. Franz Dahlem. Franz Gockel.

A lot of Franzes.

Trying to narrow it down, I type in, *Franz Berlin 1944 German Resistance*.

And maybe it does whittle a few down, but there are still a lot of Franzes, and they are all connected to Berlin, in 1944—Franz Jacob, Franz Rehrl, Franz Mett, Franz Kaufmann, Franz Sperr—hard to tell if any of them are Edie's Franz.

My name is called, my coffee is ready, and yet I stand in the corner, scrolling through the various links, skimming the information, curious, troubled, fascinated.

Edie's opened the door to a dark part of the past. It's a messy, shameful world. It's ugly. Brutal. And maybe that's what has hooked me. The ugliness and the pain and the shame.

It's how I feel. About me. About my past. About Andrew.

About failing Andrew.

Reading Edie's diary makes me realize I'm not the only one.

I'm not the only one to struggle and love and lose.

I'm not the only one to feel such guilt . . .

And suddenly it hits me—that I want to go.

I want to go to Germany. To Berlin.

I don't know where the thought comes from, and I don't really understand as I have no history in Germany. I don't even know Edie's Germany, but I'm curious.

No, it's more than curiosity . . . It feels more like a compulsion. To go, to see.

I can't imagine what I'd accomplish by going, but it's a place that has struggled and suffered, and I want to understand the suffering so I can learn how it healed.

Along with the usual phone and Internet orders, Bloom is doing the flowers for an engagement dinner party tonight on the Napa Valley Wine Train, and so the plan is for me to tackle the table arrangements while Diana conducts the interviews for the floral designer position at Bloom, as the young girl from last week definitely didn't work out.

I line up the bases for the twenty-four small centerpieces—floral wreaths of rose-hued dahlias, purple stock, and pale pink peonies with a floating calla lily in the center vase—and do one for Diana to check before she leaves. Diana studies it for a moment and then takes some greens and miniature Meyer lemons that she puts on sticks, and then tucks the greenery and lemons in the wreath, immediately adding a bright visual pop.

I ask her, "How did you know to do that?"

"It just looked too bridal or baby shower. The lemons and spiky greens give it an edge, making it more masculine which is better for a couple's event."

"Do we have enough lemons?"

"No, but do the arrangements without them, and I will pick some up on my way back. We can add them in at the end."

With Diana gone the shop is quiet. I turn on the local NPR radio station for the classical music, and get to work.

As my hands gather stems and begin to shape and arrange, my thoughts drift free. I have to return to Arizona soon, and I'm going to miss Dad. He's not the greatest conversationalist but it's been nice having this time with him. I do feel closer to him. I feel more secure as well. Hopefully the secure feeling won't go once I'm back in Scottsdale. I'll be back at work in just ten days and I'm sure Dr. Morris will be relieved to have me back. He really relies on me and I can't let him down.

But it's hard to believe that I've already been in Napa three weeks. Three weeks today, actually. I can't forget to buy my return ticket to Arizona, buy the ticket while it's cheap.

A little voice whispers in my head, *There is time to go to Berlin, if I wanted to go.*

I smash the thought.

I'm not going to Berlin.

I need to save my money and work and focus on my commitments.

But as I start the next arrangement, I find myself thinking about Edie, Franz, and Berlin. Not just the Berlin of the war, but the Berlin before, the Berlin of music, literature, architecture, and art. Her stories have teased my imagination. I want to know what she knew. I want to see the Hotel Adlon. I want to walk beneath the lime trees on Unter den Linden, and take a car to Potsdam and tour Sanssouci and walk through the gardens and have a coffee and a slice of kuchen.

As I finish the arrangement, I take a quick break, refill my water bottle and then just out of curiosity, I pull out my laptop from my purse and go to my favorite travel website, type San Francisco to Berlin, putting in Sunday's date, and giving the following Saturday as a return travel date. I check that I want a flight and a hotel package, as few flight connections as possible, and as good a price as I can get. And then I hit enter.

I hold my breath as the travel site sifts through the various fares and deals before starting to list my options. There are a lot of options. I narrow down the search by choosing the shortest duration of flight and scroll through the best fares.

I can get a twelve-and-a-half-hour flight to Berlin from San Francisco in economy, with a fourteen-hour return flight, one stop in each direction, for a little over twelve hundred dollars. If I purchase a hotel and air package, I get a special discount, with three nights free, and a significant savings on both air and hotel, making the package price just under fifteen hundred for both.

I could fly to Berlin and stay five nights for less than fifteen hundred dollars. It's a lot of money when I've got the mortgage payments on the house but my credit cards are pretty empty and I've been careful this last year. I rarely shop or spend money . . .

My fingers itch. I curl them into my palms, tempted. So very tempted.

Travel is so easy these days. All my information is stored on the travel site. I'd just have to hit enter and it'd be done.

My hands still hover above the keyboard. I want to do it. I want to go. But I don't do things like this. Andrew was the impulsive one. Not me.

I can't remember the last time I just did something crazy. For the hell of it. My life is planned. Organized. Directed. Those lists I make . . . those endless to-dos are my calls to action . . .

Abruptly, I close my laptop, put it back in my purse and get busy with the next arrangement.

My hands are busy but my mind isn't free. It keeps returning to Germany, Edie's world. It must have been terrifying and yet fascinating working at the American embassy in Berlin in December 1941. Edie was part of history in the making. She *was* history in the making.

I snip and shape and arrange even as I try to picture the American staff and journalists being put on trains and sent to the Grand Hotel in Bad Nauheim. I wish I could see the hotel. I wonder if the hotel still exists.

Finishing the arrangement I pull my computer back out, and do a quick search for the Grand but can only find historical references. I try my favorite travel site, searching Bad Nauheim and there are plenty of luxury properties, but nothing named the Grand.

I'm still debating the merits of a trip when the announcer on the NPR classical music station that Diana always streams at Bloom returns to tell us we've just been listening to Mozart, who is undoubtedly one of the greatest musicians to have ever lived, with Bach universally agreed to be the greatest.

He goes on to talk about his great works and masterpieces, and how Bach, who wrote in the baroque period, is as romantic as anything by Beethoven, Schumann, or Wagner.

The great German composers.

Edie's studies at Hoch.

Her passion for music.

And then as the piece begins, Bach's Double Violin Concerto in D minor, my eyes burn. In the violins I hear love and longing.

I hear Edie, and her love for Franz.

And suddenly I know I must go. Not for her. But for me.

I glance at my watch. It's almost noon now. Helene could swing by my house and grab my passport on her lunch break. She has a key. She's house sitting for me while I'm gone. That's all that's keeping me from actually going.

I text Helene, asking if she's taken her lunch yet.

She answers almost immediately. No, but she's just about to go.

I call her and explain that I need a favor. Can she please pass by my house on her lunch, get my passport from the important documents folder at the back of the bottom drawer in my bedroom desk, and send it by overnight mail to me?

"Are you going somewhere fun?" she asks.

"Berlin," I answer.

"Berlin?"

I can practically see her wrinkle her nose in distaste. "You don't think that sounds fun, Helene?"

"Um, no. Not unless I'm going to that big Oktoberfest thing where I'd drink beer, sing songs, and get drunk. Oh. Is that what you're doing?"

"No. That's in the autumn, and I think you're thinking of Munich."

"Right." She pauses. "So why are you going?"

"I want to go see Edie's Berlin."

"Who is Edie?"

The violin concerto plays on in the background putting a lump in my throat. It takes me a second to answer. "This rather crotchety ninety-four-year-old at my dad's retirement home."

"I don't get it."

I'm glad she can't see my face. "That's okay. I don't, either."

By the time Diana returns at one, I've booked my trip, I've mentally organized my packing list, and my passport is with FedEx, being rushed to my attention at Bloom, no signature required, arriving by ten tomorrow morning. It only cost a small fortune to guarantee its delivery, but it's worth it. I can't leave the country without it.

I'm leaving the country. I'm going to Germany. *Berlin*. Until I met Edie I'd never ever given Berlin a second thought.

This is *crazy*.

But I'm excited. And a little freaked out. This spontaneous decision making is so not me.

I wonder what Dad will say. And I can't wait to tell Edie. Not sure how she'll react, either. After all, Berlin is her city. The diaries are her stories. The memories are of a time before I was born.

And just like that, I'm filled with misgivings. Should I not be doing this?

Is it ridiculous?

But no, can't go there. Too late for second thoughts. It's a nonrefundable, non-transferable ticket. I'm too careful with money to waste $1,500 so I'm going.

On Sunday.

I think I'm having a nervous breakdown.

Diana and I put the miniature lemons on florist wire and we tuck the lemons into the twenty-four arrangements before loading the flat boxes into the deliveryman's new air-conditioned van. Thank goodness for his new van. He can finally be reliable again.

As we head back into the shop, Diana tells me about the interviews this morning. Two of the three people she interviewed were possibilities, but one was an absolute standout, and she's already asked Carolyn to come in tomorrow to work a half day and see how she does. Carolyn has a design background but no experience as a florist, however Diana was impressed with her energy and attitude, and thinks she could be a great fit at Bloom.

"I'll have to train her," Diana says as she closes the door behind us. "But that's not a big deal. I had to train you."

"This is true."

"So how much longer do I have you for?"

"I wanted to talk to you about that."

"You're not leaving soon are you?"

"Well . . ."

"Not before Saturday?"

"No. Not before the DeMoss wedding. That's a promise."

"Whew. Okay. So when do I lose you?"

"Sunday."

Diana's expression falls. "This Sunday?"

"Yeah."

"Wow." Her shoulders slump. "That's terrible."

"It's not that terrible. I'm not that good."

"No, you're not. But I like you. And just having you around has been so inspirational."

I straighten, brighten. "Has it?"

"Yeah. You're this daily reminder to brush at least twice a day and to keep flossing my teeth."

I laugh, hard, so hard that tears fill my eyes and Diana's laughing, too. I give her a hug. "Thank goodness you're a Huskie, or I wouldn't like you at all."

• • •

I leave Bloom at five and am walking to my car when a black pickup truck slows next to me. I glance at the truck. A brown and white bulldog hangs out the passenger window, tongue lolling, smiling.

Bruiser.

"Hey," I shout at Craig.

He pulls to the curb. I walk over and pet Bruiser who is absolutely thrilled to see me, although I'd be willing to bet he has no memory of me. But that's the great thing about bulldogs. They like everybody.

"How is it going?" I ask Craig, giving Bruiser's ear another scratch. Bruiser thanks me with slobber all over my wrist.

"Good. And you?"

"Great."

"You look happy."

"I am." I feel the bubble of anticipation rise, and warm me. I'm dying to tell him about Berlin. I want him to be excited for me. But he might not understand. He might not know I don't do things like this. I don't travel and jet around having adventures. If I travel, it's to a conference. I sit in meeting rooms and look at PowerPoint presentations and take copious notes. "Your aunt Edie has inspired me."

"Has she? How?"

"I'm going to go to Germany." I hesitate. "This Sunday."

"That's fantastic."

"I know." I smile shyly. "It's just for six days. I fly back in Saturday so I can spend Father's Day with my dad before returning to work Monday in Scottsdale."

There's a flicker in his eyes, an expression I can't quite read. It's only there a moment and then it's gone. "I guess we're just going to miss each other. I head to Italy Wednesday for a wine and food expo in Tuscany, but I won't be back until after you're in Scottsdale."

I'm disappointed, and I don't even know why. We hardly know each other. We've just had dinner once and talked a half-dozen times. "You're going over on your own?"

"No, Chad will be there, too, along with his girlfriend. He's planning on getting married after the expo. He was trying to keep the wedding a secret but he had to tell a few people to make sure they'd be there. Like her kids. And family. Sounds like they're all going now, and I'm happy for them."

"You like her?"

"Love Meg. She's amazing. She used to work for us. I already think of her as family."

"She's not the one . . ." My voice drifts off. I don't finish the sentence, not sure how to ask if she's the one he'd had the affair with.

But Craig knows what I'm asking and he nods. "She is."

"And it worked out?"

"True love wins."

True love wins. I used to believe that. I don't anymore.

My heart does a funny little flip and my breath suddenly catches. "I'm happy for them," I say, a catch in my voice because I'm jealous, and a little bit angry. I wanted the happy ending. Deep down, I still do. "It all sounds so romantic."

"So what's taking you to Germany?"

Nothing nearly as romantic as a wine expo or a Tuscany wedding. "Just have an itch to travel." Bruiser nudges my hand with his face, demanding more attention. I rub beneath his chin, and then around his fat jowls. He's practically panting with pleasure. "It seemed like a good time to do something new and adventurous before I'm back to being Dr. McAdams, scary dentist lady, again."

He grins. "You're far from scary."

"I'll tell my patients that."

"So Sunday . . . you're gone."

"Yeah."

"Can I take you to dinner before you go?"

"Um . . ." I look past Buster's big wrinkly face with the jutting canines and feel my insides wobble. Craig is so appealing in so many ways. If I lived here instead of Arizona . . . if I hadn't lost Andrew . . . if Andrew and I'd broken up instead of him taking his life . . .

"Your aunt Edie wouldn't approve," I say, stumbling onto the first excuse I can think of.

"Aunt Edie isn't the one asking you to dinner."

"I know, but . . . but . . ." I can't find the right words. I don't know how to tell him how desperately afraid I am of him, of men, of me, of life, of love.

I trusted Andrew. I trusted him to love me and protect me, just the way I loved him, and protected him.

And he broke that trust. And in the process, he broke me.

My mouth opens, closes. I shrug. "I like you," I say simply.

"Good. I like you. So dinner tomorrow night."

"Tomorrow night is Friday. It's bingo night. I'd hate to miss it."

His blue gaze searches my face intently. I'm not sure what he's looking for but after a moment his expression eases, and the corner of his lips lift. "In that case, I won't try to persuade you to join me for dinner, as I'd hate for you to miss something you enjoy so much."

He's letting me off the hook gently, teasing me, and I'm grateful. He's a kind man. A really good man.

But Andrew was, too.

And Andrew still hurt me. Badly.

At home, I change into shorts and a T-shirt and my shoes and go for a run.

I run and run, feeling as if wolves and monsters are at my heels.

But there are no wolves or monsters on my heels. It's just my heart crashing about my chest, thumping wildly. I'm scared.

I'm scared if I reach forward I'll lose what's behind me.

I'm scared if I stop being angry with Andrew I'll stop loving him.

I'm scared that everything will change and I'll forget who I was with him and become someone new. Someone different.

I won't be Andrew's Ali anymore. I won't be his girl. I'd become someone else's girl and I'm not ready for that. Because Andrew needs me. His ghost needs me. I'm all he has left.

NINETEEN

Edie

Today was bridge. Bill is my partner again, and I'm glad, not just because we usually win, but because I want to talk to him about Alison.

I want her to come over tonight. I need to talk to her. I need to make her understand that Franz was a good man. I'm not sure she believes me. I'm not sure she knows the risks he took, and the things he did.

Bill promises to send her a text. He says she's good about responding to texts and he'll tell her to come see me tonight, or in the morning.

I tell him I want her to come tonight, if possible. I'm not sure I'll be able to sleep, worrying.

He asks me if I'm feeling okay. He says I seem agitated.

I *am* agitated.

She must come see me tonight. I insist.

TWENTY

Ali

After my run, I shower, dress, and grab something from the fridge that I can eat at my computer. There are so many things I want to look up, so many things I want to learn before I go on Sunday.

I check the weather.

I check the distance from the airport to the hotel.

I check the currency (euros) and exchange rate. (Doesn't favor us.)

I read about the city and top attractions and I'm not surprised that nearly all have something to do with World War II.

The Third Reich Walking Tour.

Hitler's Berlin.

The Holocaust Memorial.

But there are also other tours and museums. The Potsdam palace tour. The DDR Museum. Checkpoint Charlie Museum.

It's going to be interesting. I need to get some travel guidebooks. Make a list of everything I want to see. Make proper notes so I remember the important things.

I do so love my lists and notes.

I'm online researching Edie's Berlin, wanting to find her husband Franz, and if he was a member of the German Resistance, he should be here. It ought to be easy to find him. I search for Franz Stephens but there is none. Maybe his last name isn't Stephens. I should ask her. I'll ask tomorrow.

I continue reading, and the names of Edie's friends pop up. Adam and Claus and Peter and so many others, but still, no mention of anyone who sounds like her Franz, at least, not among the notable German Resistance.

There is a Fritz, numerous Hanses, Wilhelms, and Heinrichs, Dietrichs, Axels, Rudolfs, Eugens . . .

A Roland, Theodor, Ulrich . . .

What I need is her Franz's full legal name, and his birth date. It'd help to know about his family, where he was born, where he's buried.

Tomorrow when I see her, I'm going to take my notebook, my computer, and find out everything.

I arrive at Edie's apartment just before nine the next morning, but she's not happy with me. I'm not sure what's wrong but she won't even let me inside her apartment. She stands in the doorway, blocking my entrance, shaking her head at me, her lips moving silently, as if forming words, but I can't hear what she's saying. I don't know what's happening.

"Are you upset with me?" I ask.

Her eyes are pink. Deep circles form purple smudges beneath her eyes. She looks at me as if I'm an utter disappointment.

"Edie."

I waited for you," she says. She's trembling slightly. "You were supposed to come. And I waited for you."

"When?"

"Last night. Your father said he'd text you. He said you would come and I was sure you'd come, too."

"I didn't get a message."

She lifts a hand, flaps it at me. "So go away. I don't want to talk now. It's too late—"

"Why is it too late? Did something happen?"

"I'm too upset now."

I've seen her stiff and angry and frosty. I've heard her be sharp. But I've never seen her like this. She looks frail and faded, as if she's aged ten years overnight. "I honestly didn't get a message, Edie, or I would have come. I promise I would have. You know how much I like you—"

"Don't make up stories. You don't like me."

"Oh, but I do, Edie." I give her a faint smile. "I'm not sure how it happened, but you've grown on me."

Her pink-rimmed eyes water. The tip of her tongue appears and touches her upper lip. "I stayed up late."

"I'm sorry."

"I thought something happened to you."

Oh, Edie. I move forward to hug her but she steps back, putting distance between us.

"I'm not a child," she says sharply. "I don't need to be placated."

"I wasn't trying to placate you."

"Why are you here?"

"I wanted to talk to you about Berlin. And Franz."

Her expression is impassive.

"I've booked a trip," I add. "I'm flying to Germany on Sunday, going to Berlin, and I want to visit all the places you wrote about in your diaries and I thought you could help me. You know Berlin so well and I thought maybe you could tell me where I should go, and what I should do—"

"My Berlin is gone," she interrupts. "It was destroyed in the war."

"Not everything was destroyed," I say. "And a lot of new building is happening, lots of redevelopment since the reunification of Germany in 1990."

"There's a hundred places you could go. Why Berlin?"

I look into her face, her expression guarded. She's suspicious, but also curious. But at least she's listening to what I'm saying.

"I don't know how to explain it, and I'm not sure anyone will understand it, especially as I don't really understand it, but you've made me want to see Berlin. You've made me want to know about Franz and your friends."

"But they're gone. They're all dead."

"I know. But when you talk to me about him . . . about them . . . they seem so real. They seem alive. Your stories make them live again."

E die lets me in.

We get to the kitchen and she pours me a cup of coffee, and together we sit down at her small round table, my laptop open in front of us. I get on the Internet and type in Berlin. I click on images, and photos pop up documenting the Third Reich.

Edie stiffens. She doesn't like the black and white images of Berlin dressed and draped with swastika flags and generous swathes of bunting, or the photos of crowds lining the sides of the roads, and the goose-stepping SS and the tanks.

But the photos of the Berlin parades capture the buildings and the squares and the places she knows so well.

"That," she says, tapping the screen, "is Brandenburg Gate, and the ornate building on the far right of Pariser Platz is Blücher Palace, the US embassy. It's where I worked in the chancery. I was supposed to assist one of the officials for a week but I ended up getting hired full-time when they realized I was fluent in four languages, and passable in Russian."

I click on another photo that is of Blücher Palace in the rain and Edie studies the image intently. "That's where I worked. That's where I went every day for two years." She looks at me, eyes clear, bright. "There was no American ambassador at that time. Ambassador Wilson was recalled in 1938 in protest over Kristallnacht. I was still studying at the Hoch during that period, but I wasn't happy in Frankfurt. I wanted to be in Berlin. To me, everything important seemed to be taking place in Berlin."

"But wasn't Britain already at war with Germany? Didn't that scare you moving to Berlin?"

"Britain and France didn't declare war on Germany until after Germany invaded Poland, in September 1939, and the US didn't enter the war for almost another two years, so being an American, especially an American working for the US embassy, meant I was quite protected. Quite safe."

Edie is talking again about the old American embassy in Berlin, and the other embassies, and how they were once in the Tiergarten area but were forced out as the Tiergarten was emptied and bulldozed for Germania.

She's talking so fast I can barely keep up with her. "What is Germania?" I interrupt.

"Hitler's vision for Berlin . . . his dream capital that was absolutely hideous." She shudders. "Thank goodness it didn't happen, but so very many beautiful old buildings were demolished to make room for this futuristic capital. Such a shame. Although, with all the raids on Berlin, I doubt many of those beautiful buildings would have survived the bombing."

"What was that like? The bombing?"

"Frightening, at first, and then merely mind-numbing, because like everything else, one gets used to the sirens and the blackouts and the dashing to the shelters. There were some nights, near the end, when I was just too exhausted to race to the shelter. Better to die in my bed."

"Franz let you do that?"

"Oh, no. Never when he was at home. But he was rarely at home during that last year, always being sent here and there on secret missions. I'd be alone for weeks at a time, and it was in those long stretches that I'd just . . . give up."

I look into Edie's face, seeing the deep wrinkles, the high protruding cheekbones, the eyes that look more gray than blue this morning. Her skin is so thin you can see the faint blue veins beneath and yet she still has a steely core. I can feel her resolve. "I can't imagine you ever giving up."

"We spent years hungry, and cold. Everything was rationed. Everything was a struggle, but for me, the blackouts were the worst. The blackouts were suffocating. You step outside at night, and there's not a single light anywhere. No car lights, no street lamps, no gleam of light from a building. If the moon was obscured, or if there should be fog or mist, I'd feel absolute panic. The danger was real, too. In the pitch-black night that lasted until dawn, you'd fall into holes, run over other people on the sidewalk or street, trip over debris, because you couldn't see anything. Absolutely nothing. You could put your hand out in front of your face and not even see your fingers. It was that bad. And with the bombings, the city landscape was constantly changing. One day there's a building on the corner. The next, there's just a ruined building and a hole yawning in the middle of the street."

Her voice fades and she stares at my computer screen with a picture of a burned-out building. "I don't want to see that." Her voice quavers. "Take that away."

I close the laptop. "You kept no diary during that time?"

"Oh, no, I did. But it disappeared during the early spring of 1944. The building next door to ours was destroyed in one of the air raids and Franz insisted we move to his sister's for a bit. I didn't want to go, but he was worried about my safety, and so we packed a few things. Locked up the place." Her voice fades. "And that was it. We never returned to our home again."

"Why not?"

"Terrible things were happening in our neighborhood. Franz thought it was too dangerous. He thought if I stayed there I might get involved."

"So where did you go?"

"The Adlon for a month, and then to friends. We bounced from place to place for a while, waiting, waiting for the war to end so we could go home."

"But you never did go back."

"No."

"What happened to everything?"

"I don't know. I doubt the building survived the war. Berlin was bombed many times between November 1943 and March 1944. I think there were sixteen or seventeen air raids. And then later, after the war ended, the Russians ransacked or confiscated everything they could get their hands on. Where we lived in the Mitte ended up in the Russians' hands, and once the wall went up, it was impossible to get in, or out. I tried to visit with Ellie in 1978 but the wall was up. We couldn't get the necessary visas to go to the other side."

"I can't imagine staying in Berlin with all the air raids."

"I suppose I could have gone to the country more, gone to Franz's family more. Many of the wives did just that. They went to stay with relatives outside the city, where it was safer, but I hated to leave Franz alone."

"Yet he had his assignments . . . you said he'd go off for weeks and leave you alone."

"But Franz was all I had. There was no other family—" She breaks off, looks down, and fusses with the lace doily beneath her coffee cup. Her hand trembles as she turns it. "Well, Franz had his family, and his younger sister liked me, but his mother wasn't sure about me. I don't think she trusted me. I don't think she believed I was a good influence."

"And the Adlon . . . it stayed open throughout the war?"

"It did. It was one of the few that survived, through the war." Her expression softens. "I so loved the Adlon, too, and yes, it was a splurge, but it was also the center of everything. Drinks and dinners before the war, and then even during the rationing, you could still go there for a civilized meal. For conversation."

She's quiet remembering. "It was, perhaps, the only civilized place left in Berlin in 1944. During my last year in Berlin, during that final summer of 1944, the Adlon remained the center of everything for those like me, who were married to prominent Germans—"

"Nazis?"

Her shoulders twist. "If you weren't a 'loyal' Nazi, you were gone. Dead. So for those who were officers or who'd been aristocrats, the Adlon was a refuge from the war. It was one of the few places one could go for hot water and a telephone. I could leave a message there, too, and during the People's Court trials in August 1944, it was my only connection to Berlin when I was in Switzerland."

"When did you go to Switzerland?"

"In July."

"But wasn't the attempt in July—"

"Yes. Which is why the Adlon was so vital. Those calls to friends and from friends were my only real way of knowing what was happening, versus what the German propaganda machine spit out. And what the German propaganda machine spit out—just like the People's Court—was lies. They both operated under the principle of controlling the country, the people, with fear, and terror. If you are aggressive enough . . . violent enough . . . you will control the masses because most people buckle to fear and intimidation. They can't help it. Fear is destructive. Corrosive. One doesn't want to hurt, or be hurt. One doesn't want to suffer."

There is so much she's saying that I'm struggling to process it all. There are so many questions I want to ask, but I can't remember them all. "But your Franz and his circle of friends, they weren't afraid?"

"Oh, they were afraid, very afraid, but eventually they were more afraid of not taking action. They were afraid that they'd fail their ancestors, their country, the noble German blood in their veins, if they didn't act. You see, many of those who took part in the July twentieth plot were either military officers or descended from nobility. They were nationalists, loyal to Germany. I don't know that their motives were pure. I doubt they were truly altruistic—except for the pastors and priests—but the others, they were Prussian Wehrmacht soldiers and officers. They were aristocrats and the educated upper class. They'd come from affluent families and comfortable lives. And maybe that's why they failed. They were smart but not hardened. Idealistic intellectuals, and impractical, ill equipped for the reality of the Nazi philosophy of blitzkrieg, total war."

While she was talking I'd opened my laptop again and typed in the words *July 20th Plot* in the Internet search engine and links popped up—the German Resistance, Failed Coup, Claus von Stauffenberg.

Edie leans forward, points to a black-and-white photograph of a handsome young man in uniform. "Claus," she says. She leans even closer and reads the caption, and then sits back. "Terrible," she murmurs, "terrible."

"Tell me," I say.

"*Sippenhaft.*"

"*Sippenhaft?*" I repeat, the term unfamiliar, but then, so much of this is unfamiliar. We're taught European history and World War II, but our history lessons are divided between the war in the Pacific and the war in Europe.

"It's an old Germanic custom, and the Nazi authorities took advantage of this 'German' custom to punish those who betrayed Germany."

I'm still confused, so I type in a version of the word and the search engine corrects me, then pulls up the definition for *Sippenhaft*. I skim the definition, discovering that the word translates to "kith and kin imprisonment" for everyone connected to an individual suspected, or accused, of being disloyal. Kith and kin being family, friend, or neighbor.

"So who was punished this way?" I ask, turning from the laptop to Edie.

"The families of those involved in the July twentieth assassination attempt, beginning with Claus' family. In the weeks following the failed July twentieth coup, all of Claus' family was arrested—his wife, his children, his brothers, his mother, mother-in-law, cousins, uncles, and aunts, as well as all of their spouses and children."

"So everybody?"

"Yes."

"But not you?"

"I was away."

"Switzerland," I say softly.

She says nothing, but her silence speaks volumes.

"Did you know what was going to happen?" I ask.

She shakes her head, lips pressed tight. Her eyes are pink around the edges. She looks frail again. Tired.

No, not tired.

Sad. Terribly, terribly sad.

My chest aches. I ache. I think of Andrew. I think of how I was gone when he died . . . off to get ice cream.

I think of Edie and how she was sent to Switzerland.

I struggle to hold in the emotion. I can't cry. Not here, not in front of her. This is her story. And this is also what I want to know. What I need to know.

"If you'd remained in Berlin, you would have been arrested," I add quietly.

She nods once. "Yes, but I don't think I would have suffered as much as the Stauffenbergs and other German aristocrats. You see, Propaganda Minister Joseph Goebbels had long resented anyone who came from nobility, and it infuriated him that Colonel Stauffenberg was nobility. But as I'd said, many of the Wehrmacht officers were aristocrats. That was the Prussian way. Nobility was tied to leadership, and Prussian Germans prided themselves on their military leadership. So Claus' actions were despicable to the average German, and particularly offensive to the Nazi leadership who were not from an aristocratic background. I think it's Goebbels who referred to the German aristocrats as 'blue-blooded swine,' so the most obvious solution for Goebbels and Himmler was to exterminate all the aristocrats who shared the same 'bad blood' by imposing *Sippenhaft*, wiping out the individual and his entire family."

"Wiping out women and children, too?"

"Yes, but in this case, the children weren't killed or imprisoned, like so many of the women and mothers, but instead they were taken from their families when the mothers were arrested and placed with new families, because these children were, after all, bright, healthy Aryan children. Blond, blue-eyed, genetically desirable.

They were given to others. Prussian children . . . these Aryan children . . ."

Edie is quiet a long time. I wait for her to continue, my heart beating very fast because I do not know what she will tell me next, and yet I know it won't be good. It can't be good. Nothing that happened during that horrible war was good.

But Edie doesn't add more, and I can't stop thinking of the children taken from their mothers. I picture the Aryan babies and toddlers, the young boys and girls, and then those blond, blue-eyed children morph into the photo of Anne Frank, and pictures seared into my memory from the movie *Schindler's List*.

I see flashes of images, photographs and impressions of the war. The Jewish women and children on train platforms. The SS guards marching. The barracks of the concentration camps. The "showers."

"Did the Germans know what was happening during the war?" I ask, sick. Queasy. "Did Franz know what was happening?"

"I believe Franz knew more than most, yes."

"But he didn't tell you?"

"He was careful not to say too much. Most of the men were careful not to share very much. Adam was one of those who was very private. His wife knew virtually nothing. Claus' wife knew some. I think Peter's wife, Marion, knew the most. She was more involved than most wives and women, but even the most ignorant among us, still knew our men were committed to saving Germany. You couldn't *not* know, what with the frequency and duration of the meetings. Of course, none of these men called themselves 'the Resistance.' They weren't 'resisting,' they were attempting to remove Hitler from power and put a new government in place. They had a whole new cabinet and all the necessary government ministers ready. Everyone was ready. They just needed Hitler dead."

"So Claus made the attempt."

"And it failed."

I exhale slowly.

I know this next part from history. It's in the books. It's documented in newspaper articles and archives. In Internet encyclopedias and memoirs. I've been reading them all. I know who dies. I know who survives.

And yet listening to Edie, hearing her describe these men, and their goals, and knowing they all had wives and families, I feel . . . pain.

I want them all to survive. Not just Franz, and Franz and Edie's friends, but the 170,000 Jews that called Berlin home up until 1930 when the persecution began.

Indeed, I want to go back in time and change it all. A world without war. A world without suffering . . .

"You'd make an excellent history teacher, Aunt Edie," Craig says, from the doorway.

Edie and I both jump, startled.

My heart is hammering and I'm still feeling emotional. Undone. But Edie's surprise gives way to pleasure. She smiles at him. "Well, I was a teacher," she answers. "A very good teacher."

"And from all accounts, a very strict teacher," he adds.

"Yes, well, that goes without saying," she retorts, hands folding neatly on the table. "I didn't think I would see you until later."

"My meeting finished early so I thought I'd come over and see if you needed any help, or just company." Craig glances at me. "But apparently you've already got great company."

My pulse is still a little too fast, and I'm not sure if it's the stories, and the past, or the sudden appearance of Craig. Either way, I self-consciously stack my notebook and laptop and slide them into my purse. "I should go see Dad, and then get to Bloom. Today is my last day."

Edie looks at Craig. "She's going to Berlin. She's staying at a hotel on Torstrasse, in Mitte. It's very central to everything."

"So you approve, Aunt Edie?" he asks.

"Yes. I think the trip will be good for her," Edie answers with a decisive nod.

"I think it's a great idea," he says. "It's a wonderful city, one of my favorites in Europe."

I stand and reach for my bag. "You know Berlin well?"

"I visit the city at least once a year." He glances at his aunt. "I've tried to take my aunt with me, but she refuses every offer . . . just as she's refused to discuss Germany. I think Chad and I are both a little bit envious that she's shared so much with you."

Edie rolls her eyes. "You and Chad were never that interested in my past, which is why I haven't forced you to listen to my stories. You are good nephews, and you take care of me, but when it comes to you young men, my past is ancient history."

"I don't think that's true, or fair," Craig answers, but he's smiling.

"Pssh." She gestures, waving him off, but she's smiling, too.

Craig turns to me. "Need any recommendations? Hotels? Restaurants? Things to do?"

"I've got the hotel booked, along with some half-day tours. I'm most interested in visiting the memorials and seeing some of the places Edie has talked about." I glance at Edie, adding almost shyly, "I'm going to take lots of pictures. I thought it'd be interesting to try to document Edie's Berlin, show her how the city has changed since she was last there in the seventies."

Edie looks startled. "You don't need to do that."

"I know, but you've made me curious. And you've made me care . . . about you, and Franz, and your friends."

"It should be an interesting trip," Craig says.

I nod. "I think so. I'm really excited." There's a lift in my voice, an energy I haven't felt in God knows how long. I'm going to do something different, and it's a little scary, but scary is good. It's a challenge. And a purpose.

The scary is nudging me into action.

The nudge might even shift the balance and weight of the world.

Or maybe just shift the balance and weight within me.

"Which hotel?" he asks.

"The Mani."

"It's in the Mitte," Edie speaks up. "I don't know the Mani, but I would think anywhere in the Mitte is good. "

"You know that area, Aunt Edie?" Craig asks.

"I know the area from when I lived in Berlin. Everyone did. It's the center of the city and close to Museum Island and so many of the important buildings, including the lovely old apartment building Franz and I were living in until the raid in March 1944. That bombing wiped out our building and much of our neighborhood."

"Were you able to visit your old neighborhood in 1978 when you went with Grandma?" Craig asks.

"No. My old neighborhood was on the other side of the wall." Edie looks at me. "You know the wall cut through the city, and the Mitte was on the East German side, and I wasn't allowed to travel from West Berlin to East Berlin. Not then."

"But the wall is down now," I say.

"Yes." Edie is silent a moment. "I wonder what my neighborhood looks like now."

"I will take pictures."

"There's no need—"

"But I want to. I'm curious, too."

We are both quiet for a moment and then I muster my courage and ask her about something I've been wondering ever since I read the diary of Edie's internment at Bad Nauheim. "Edie, you've told me about the Adlon, and the bombings, and Franz's friends. But you never told me about your music. Whatever happened to your music, Edie? You'd gone to Germany to study. What happened after the war?"

She shrugs. "I was done with it."

"Done with it?"

"Yes, I put it behind me."

"Studying it, you mean?"

"Studying, playing, listening—I was done. *Alles. Das ist alles.*

I didn't want music anymore, not the way I had before." She pauses and her jaw tightens, her throat working. "How could I play . . . write . . . listen? I'd lost them all. Franz and my beloved friends . . . Claus, Adam, Peter . . ." Her voice fades and her eyes tear. "Johann, Wolfgang, Ludwig, Richard." Her lips tremble. "I loved them, and then they were all gone."

TWENTY-ONE

Edie

Alison leaves and Craig walks her up to her father's apartment. I remain at the small breakfast table in my apartment after they are both gone and I cry. I don't ever cry, but I cry now.

I miss my music. I miss my loves. I miss my life.

I am old now and have so little time left. One of these days I will wake up like Ruth and not remember.

I would rather die than not remember.

I must remember, otherwise, they never mattered . . . might as well have never existed.

It takes me a long time to calm myself, compose myself. Alison has no idea how much she's upset me. I know she didn't mean to upset me. It was a legitimate question. It's one my family never asked. They must have simply assumed . . .

If I were younger, I'd go to Berlin one last time.

I'd like to see the new Berlin with the wall down.

I didn't like Berlin in 1978. My sister was repulsed by the checkpoints and soldiers with their automatic rifles, but for me, the shock and horror was visceral. It was as if I'd been thrust back into the war all over again. The uniforms. The guns. The fear.

Standing at Checkpoint Charlie in 1978, the terror returned.

I was afraid, and the anxiety didn't lessen during the five days we spent in Berlin. I couldn't wait to leave. We never went to Potsdam. Didn't visit the gardens or summer palace. I couldn't. How could I enjoy Berlin when I couldn't breathe?

TWENTY-TWO

Ali

It's Saturday morning. Tomorrow I leave for Berlin. Today is my last day in Napa and I'm spending the morning at Bloom, giving Diana a hand with the last of the wedding bouquets and boutonnieres. We did the centerpieces yesterday—she, Carolyn, and I—and Carolyn's good, a natural. She's only been at the shop a few days, but with her design background and artistic eye, she has a flare for color and shape. She also makes Diana laugh. I'm glad to know that when I leave, Diana—and Bloom—will both be fine, although privately it's a bit deflating to discover I've been so easily replaced. I'd kind of liked being Diana's saving grace. Now I'm just a dentist again.

Once the wedding flowers are off, I turn my attention to a special project. It's a small good-bye gift to Edie and Ruth. I'd make one for my dad, but I don't think he'd notice, or care.

Carolyn offers to give me a hand. I tell her I've got it, and I do, because I want this to be from me. I want to give something to Edie, something to thank her for her time and her stories. She's become my friend, although I'm not sure what she thinks of me, and that's okay, too. Edie doesn't have to like me. I'm the one that's benefited from knowing her.

As I fill the pair of tin window boxes with soil, and then add each of the flowers, Carolyn sweeps the shop floor and then gets busy cleaning the large front window. She's humming as she works. I smile to myself, watching her.

She reminds me of my mom. Busy, kind, warm.

Happy.

I used to think Andrew was the same way. Now I know there was more going on beneath the surface. He had problems—thoughts—fears he didn't feel he could share with me. I wish I'd known. I wish he'd let me in, allowed me to help.

Did any of us know he was unhappy? I don't think so, and my mom—the former teacher—was so very perceptive.

But I can't blame her, or any of the others. No one was closer to Andrew than me. I slept in the same bed . . . cooked dinner with him . . . ran for miles at his side . . . we even showered together.

How could I not know that Andrew was unhappy?

How could I have missed all the signs?

It makes me mistrust myself. Doubt my judgment. And in my work, my judgment is everything.

I finish the two arrangements, galvanized window boxes I've filled with zinnias and dwarf dahlias in a riot of orange, red, pink, and purple.

I call Dad before I leave Bloom, and ask him if he still wants to do dinner and bingo at the home, or if I could possibly take him out and do something special. It is, after all, my last night in Napa, and we have yet to go to any of the restaurants that he and Mom used to love. But he's not interested in going out. He likes staying in, claiming it's more comfortable and less stressful.

"So dinner in the dining room?" I ask him.

"Where else?" he barks.

I make a face. He really could try to be a little nicer. "So what time should I meet you?"

"What time will you be here?"

"I've something for Edie, a gift I've made. I'll go by her room first, and then I can be downstairs by six or six thirty."

"I don't want to wait for you. I don't like standing around waiting. Let's just say six thirty."

"In the dining room."

"With all the boys?"

I suppress a sigh. No use arguing with him. He is who he is. I'm not going to change him. "Whatever makes you happy."

With the flower boxes in the trunk of Mom's car, I go to the bank, withdraw money, stop at the dry cleaners, and then swing by Copperfields Bookstore to pick up the travel books they ordered for me on Berlin and Germany.

It's almost five thirty when I arrive at Napa Estates, and I take Ruth's flower box to her first since I'm not sure when Memory Care actually serves patients their dinner, or what their visiting-hour schedule is. The TV is on in Memory Care's lounge. Half of the residents are asleep. The other half stare blankly at the TV. I find Ruth sleeping in a recliner in a corner by the window, the late-afternoon light slanting across the floor, streaking her lap. She looks very small, almost like a child. Her mouth gapes open and she's snoring very softly. If I had a blanket I'd pull it over her legs, tuck it around her waist.

We come into life helpless. We age and time renders us helpless. Hopefully in between we are loved. Hopefully we have good people around us.

There's a small table at Ruth's elbow and the nurse gives me permission to place the window box on it there—but only temporarily since the flowers and plants aren't all edible—but at least Ruth will see it when she wakes.

This will be me one day, I think, as I lean over to kiss Ruth on the forehead. One day I won't do anything but sleep and stare at the TV.

Thank God I'm trying to live life now.

Returning to the reception desk in the lobby, I retrieve the second window box and head for the elevator.

I'm a little bit nervous as I exit the elevator on the second floor and walk to Edie's room. I hope she'll like the flowers. I wanted to do something for her, give something to her, as she's given so much to me.

"I brought you something," I say, when Edie answers the door. "I thought you might enjoy a little bit of color."

She glances down at the window box.

"I made one for Ruth, too, but the nurse isn't sure they can keep it in the Memory Care lounge since some of the patients eat flowers and leaves and things, but maybe Ruth can enjoy yours on the weekends when she comes here for a cup of tea."

Edie looks up at me, frowning.

She doesn't like the window box. She doesn't understand the significance.

"You said dahlias were—"

"Show-offs," she says shortly, interrupting me. "I remember. I'm old, not dead."

I smile, and it just keeps growing, the smile filling me, and taking over my face, making my cheeks feel fat and my jaw ache.

"My mother loved dahlias, too," I say. "And you have a perfect spot for a window box—right in that window in your kitchen, where it gets lots of light."

"We're not allowed to hang things from our windows."

"But it goes in here, in the kitchen, on the inside. It's an indoor garden, and the flowers have their own little watering tray already tucked down in the bottom of the window box."

"And how do you propose I hang that thing in my window that 'gets lots of light'?"

"I'm sure Craig could figure out a way. If he can remodel that house—"

"I'm not going to call and ask Craig to come here to hang a window box."

"You don't have to ask him. I'm sure he'll offer. He loves doing nice things for you."

She harrumphs, and steps back, opening the door wide. "Come in," she says, grumpily. I hope this is just an act. I hope she's pleased by my gift. Hard to tell with Edie, though. "And I suppose Craig wouldn't mind hanging it up. We'll find out. He's supposed to be here soon. He's bringing us dinner."

"*Us* dinner?"

"Yes. *Us*, dinner." She gives me a look, eyebrows arching, lips pressed thin. "It's your good-bye dinner. A bon voyage thing."

Dad appears at Edie's door at six on the dot. He's put on a navy plaid button-down shirt and is looking decidedly handsome. "What are you doing here?"

"I have a dinner party to attend."

"Where?"

"Here."

"Here?"

"Yes, now may I come in?"

Still confused, I give him a hug as he enters Edie's apartment. "But what about your buddies, Dad? Are they coming, too?"

"Do you want them here? I could invite them up. After all, it's your good-bye party."

I glance from Dad to Edie. "You knew about this?"

"It was my idea," she says smugly. "Fortunately, your dad knows how to keep a secret."

"Yes, he does," I agree.

Craig arrives ten minutes later with bags of Chinese takeout.

"Bill, Ali," he says to us, before kissing his aunt's cheek. "Hope I haven't kept you waiting long. There was some traffic."

"No problem at all," Dad says.

I watch Craig carry the white paper bags to the kitchen. "When were you roped in?" I ask him, reaching into the cupboards for plates.

"Probably the same time Aunt Edie roped in your dad," he answers. "And we have all my aunt's favorites. Peking duck, Hunan beef, Shanghai dumplings, green beans, garlicky bok choy, lo mein, and fried rice. Did I forget anything?"

Edie smiles at him. "No. Sounds as if you got the order right."

We don't actually end up eating at the table, but instead sit on her pair of love seats, Dad and I squished together on one, with Edie and Craig on the other. We use the throwaway chopsticks and balance our plates on our laps. Everyone handles the chopsticks pretty well but Edie is probably the most comfortable. I don't know why I'm surprised. I know she's well traveled but I forget how much she's lived.

Over tea and fortune cookies, Edie says she's been thinking about my upcoming trip all day. "You can't just go to Berlin to see the memorials. You can't go to only see the scars. They are there. And they are ugly, so ugly that if you look at them and just at them, you will be completely repelled. So if you go, you must go to see all of it. You must go and see the beautiful things and the Berlin so many of us loved so dearly."

Edie studies her fortune cookie, which she hasn't yet broken. "Berlin is an old, old city, dating back to 1237, and the capital of the German kingdom of Prussia. Prussia was known for its leaders, its army, its courage. What happened in the twentieth century is dreadful—amoral—but it is just one piece of Prussia's history. So when you go, look for Prussia. Look for the art and architecture, as well as the culture that makes Berlin unique."

"But the Berlin you loved is gone," I say. "Both the Adlon and the opera house . . . ?"

"Yes, the Adlon and the Staatsoper Unter den Linden were destroyed in 1945 at the very end of the war, but I understand the East Germans rebuilt the Staatsoper in the 1950s and when you were showing me pictures on the Internet we saw that there is a new hotel named the Adlon where the original once was. Craig said he's stayed there before. It's nice, isn't it?" Edie looks at him for confirmation.

"Very nice," he agrees. "It's one of my favorite hotels in Berlin."

"Expensive," my dad says.

"Five stars. Luxury."

"But it's not my Adlon, no," Edie adds. "But I still think it's worth a visit, if only to have a cocktail and toast Herr and Frau Adlon who were so very kind and courteous and brave throughout the war. I adored Herr Adlon. But we all did. And the way he died, the way—" She breaks off, shakes her head. "Don't want to talk about that. His memory deserves better." She straightens her shoulders. "But do go, and have a drink, or a lunch, and then have a walk down Unter den Linden and savor the dappled shade and sunshine."

I rise and go to my purse to retrieve my notebook and pen. "What else?" I ask, ready to take notes.

"If you can, you really should go to Potsdam. It's just outside the city and for hundreds of years it was the home of the Prussian kings and you can still tour two of the palaces, Sanssouci, with its extraordinary gardens, and the Cecilienhof Palace, which is actually not very old as palaces go, and looks like a hunting lodge, not a palace, but it's famous today as the place where Churchill, Stalin, and Truman met for the Potsdam Conference in July 1945. If you're short on time, I would recommend Sanssouci for the palace and gardens, and then stop for some cake and coffee late afternoon at one of the *Konditoreis* at the little square across from the palace. Germany is famous for its bakeries and you should try as many sweets and pastries as you can."

"Do you have a favorite I must try?"

"All of them!" Her eyes sparkle as she laughs, the laugh surprisingly girlish. "Germans love their sponge cakes with layers of fruit and whipped cream, as well as the rich chocolate Sacher torte, and almond-flavored sweets. But for me, there is nothing like *Zwetschgenkuchen*, straight from the oven. I spent many years trying to find a recipe to make a proper plum tart, but nothing ever tasted as good as the buttery, tart but sweet *Zwetschgenkuchen* I had in Germany."

"Anything else?"

"Drink. Beer. Wine—"

"Wine," Craig emphasizes.

"Eat," she continues still smiling. "Listen to music. Go to the opera. Meet people. Make friends. Enjoy." She smiles almost wistfully. "Enjoy yourself. That is what you must do if you go. Do not be the timid American tourist, afraid to venture out. If you are brave enough to go, then explore. Take it all in. Make it yours. That's what I would do."

Then that is what I will do, too.

D ad excuses himself at ten to eight as he has a program he watches at eight and he doesn't want to miss it. I offer to walk him back and he frowns at me. "Why? You think I need protection?"

I just shake my head and kiss him good-bye, telling him I will come see him in the morning before I go, and then for a bit it's just Craig, Edie, and me, making small talk over my cups of tea.

Then Edie rises and starts for the guest room.

"Do you need help, Aunt Edie?" Craig asks.

She stops, turns around. "Can you get one of my boxes down? I want the Berlin years."

"Of course I can. Come sit back down."

But she doesn't sit back down on her loveseat. She comes to sit next to me on mine. Craig hands her the box and she takes off the lid, and carefully goes through the small boxes and bundles of letters and envelopes until she comes to a dark brown leather book on the bottom. She draws it out, running a light hand across the dark leather cover as Craig sets the box on the coffee table.

"Haven't looked at this one in years," Edie says. "Not sure I want to look at it now." She traces a scratch in the leather then looks at me. "This is the last one, the diary I kept the summer of 1944. As you know, I'd always kept diaries, but after this one, I stopped. I couldn't write."

I hear heaviness in her voice, and sorrow.

"Too much to say?" I ask gently.

She gives her head a nearly imperceptible shake. "Because there was nothing to say. The war said it all."

I'm determined not to be emotional. I'm determined to be calm and matter-of-fact but I know what this diary is. I know what it represents. The summer of 1944 was the summer of the July 20 assassination attempt. The attempt failed and all those involved were rounded up, tortured, and killed.

Edie runs her fingers across the scuffed cover again and again. Craig and I both watch her, neither of us speaking.

"I learned during that trip to Berlin with my sister, back in 1978, that Franz wasn't buried anywhere." Her voice cracks.

"None of them were. They were executed and cremated and the ashes were scattered . . . blown by the wind. But if the Gestapo and the People's Court thought they'd punished the traitors by discarding the ashes, they were wrong. *Wrong!*"

She lifts her head, looks me in the eye. "All they did was free the men, returning them to their land."

Her voice quavers. "You see why I have not spoken of Germany for all these years. It is impossible. My friends were not Nazis. My friends were those the Nazis despised—the artists, the intellectuals, the students, the Jews, the Gypsies, the Poles, the aristocrats. My Germany was all of those things and then it was gone. Just as my Berlin was not the Berlin I found in 1978. That Berlin sickened me. She was once so beautiful and to see her divided, punished with that wall and barbed wire—"

"But that's not the Berlin Ali will find," Craig says quietly. "The wall is gone. The ugly empty scar of Potsdamer Platz has been given new life with a bold redevelopment project."

"Those glass and neon buildings you showed me," Edie sniffs.

"There was no way to go back and re-create what was lost during the war. Better to move forward, integrating the old with the new." He looks at me, and smiles. "You're lucky I have my Tuscany wine expo or I'd go to Berlin with you."

TWENTY-THREE

Edie

Alison and Craig washed and dried the plates and teacups and saucers, putting them away. Craig is walking Alison out now, and there's nothing for me to do.

It was a good night. I enjoyed myself. Interestingly enough, tonight Alison didn't even annoy me.

I take a damp dish towel and wipe the counters one more time, determined to ignore the flower box with the cheerful dahlias and zinnias on one of the counters. Craig promised to hang it for me this weekend. I told him not to bother. He laughed and called me a sourpuss. I told him he was disrespectful.

Alison listened to us; she's always listening and watching. She's such a strange girl but she's growing on me. A little.

I turn to my window box.

I like it. I do, especially the spiky pink dahlias with the yellow peach glow in the center.

Glamour puss.

Show-off.

I hang the towel up and face the window box. Bob used to buy me flowers. He knew I liked them. Franz didn't buy me flowers, but that was because there were no flowers available. Or chocolates. Or sweets.

If one went out into the country, you could get something special—like milk and cheese, but in the city, we had so little. The rationing was so severe. We tried to make it a game but it wasn't easy. Near the end, nothing was easy.

But then, the end for Franz and me came so fast I didn't even know it was the end until it was too late.

Most of those committed to the Resistance were married men, men with wives and children and responsibilities. But they were also responsible for Germany. They were, after all, Germans and this wasn't the Germany they knew and loved.

They couldn't look the other way. They couldn't stay silent. Do nothing.

We, the women who loved them, understood. This is why we loved them. This is why we risked our lives, too, because nobody was safe.

None of us wanted pain. We didn't want to die. We didn't want to be tortured. But a man has a conscience, and a relationship with God, and that relationship with God requires one to act.

To do.

I didn't know that anything had been planned for July 20.

I didn't know anything immediate was in the works.

I did know Franz was tense. Tired. He wasn't sleeping much, and was constantly working, and traveling, and in secret meetings.

And then he told me I needed to get away from Berlin and get some fresh air and sun. He said I should go to Switzerland, and perhaps some of my old friends from the music conservatory who were in Switzerland could join me at one of the lake resorts and relax with me, and then he'd join me at the end of the month.

I thought it was very extravagant. We didn't have a lot of

money. It would be costly to take the train so far and stay in a hotel, but I loved the idea of good food, and sunlight. Best of all, there would be no blackouts.

I didn't know it was the last time I'd see him. I didn't suspect anything since Franz was always traveling and working and saying I needed more milk and fresh fruit and meat. It didn't cross my mind that once he put me on the train for Zurich all hell would break loose.

I'd only been in Switzerland two days when word reached us on the morning of the twenty-first that there had been an attempt on der Führer's life. It had failed and the traitors were being arrested by the dozens and they would all die.

I remember feeling as if my legs would give way. I remember collapsing into a chair, and Maria from the hotel's front desk rushed to me, and called for help.

She didn't know what had happened.

She didn't know what I knew.

Franz, Adam, Peter, Helmut, Hans, Claus—they would all be arrested. I didn't even know if they'd get a trial. Hitler and his monkey "People's Court" didn't believe in trials.

It was a day later that we learned Claus had been shot.

The others were being interrogated. They would eventually die a horrible death, slow strangulation—

I stop myself there, unable to finish the thought. I still can't bear to remember the details.

They were good men and women, and ordinary men and women . . .

Men like Franz who became extraordinary for speaking out, standing up, showing courage.

I was a good woman, an ordinary woman, too, but when I returned to the US, no one knew that anymore.

No one could believe that, not after the war.

TWENTY-FOUR

Ali

I'm packed and the suitcases are in the trunk of the car. I turn off the lights, lock the Poppy Lane house's front door, thinking this is a very nice house, in a very nice neighborhood. I wish Mom and Dad were still here. It feels like home.

I give the house a last glance and then I'm off. I won't be back until Saturday night, and then I'll be here just a day, just long enough to have brunch with Dad for Father's Day, and then it'll be back to the airport to fly to Phoenix.

My time in Napa is essentially over.

It's been a good three weeks. And Dr. Morris was right. I needed the break.

I need to be in San Francisco by two, which gives me an hour to spare. I stop by Napa Estates to say good-bye to Dad. He's not very chatty. He's focused on getting downstairs for breakfast with "the boys."

"Can you please act like you'll miss me a little bit?" I tease him.

"Of course I'll miss you. But I won't be sitting around missing you. You're off on an adventure. You're going to have a great time."

I hug him good-bye. "Just be careful while I'm gone, and watch out for those man-hungry single ladies. I don't want to come back next week and find out you're married."

"Don't worry. I avoid those women at all costs," he says.

I give him another hug, holding him tighter than he probably likes. I don't feel as if I know him well. Perhaps I never will. But maybe that's okay. Maybe we don't need to share our innermost thoughts and feelings. Maybe it's enough to share a meal, a game of cards, an afternoon on a Sunday. "But Dad, maybe you don't need to avoid women altogether. Mom wouldn't want that. Mom would want you to have companionship—"

"We don't need to talk about this. I'm not ready to think about any of that. Besides, I'd never love anyone the way I loved your mom."

"Maybe you don't have to. Maybe just being some nice woman's best friend would be enough."

He breaks free, gives me a stern look. "Thank you, Ann Landers. You can go now."

I stop by Edie's room and knock lightly on the door. She and Ruth usually have brunch together around eleven. I imagine Edie is getting dressed now.

She opens the door, and she's in one of her nice Sunday outfits, a gray and white knit skirt and matching white knit top.

"You're probably sick of me," I say, smiling at her.

"I am," she agrees. "But since you're here, come in. I've something for you, for your trip. I'd meant to give it to you last night but completely forgot."

I follow her into her living room where she hands me a plastic bag with some treats for my trip—chocolates and packages of cheese and peanut butter crackers—because she's heard they don't serve a lot of food on flights anymore and thought I might get hungry, if not on the flight, then maybe at the hotel when I'm wide awake with jet lag.

"Thank you," I say, touched. "That is so nice of you."

"I told Craig to buy them. I don't drive anymore. I've given up my car."

I know.

Maybe that's why I can't stop looking at her, and smiling at her.

"Have you packed an umbrella?" she asks. "The weather can change quickly in Berlin, and you don't want to pay those high European prices for an umbrella once you're there."

"I have one. I bought one. Here."

"Good." She folds her hands in front of her. "The last time I was in Germany the dollar was very strong, and so it was much more affordable. It's not that way anymore from what I understand."

"That's true."

She asks if I've packed a coat—I have. She wants to know if I'm taking anything sharp for evenings (her words, not mine) in case I go to dinner or the opera, and perhaps a couple cardigans for the daytime if the weather is cool. I told her I have.

She says that in her time, everyone rode bicycles all over Berlin and girls had no problem riding bikes with their long skirts, but she thinks trousers or capris might be easier for me. I tell her I haven't ridden a bike in ages and I'm not sure I'll have time to ride one while in Germany, but I promise to take lots of photos and look up all the people and places she's mentioned. "And I wrote down the addresses, too, of your old house and your friends' houses. I'll go take pictures of whatever's there. It might be old. It might be new. Hopefully you won't be disappointed—"

"Me? Why should I be disappointed? This is your trip, not mine."

"But I want to go for you—"

"I don't believe that. Nor should you." Her gaze meets mine, fixed, steady, even as one of her hands moves lightly over her lap, skimming the soft knit fabric. "This trip isn't about me. Which makes me wonder why you're going. What is it you're looking for in Germany? And why Germany?"

For a long moment there is silence.

I don't know what to say. And I don't know what to say because I don't know the answers to these questions. I'm not even sure why I feel so compelled to go—now. But there is an urgency, and a need to know. To see.

But know what?

See what?

"You loved Germany," I say at last. "You loved your music studies and the people you met. You loved Berlin."

"Yes."

"And then it was all gone."

"Yes."

My chest tightens and a lump fills my throat. It hurts to swallow. "The war . . . the chaos . . . the deaths, and betrayals . . . you couldn't stop it."

"No."

"You couldn't change it."

"No."

"And yet you still love Germany."

"Even though Germany broke my heart?" Her thin shoulders twist. She doesn't wait for a response. "Disappointment is part of life. We can't escape it. Ever."

"I just want to understand it better."

"*It?*"

"Germany. The war. The losses. All of it."

"You might be disappointed."

"Why?"

"Germans do not like discussing the war. They do not like being confronted with their past. I discovered in 1978 that younger generations were determined to distance themselves from the past.

They have no desire to be burdened by the older generation's failings and atrocities."

"I'm not going to judge, but to learn."

"Then maybe this might be helpful." Edie slowly rises and goes to the kitchen, returning with the diary with the scratched dark leather cover. "Take this one with you. It might help answer some of your questions, or at the very least, give you a perspective you might not get otherwise. But maybe wait to read it, wait until the end of your trip, until after you've seen the city for yourself. I think that's better. Yes, I think that's best."

"I'll wait until the end. I promise. And I'll take lots of photos, and show you everything when I come back."

"You are lucky to go and see this new shiny Berlin without the weight and suffering of its past."

I hear the wistful note in her voice. "Do you wish you were going with me?"

"No. I'm tired. Just keeping Ruthie entertained is exhausting enough."

I smile. "She's lucky to have you."

"I'm lucky to have her."

"You've never regretted not marrying again?"

Her sparse eyebrows shoot up. "I did marry again. Stephens is my second husband's name."

"What?"

"I was twenty-four when Franz was killed, too young to remain alone for the rest of my life. I wanted what you still want—a husband, children—and I found a perfect gentleman in Bob Stephens. We met in 1947, at an event at the San Francisco consulate, and were married the following year."

"Edie, I had no idea. I thought Stephens was Franz's last name."

"Franz's last name is Franz. Well, von Franz. His given name was Tor. But you know that—"

"I've never heard this before."

"Nonsense. You weren't listening—"

"I've listened to everything you've told me."

"Then you'd know his name was Major Baron Torsten von Franz. But I never called him Torsten. He was always Franz to me. When we married I became von Franz, but when I remarried, I took Bob's last name."

I want to write this all down so I look around for my purse and notebook but I left both in the car. "No wonder I couldn't find him in my research. I had Franz's name all wrong."

She starts down the hall and gestures for me to follow. We enter her bedroom and approach her nightstand. She lifts one of the silver-framed photos and holds it out to me.

I'm expecting a young handsome blond man, someone dashing, with piercing blue eyes and a chiseled jaw, but the man in the photo is middle-aged with a buzz cut, a wide mouth, and ears that don't quite lie flat. But he looks affable, and he has nice eyes.

"This is Bob," she tells me. "He was a career army man."

He looks like a Bob. He also looks kind, which I imagine is just what Edie needed, but I want to see Franz—correction, Torsten. I want to see who inspired such great passion and devotion in young Edie.

But Edie's still talking about Bob. "He saw considerable action in the Pacific during World War II. Like me, he spoke several languages, different languages—Korean, Japanese, Mandarin, some Cantonese— and so when the US entered the Korean war, even though he'd just retired, they asked if he'd go and serve as intelligence. They trusted him, and needed him. I understood why he went—he, like me, believed it was essential to stop dictators and the spread of Communism, but it was not easy to let him go." She pauses. "But I did."

I glance back down into Bob's affable face, with his protruding ears and wide easy smile. "Tell me this story ends happily."

Her lips press. Her shoulders lift, and fall.

Dammit.

I take a step away, frustrated. "You tell the worst stories, Edie. They are so *sad*."

"They didn't happen to you."

"No, but it's horrific. You've lived through unimaginable tragedies and now you're going to tell me your lovely, kind second husband dies in Korea?"

"Just because I loved twice and lost both times, doesn't mean you will."

"That's not the point."

"But I think it is the point. It's what's in the back of your mind." She returns the frame to her night stand. "And if, on the unlikely chance, it did happen again to you, you'd recover, Alison. Why? Because it's what strong people do."

"Maybe I don't want to be strong!"

"It's too late. You were born with resolve. You yourself said you've always had goals, you need lists, you like to accomplish things, so accomplish things and live your life. That's what you are meant to do."

My heart still pounds. I feel queasy. "I thought you loved Franz so much."

"I did."

"But you have no picture of him, nothing here, next to your bed."

"There were no photos to frame. I left Berlin mid-July 1944 with a small suitcase for a couple of weeks in Switzerland. I didn't know I'd never return. And by the time the war was over, there was no way to get anything back. Franz was gone. His family scattered, their home and town now in the Russian sector. Once the wall went up, there was no information available, no one I could contact. My world, my Germany had vanished."

"Wasn't it difficult to replace him?"

"He was never replaced. You don't replace someone like Franz, and yet at the same time, I was twenty-four, and he was gone. He wasn't coming back. What was I to do? Never care for anyone again? Never need anyone again? Never crave companionship or tenderness? I was too young to be alone for the rest of my life."

"So you fell in love—a second time."

"Yes, because Bob was nothing like Franz. I didn't want to love someone like Franz, and I don't think I could have. Bob was older, and mature, and so very protective of me."

"Not that protective if he went off to Korea leaving you behind."

"We both knew Korea would be dangerous, but I don't think either of us expected him to die there. He was intelligence. He wouldn't be on the front line."

I glance down at the cluster of photos on the table, seeing him tucked between the old-fashioned black-and-white photo of two little girls in matching sailor dresses with ringlets and huge white silk bows in their hair, and a picture of Edie with her blonde, teenage nephews, Craig and Chad.

Bob is still smiling into the camera. He's not a handsome man. He doesn't look dashing, but he does look kind.

"Edie, I just can't believe he'd leave you for war."

She shrugged. "He wouldn't have gone if I'd asked him to stay."

"No?"

"He asked my opinion. He wanted to know what I thought. I understood why he felt compelled to go. I respected his sense of duty and honor." She hesitates. "And to be honest, I thought he'd come back. I was sure he'd come home. I didn't think I'd lose him."

"Did you feel guilty?"

"Angry, shocked, guilty and . . . heartbroken. Heartbroken," she repeats. "I received the telegram on Christmas Day. I've never wanted to celebrate Christmas since. And perhaps the greatest tragedy is that it was a non-combat accident. He was in the same jeep with General Walker. Their vehicle was struck by a speeding truck. It could have happened anywhere . . . here, there. It wasn't enemy fire, or friendly fire. It was a speeding truck."

I don't know what to say. I don't have the words. But I would like to hug her.

I'd like to tell her how much I admire her as well as her tremendous courage and strength, but she's holding herself tall, and still, and there is too much distance between us, between our generations.

I don't know if there ever would be a right time to close the distance. I'm not sure I'd even know how to close the distance. Edie is a prickly old lady, with fierce spirit and an iron core, someone who doesn't invite praise or compliments.

And I like her all the better for it.

I hope one day to be just as fierce and prickly as dear feisty Edie.

"I'm sorry," I finally murmur.

"I am sorry, too," she answers. "Just as I wished for many years that there had been a child. But just as with Franz . . . it wasn't meant to be."

"I don't think I could handle what you've been through."

"It was difficult, but how could I ever feel sorry for myself when I still had my family? When I knew my mother and my sister were safe? When our home wasn't bombed, our possessions weren't confiscated? How could I give up, or complain, or feel self-pity when so many others . . . when *millions* of people . . . were starved? Murdered?

"What happened might have been seventy years ago," she adds, her voice growing stronger. "But it was real. It wasn't just something made up and put in a book. It was life. *My* life. The lives of those all around me."

"It's unthinkable to my generation."

She laughs, a low hollow sound. "As it once was to mine."

TWENTY-FIVE

The KLM jet touches down with the slightest of bumps, a smooth landing following a smooth flight. I slept most of the way and so far the entire journey feels deceptively easy, making me wonder as I pass through customs, why I've waited so long to travel.

I haven't been out of the country in years. There wasn't a lot of time, not with school and then work, but I suppose we could have tried harder to make time. Andrew was always itching to get on a plane, go somewhere exotic, be adventurous, hike, explore. Machu Picchu. Patagonia. Zambia. Bali. Marrakech.

It didn't happen.

Instead we worked, and worked, and he ran, and ran.

We did have a trip booked for our honeymoon. We were supposed to go to the Amalfi Coast for ten days, and we had the flights into Rome, and the train to Naples where a driver would take us to our hotel in Positano.

My mom handled cancelling the honeymoon since Andrew's parents were too distraught. She also helped organize sending copies of his death certificate to get the money back from the airline when they weren't going to refund. They had only wanted to offer a ticket against future travel. Mom, who doesn't ruffle easily, lost it with the customer service agent for not understanding that there would be no future travel for Andrew. "What part of dead do you not understand?" she snapped.

Now here I am, fifteen months after his death, in the back of a cab heading from the Berlin airport to my hotel.

Sunshine fills the cab. The streets are wide and clean and the traffic isn't too bad since the morning rush is over.

The taxi driver tells me in excellent English that the weather is supposed to be nice most of the week, with maybe just a little rain Tuesday and Wednesday. "You're lucky you weren't here last week," he adds, looking at me in the rearview mirror. "It rained for a week straight, and was cold. The tourists weren't happy."

"Have you always lived in Berlin?" I ask him.

"Yes. But not the DDR. West Berlin."

He's hair challenged with crooked teeth and could be anywhere from mid-thirties to his late fifties. "So you were here when the wall came down in 1989?"

"Yes."

"You remember it?"

"*Ja.* Oh, yes. I was twenty-one, and it was incredible. Unbelievable. We met on the top of the wall, East Berliners, West Berliners. We shared beer and wine and we were all hugging and dancing in the streets. Who would have thought the wall would ever come down? Not in my lifetime." His gaze meets mine in the rearview mirror. "But then, my mother said back in 1961, no one thought a wall would ever cut through the middle of Berlin in the first place. Life is strange. No one can ever predict what will happen."

"Your mother was a Berliner, too?"

"*Ja.* But her family was all on the other side. The wall went up very fast. One day there was a barricade, but then in the following night, it became cement and stone, topped with barbed wire. There were guard towers. Soldiers with dogs and guns." He shook his head. "My mother was cut off from her family. Eventually she could get a day pass to go visit them, but just for a day. Lots of police and security to get in, and even more to get out. It was depressing for her to go visit, too. The shops weren't so good. The opportunities weren't so good. The new buildings and architecture not good. Even the air, not good since it was hazy and gray from brown coal. The haze hung over the city, like a . . . depression.

"A depression," he repeats, nodding before shooting me another quick glance in the mirror. "It was hard for my mother to see her mother and aunts and cousins with less. Gradually she stopped going over, maybe just visiting once a year, and then once every couple of years."

"Did she ever stop her visits?"

"When her mother died."

"You knew your grandmother, though?"

"I met her when I was little, once or twice, but my mother was afraid to take me, just in case she couldn't get back. There was always so much fear. Maybe this time she gets denied at the border. Maybe this time she's trapped—" He breaks off, points out the window. "The new Reichstag, rebuilt after the reunification. Beautiful, yes?"

It is a magnificent building topped with a huge dome. I'd seen photos of it in my Berlin travel guide.

I'm staring out the window, watching everything. "The Tiergarten." He gestures. "And the Zoo. A very big park for the people. Nice for walking and family outings. I think it might be bigger than your Central Park in New York. That's what a tourist told me. Not sure if it's true."

"Victory Column," he adds. "And there. See? *Brandenburger Tor.*"

I know that one from poring over the photos with Edie. Brandenburg Gate. Which meant the Blücher Palace, which was once the American embassy, is just on the other side, and the old Adlon Hotel would have been another block east, with the opera house another couple blocks down Unter den Linden.

I feel a bubble of excitement and pleasure. I've never been here but I feel as if I know it, which is strange and fascinating, as I never felt any interest in Berlin, or this part of Europe, until now.

Thanks to my American education, I'd imagined Berlin as a vast industrial city, just as northern Germany was all smokestacks and autobahn and smog.

Not sure why I thought that.

"The Holocaust Memorial is over there." The taxi driver nods to the far side of the Brandenburg Gate. "Some people like the design. Others hate it. Me, I am not a fan. Too much concrete."

I lean forward to try to get a better view, but can see nothing from here. We are blocks away and nothing is visible around the gate and buildings. "I'd heard it was supposed to be a forest."

"All I know is that it was *sehr teuer*. Very costly."

The driver continues to point out various landmarks along the way to the hotel, but the names and places blur. I slept for about four or five hours on the plane but I'm starting to feel the jet lag now. I could use coffee and a shower after my all-night flight, and maybe even a brief nap.

We reach my hotel, the Mani, on Torstrasse, and I pay him for the ride, tipping him generously since he'd been quite helpful and I appreciated the tour.

I've arrived at the hotel before the official check-in time but the front desk expedites my check-in so I can get to my room. The Wi-Fi is free and should allow me to get on my phone and I check that out first, and yes I'm able to get on my e-mail, send text messages, and Skype . . . not that I have anyone to Skype with.

I do have several new text messages, though.

Craig Hallahan wants to know if I've arrived safely. (Yes, Craig, thank you.)

And Helene from the office texted to say that Dr. Morris has shingles and won't be in the office for the next week at the very least. I'm not to hurry home, but she thought I'd want to know. (Thanks, Helene, for the bad news.)

I drop the phone and close my eyes, tempted to nap. It'd be so easy to give in to sleep but it's just noon now and it's bright and sunny outside. I should go out and stretch my legs, and get my bearings. I've signed up for a city tour for tomorrow morning, with a walking tour in the afternoon, and then I'm off to Potsdam Tuesday for a palace day trip, and then Wednesday I'm going to visit the Holocaust Memorial, the Berlin Wall Memorial, and the Memorial to the German Resistance. I'd hoped to maybe attend an opera or symphony at the Opera House but I haven't purchased tickets yet and right now am not sure I will. I don't want to be booked up every minute of every day. I'd like to be able to sleep in and have time to wander, and sit in cafes and people watch.

And so instead of jumping up and going out to explore, I close my eyes and give in to sleep. There is something so decadent and delicious about sleeping when you're not supposed to be . . .

I wake up hours later. I only know it's hours later because the sun has shifted, the bright rays gone, the foot of my bed bathed in pale gold light, the light of late afternoon.

I've slept deeply and I'm groggy.

It requires effort to rise. My head thumps, heavy, reminding me that my sleep cycles are confused and I haven't had enough caffeine today.

I shower and dress, transferring my wallet and camera phone into a tote bag. I tuck in my map, a small dictionary, and travel books, and then add my notebook, too, where I've made note of everything Edie talked about. I've a list of the things I'm to visit and see. My goal is to take a picture of everything—or of the place something should be—and share my photos with her when I return.

Thinking of Edie makes me think of Craig, and I'm conflicted when it comes to Craig. He's interesting and smart and ridiculously attractive—three reasons why I need to keep my distance. I'm still struggling with losing Andrew. I'm not ready to feel anything for anyone.

And yet, as I take the elevator down and nod at the girls at the front desk, I feel a giddy burst of possibility.

I'm in Berlin. I'm having an adventure.

I'm doing something wildly impulsive.

The impulsiveness is exciting and frightening, and the adventure itself is actually bittersweet. Andrew would have loved this. He would have loved to be here with me, on a quest with me.

After all, Andrew was the free spirit. It certainly wasn't ever me.

I walk for over an hour, turning down narrow streets and winding through residential neighborhoods. The late-afternoon sunlight gives way to lavender shadows. Lights turn on and every couple of blocks cafes dot the four corners, tables and chairs spilling out onto the streets. The tables are full, singles and couples and families out for dinner, and even though it's a Sunday evening (or is it because it's a Sunday evening?) no one seems in a hurry to leave.

Hungry, I loop back to my hotel, and start looking for a place to eat. There are Italian restaurants, Indian and Russian restaurants and Japanese sushi spots, but none of those appeal. It's my first night in Berlin. I want German cuisine.

I come across a place with an empty table beneath the front

awning. I scan the chalkboard menu: *Bier, Schnitzel, Wurst.* Perfect. I seat myself, hoping I'm doing the right thing. The waiter approaches with a small menu. I have already practiced my German for the occasion. "*Ein Bier, bitte,*" I say, pleased I've remembered the right words.

My pronunciation—or accent—must give me away. "What kind of beer?" the waiter asks in English.

"A good German beer?"

The waiter all but rolls his eyes. "Pils, an Alt, Kölsch, Weissbier . . . ?"

I have no idea if those are names of beer, or labels. I glance around me, point to a tall glass on a table kitty-corner to my table. "Like that one."

"Pils."

"Yes. *Danke schön.*"

His eyebrows lift satirically. He walks away, clearly not a fan.

Okay, not the friendliest German I met today, but at least my taxi driver was very nice.

I sleep better than I expect, and the next morning, fortified with the hotel's breakfast buffet and several cups of cappuccino, I'm ready to meet up with my bus tour.

The young man at the front desk gives me directions to Alexanderplatz where I'll meet my bus. It's a hop-on, hop-off type tour that you listen to with a headset. If you don't get off the bus anywhere, it's a two-and-a-half-hour tour. I'm not planning on getting off anywhere today.

The tour is a good overview of the city, and I learn things I didn't know. I'd thought I was fairly clear on some of the key dates and details but after listening to two and a half hours of history and facts, I'm overwhelmed by the number of gates and tors, plots and plazas, boroughs, localities, and municipalities that have been included and then excluded by various political machinations and administrative reforms.

The tour tries to give a sense of history, while sharing contemporary facts, such as the huge administrative reform in 2001 that swallowed everything up into one big city with twelve boroughs. Each of the boroughs has its own government which must answer to Berlin's city and state government (since Berlin is both a city and one of Germany's federal states.) I get that. But then when the narrator goes on to explain that each borough is made up of several localities, or sub-districts, that often have a strong historical identity as a village or an independent town, and that within each locality is another cluster of tracts that somewhat compare to neighborhoods, I tune out, no longer able to listen.

I put away my notebook and guidebook and map and just gaze out at the domes and parks and bridges.

It's impossible to learn everything about a city this old in one tour, which is why I'm signed up for the afternoon walking tour. I'll have a live guide this time, and I'll be able to ask questions when I don't understand something.

It's five thirty when I finally return to the hotel, feet aching, and I'm definitely feeling the jet lag now and would love a nap but can't do it today or I won't sleep tonight.

I sit at the small desk in the corner of my room and check messages and e-mail. I've a text from Dad wanting to know if I got in safely. I can't believe I didn't send him a message yesterday. I answer him and then send a message to Helene, asking how Dr. Morris is today. For a moment I'm tempted to send a message to Craig, telling him how amazing Berlin is, but that wouldn't be smart. I can't encourage him. I shouldn't reach out to him. I shouldn't want to reach out to him. He lives in Napa, I live in Scottsdale. Nothing is going to happen.

I eat an early dinner at a restaurant a block from the hotel, and go to bed early, desperate for sleep.

In the morning the hotel doorman hails a cab for me, sending me to the meet-up point for this morning's Potsdam and Dresden palace tours. It's not until I'm actually on the private bus, heading to Dresden that I discover I've booked the wrong tour. We're not going to Potsdam today. That's a separate tour entirely, a four-hour tour. Today's trip to Dresden is a ten-hour tour, with two hours' driving each way.

I'm regretting my haste in booking the palace tour. Being impulsive doesn't always pay. But my frustration begins to melt as our guide takes the microphone and begins to tell us the history and significance of Dresden, the former royal residence of the Saxon kings, and a city famous throughout Europe for its culture and architectural splendor.

But there's a dark side to the beautiful baroque city. In February 1945 the Allied forces targeted Dresden, bombing the historic city for three straight days, unleashing nearly four thousand tons of explosives and incendiary bombs, destroying much of the city's famed beauty, and killing nearly 40,000 of its civilian citizens.

Suddenly Edie's Germany comes into focus.

I'm reminded all over again of why I'm here.

To not just trace her steps, and support her story. But to find truth. And meaning.

We're back in Berlin at seven that evening and I catch a cab for my hotel. It's not yet dark so I could walk the thirty minutes back to the Mani, but I'm tired. I've had enough activity for the day. I've taken at least fifty pictures and I'm looking forward to getting back to my room, having some dinner, and downloading the photos onto my laptop.

It was a good day. I'm glad I went to Dresden but I'm also glad to be back in my room to process everything I saw and learned today.

The travesty of war weighs heavily on me. I feel for the people of Dresden, and then I catch myself—but what about the Jews?

And the Poles and the Czechs?

What about everyone who was different?

Those that were disabled, homosexual? The very religious? They were all killed, too. The suffering staggers me. I can see why people do not wish to talk about the war. I can see why Germany is conflicted about its past.

How does a country come to terms with its history? Its madness?

I wonder how the passing of time affects the different generations. I wonder what the young people are taught in school. I wonder if they try to talk with their grandparents and great-grandparents about the war. About the Third Reich.

There aren't many who lived through the war that are still alive. Edie's generation is almost gone. What does that mean for the future?

Does it mean one can forget?

I suddenly think of Andrew and our last day together. The run. The meal at the Yardhouse. Walking back home together, holding hands.

Did he know all day what he was about to do?

Or was it all impulse?

But in the end, I suppose it doesn't matter. Because whether it was planned, or impulsive, it doesn't change the outcome.

TWENTY-SIX

I know I'm not supposed to read Edie's diary yet, but I'm tempted to open it and read just a little.

I want to hear her voice. I want to feel her here with me.

But she is here, I remind myself. She's the impetus for this trip. Her passion inspired me.

I slip the diary into my bag and dress, heading out for the half-day tour of Potsdam.

Fortunately, I get it right today, it is a tour today of Potsdam and while I enjoyed walking through the palace of Sanssoucci, it's the extensive palace gardens that thrill me. I wander beneath the big trees, around the fountains and lakes, through the grounds that are both serene and magical. My mother would love the gardens. As I walk I can almost feel her with me.

Or is it Edie?

Maybe it's all of them . . . those that have loved this place. Maybe their spirit is still here, protecting. Loving.

I like the thought. It's a happy one.

After the tour we explore historic Potsdam, have a break for lunch, and I go to a Konditorei and order a slice of plum cake and coffee, in honor of Edie, and sit outside eating slowly, watching the tourists cross the cobbled square. At noon the clock chimes and bells somewhere ring. A warm breeze rustles the leaves of the trees, lifting a tendril of my hair.

I pause, fork in hand, and listen.

And feel.

Despite the tourists and the chatter, there's a lovely stillness here, a sense of depth and time. I can see Edie and Franz at a table in the historic plaza, talking, laughing. I can picture him leaning forward to kiss her. I can see her hand reach up to cup his face.

Love changes one. It transforms.

Love always protects, always trusts, always hopes . . .

Those last words aren't mine. I recognize them from the passage my mother was going to read at our wedding, the popular passage from Corinthians that is often read at weddings. But that's not why my mom wanted to read them. She said these were not just words, or good advice. They were the words that inspired her daily.

Love keeps no record of wrongs . . .

If I loved Andrew as much as I say I do, then I can't stay angry with him anymore. I can't blame him for leaving me, or blame him for hurting me. I can't blame myself, either.

Love never fails . . .

I did love him, and love—true love—never fails.

Maybe it's time to forgive him. Maybe it's time to forgive myself.

The tour to Potsdam has energized me. I walk after the bus has dropped us off, map in hand, enjoying playing tourist.

The Potsdam guide told me I have to go to the Fassbender & Rausch chocolate shop to see the incredible chocolate displays, including a giant teddy bear and some of Berlin's most famous landmarks like a huge chocolate Brandenburg Gate. Apparently it's a good place to pick up souvenirs and take photos, and if I do go, I must stop at the cafe attached to the shop since the hot chocolate and chocolate cake are to die for.

The guide is right. Fassbender & Rausch is incredible and while I can't find room for another dessert, I do buy gifts to take home, handmade truffles and chocolates for Dad, Edie, Ruth, and everyone at the dental office. I also take lots of photos.

I nibble on some caramel-filled chocolates and start walking back towards my hotel with my guidebook in hand. I follow the sidewalk that parallels the river, which is the west side of Museum Island, passing first the handsome *Berliner Dom*, a cathedral that looks as if it's hundreds of years old but actually only dates back to 1905, and then walking past gardens, before crossing the bridge at Schlossplatz, to end up at Hackescher Markt.

It's a gorgeous afternoon—sunny and bright but not too hot—and I'm in no hurry. I buy a bottle of water at one of the little stores and wander in and out of the various shops and boutiques. My attention is drawn to a black and neon pink T-shirt in a souvenir shop: *Good Girls Go to Heaven, Bad Girls Go to Berlin*. Don't think I'll buy it, but it makes me smile.

My guidebook suggests I head over to the Hackescher Höfe, or courtyards. It's a heritage site that has been restored, filled with shops and restaurants, along with several memorials, including the Otto Weidt Museum and further back in the same courtyard, the Anne Frank Center, the sister museum for the Anne Frank House in Amsterdam.

I visit both exhibits, and they are sobering.

I stop for dinner on my way home at a restaurant not far from the hotel. The evening is warm and everyone sits outside. I'm able to squeeze into a corner table. I order dinner and a glass of wine and while I wait, I pull out Edie's diary. I've been here for four days now and I've seen Berlin—new and old, historic and social—and I'm ready to read the rest.

I open the cover of the diary. A number of pages have been torn from the front.

I smooth the first page, noting the date. July 1944.

I'm just about to start reading when the woman next to me accidentally drops her phone which bounces towards my feet. I pick it up, and hand it back and she thanks me in German, "Danke schön."

I respond with, "Bitte."

She smiles. "You're an American," she says in English.

I grimace. "Is it that obvious?"

"That's okay. I wasn't born here, either." She pockets her phone and smiles at me. "But Berlin is international. Everyone is here. It's the place to be."

She speaks flawless English, but there is an accent. I'm trying to place the accent. "You're a tourist, too?"

"No. I live here now. I got citizenship last year, but I was born in Israel."

"You're Jewish?"

"One hundred percent," she retorts, raising her glass of beer. "There's a lot of us in Berlin, now. A lot of Jews emigrating to Germany, mostly from Russia and Israel, but also America. One of my good friends is from Portland, Oregon. She moved here to study and stayed. Another friend is a photographer from New York. He's become a German citizen, too. Higher education is free here, for citizens, and Berlin is very safe. We don't feel threatened here. We aren't persecuted."

My disbelief must show because she adds, "Look it up. You'll see that under German law of 1949, any Jew, or the descendant of such a Jew, forced to flee the Nazis, has the right to become a naturalized German. And since 1990, Berlin's Jewish population has grown by forty-five thousand to fifty-five thousand people, depending on your source. That's a lot of people in twenty-five years." She stands and places a handful of euros on the table, along with some coins. *"Auf Wiedersehen. Bye-bye!"*

"Good-bye."

I watch her walk away until she disappears into the crowd spilling out onto the pavement, and then I return to reading.

July 15, 1944

Franz has put me on the train to Munich, and from Munich I'll continue to Zurich. The train is very crowded and uncomfortable. Many people stand or sit on their luggage since there are not enough seats. It is very hot and with so many bodies crowded into such a small space, the stench of sweat and unwashed bodies is overpowering.

I knew there would be soldiers on board but these men are not the arrogant soldiers I first encountered in 1937 and 1938. They are mostly silent, and still, leaning against the wall, watching the world pass without saying a word.

But then, almost no one speaks, and there is certainly no laughter.

People are tired, and hungry. Hitler's masses are still loyal, but they are exhausted by the years of rationing and bombings and blackouts.

July 17, 1944

Missed my connecting train in Zurich after an intense border crossing where the SS scrutinized my passport before finally allowing me to leave. In Zurich I needed another train and then I had to take a bus. The hotel in Ascona gave away my room when I didn't arrive yesterday as scheduled.

They recommended the villa just above the lake, which rents rooms but it is very expensive and I can't afford more than a night there. I will stay a night so that I have somewhere to sleep but must find something else.

July 18, 1944

The villa was very lovely as one might imagine, quite luxurious with many foreigners. Ascona is part of Ticino, the Italian-speaking region of Switzerland and located at the northern end of picturesque Lake Maggiore. Ascona is very serene and pretty, and as far from the chaos and conflict of Berlin as one could desire.

Hard to believe that war consumes the rest of Europe. And while food is still rationed here, it is of much better quality and quantity than one could find anywhere in Germany.

July 19, 1944

Have switched to a smaller hotel on the lake. It is much more affordable and quieter, too. There are no grand spaces here, but I am quite fond of the small but lovely terrace overlooking the lake with chairs for sunbathing.

After checking in, the hotel front desk allowed me to use their phone to call Franz's office, but his secretary said he was out. I asked her to let Franz know I'd made it safely but changed hotels and I'd call again tomorrow.

July 20, 1944

After breakfast I tried to reach Franz again at work. I'd just missed him. Apparently he'd been in this morning and had just stepped out for lunch.

His secretary, who is not the friendliest woman in the first place, sounded annoyed to hear from me again. She was rather sarcastic when I mentioned that I was in Switzerland on holiday. She said it must be nice to be on holiday while everyone else is being bombed to bits.

I hang up, not at all convinced that Egbert will do anything.

I didn't hear the radio announcement myself. I was in my room, in bed resting, when the German woman on my floor pounded. She'd come to tell me that there had been an attempt on der Führer's life today but he'd survived—thank God.

I didn't know what to think, my mind was a whirl and I immediately turned on my radio. The neighbor stayed for a while, talking nonstop. She is very emotional and cried, saying how lucky we are that Hitler survived. She says God must have His hand over Hitler's head. The whole time she sat with me, I was in agony.

Who was part of the assassination attempt? Was this what Franz was working on? Or is this something else?

Please God let this be something else . . .

July 21, 1944

Didn't sleep last night. Couldn't. Haven't eaten, either. Can barely sip some watery tea. Another radio announcement saying something about Hitler returning to work with just some cuts and superficial burns. The enemy was behind the attempt. Finally, after one, in the middle of the night, Hitler himself speaks. He talks of a small group of stupid soldiers behind the attempt, as well as a larger government coup, and mentions

Count von Stauffenberg. Everyone associated with the attempted coup would be ruthlessly hunted down and "exterminated."

I think I must have fainted as I opened my eyes and I was lying on the floor, not far from the radio. I didn't get up for a long time. My arms and legs wouldn't move. It was as if I had no bones. No muscles or tissue. I was nothing but panic and the roar of blood in my ears.

Franz is in trouble. Franz must come and join me now before it's too late.

July 22, 1944

My German neighbor returns today, gloating. News reports today say that Claus von Stauffenberg's entire family has been arrested, and his wife and children have been murdered. The reports so far are unconfirmed and I pray it is just rumor. I can see Nina's face and the children now. They have the most beautiful children. The boys were all so loving and I remember how just last year I bounced Valerie on my knee. She was just two at the time and the sweetest of things. I can't believe they're all gone. I refuse to believe it. The secret police can't be that cruel. But why doesn't Franz contact me? Why can't he send word that he's safe? I need to know he's safe and has a plan to escape.

German papers in the reception today, headlines shout that the German revolt is over. I read and reread the lines: "The attempt of the small clique of conspirators to seize power in Germany was nipped in the bud without difficulty . . ."

There are other reports swirling around Rome. The Stockholm press claims that the attempted coup took place at Obersalzberg,

*during the regular afternoon staff meeting. The bomb apparently
went off before Hitler had fully entered the room.*

July 23, 1944

*Had a message from the hotel reception that a Marion von
Wartenburg telephoned. She didn't leave a message. I tried to
phone her back but there was no answer.*

July 24, 1944

*Haven't been able to reach Marion yet. Afraid to call anyone
else. Can't get information here in Ascona. Want to call Missie
but I don't know where she's staying. I've thought of ringing
the Adlon—she might be there—and possibly they could get a
message to her. Missie would know what's happening. She's
very close to Adam, too, and would know far more than Clarita, whom Adam has shielded from the discussions, planning
to protect her and the children. Am terrified though that I will
just make things worse . . . can't arouse suspicions. But don't
understand why Franz hasn't contacted me. Makes me fear the
worst. Please God, let me know he's okay.*

July 26, 1944

*Reached Marion this morning. She was very calm on the phone,
but very vague, referring to the past few days as "distressing
events" and how Berlin was a very sad place right now. It
wasn't until the very end of the call that she mentioned that
Peter and a number of others had been arrested July 21st and
22nd, and more arrests had taken place that day. The men were
to be tried soon and she planned to attend Peter's trial, if she'd*

be permitted. Marion studied law, has a doctorate degree in law and training as an assistant judge. If she is not allowed in court, then the court is a mockery. But perhaps it is better if she stays away. Peter was Claus' cousin and if the Gestapo apply Sippenhaft . . .

Marion doesn't say that Peter is doomed, but it's understood. He was too close to Claus, which makes me think of Claus' older brother, Berthold. He is doomed, too. Now it's impossible not to race through the list of friends who gathered this past year at Peter and Marion's apartment. Are they all doomed, then?

Instead I ask about Franz.

Marion is silent a moment. "I'd hoped you'd have news for me," she says. "Nobody has seen him in days."

It's as I feared. He's either been arrested, or he's . . . dead.

I don't remember the rest that was said. My mind went blank.

July 29, 1944

Missie phoned from the Adlon. She sounded so cheerful during the call. She's still working at the office but had a lovely lunch with the girls. Melanie is in the city on her own, which I grasp to mean that Gottfried's been arrested. She chatters about nothing and yet in her chatter is everything. I tell her I'm very much on my own, too, so I hope she'll have a cup of tea for me. She promises to call if she has news but it might be difficult since Goebbels has declared Totaler Krieg on those who are disloyal, and now that it's all-out war, there probably won't be opportunities for the girls to get together the way they used to.

I hang up and lie on my bed and wish, oh how I wish, I'd never let Franz put me on the train two weeks ago.

August 1, 1944

More arrests in Berlin today, Melanie among them.

August 4, 1944

Missie phones. She casually mentions an embassy dinner years ago where we first met and were introduced to Ambassador von Hassell. She's only mentioned him because something terrible has happened to him. She doesn't say that, but I know it. That's how this works now. Every name, every friend, every connection is a casualty. What were we thinking, believing we could change things? What brash, naïve folly was this?

August 8, 1944

The radio and newspaper are filled with the news that eight Germans, including Peter, have been tried before the People's Court and found guilty of high treason. All eight have been hanged already.

Peter's gone. My thoughts are with Marion. I pray she's safe.

I'm beyond heartsick. I feel physically ill. Can't write more. This is a nightmare I'll never wake from.

August 9, 1944

The Allied radio is giving names of others rumored to have participated in the July 20th attempt, including those not yet arrested or charged.

Don't the Americans and British understand what they're doing? They're naming people who could be innocent. They're signing the death warrants with every name they mention. It is too much.

August 11, 1944

Still not well. Terrible cramping. Worried. Wish I could reach Franz. Need Franz. He should have never sent me here, away from him.

August 12, 1944

The Allies have captured France.
  And I am bleeding.

August 16, 1944

Have returned to the hotel after five days at the hospital. There was nothing they could do. I have instructions to rest and stay in bed. I'm to be calm and not get excited. I am not calm, but I cannot imagine getting excited. I have lost the baby and there is still no word from Franz.

August 19, 1944

I go down to the hotel's front desk and they help me phone Claudia. Claudia has not seen Franz in weeks . . . maybe longer. The last time she spoke to him was the day after he'd driven me to the train station. He'd stopped in at their apartment and stayed for dinner. It had been quite a nice evening. He'd told her he was hoping to join me in Rome for his medical leave sometime in August. She'd thought that perhaps he was already with me . . . ?

He's not here, I tell her.
She is silent. There is nothing she can say.

August 20, 1944

Lay awake all night, wondering, worrying, talking to Franz. I told him about the baby. I told him I was scared. But most of all, I told him I loved him and would always love him.

August 21, 1944

The German news continues to contradict itself. The dates of the trials and executions are not consistent. It makes one hope. I'm afraid to hope.

August 22, 1944

Adam's Clarita arrested now. She didn't have a chance to see Adam, either, before her arrest.

August 23, 1944

The German news today published a detailed account of Adam's trial and execution. He was executed yesterday without being allowed to speak to Clarita. Too heartsick to write more.

August 24, 1944

The news reports claim that the Allied forces have entered Paris. They say Paris will be liberated. I should be glad for Paris and yet I grieve for my friends in Berlin.

August 25, 1944

*Missie called today, no message. I don't know where to phone
her. Afraid to phone her. Afraid to hear what she might say.*

August 26, 1944

*Rumors swirling that all those arrested are being tortured. I'm
not surprised. Just sickened. Can't bear this. I can't. I'm afraid
I'm going to lose my mind.*

August 27, 1944

*The nice young woman from hotel reception came to see me today.
Her name is Fabiola and she told me that the staff at the hotel is
worried about me as they haven't seen me for a few days and they
say in the kitchen that I do not order food. She asks if I am eating.
I say I cannot eat. She asks if I'm unwell. I tell her that I am fine.*
   She leaves.
   But I am not fine.

August 30, 1944

*Maria phoned. She left a brief message with the hotel's front
desk:* Franz trial next week.
   *I immediately start packing. I must go. I must get to him.
There is no way to get to him.*

August 31, 1944

*No one who has gone to the People's Court has been pardoned.
No one goes to the People's Court and lives.*

But if Franz is executed, I don't want to live.
Without him, there is nothing for me anymore.

September 2, 1944

Every day I wait for word from Berlin.

Every minute of every day I think about Franz. I pray for him. I pray for him to have strength. I won't let myself think about what they have done to him. How they must have tortured him. I pray that he has been strong. That he has God.

September 3, 1944

I am ready to die. Ready to escape this madness.

September 4, 1944

Maria called late. She phoned from the Adlon. Trial postponed while they gather more evidence, but a dozen have been executed this week alone.

"That means there's hope," I say. "If they can't build a case . . . if they need more evidence."

"I wish that's what it means. But usually a trial is postponed so they can conduct further interrogations."

"Torture," I say.

"I'm sorry."

September 8, 1944

I pray now for Franz's death.

I can't bear to think of them torturing him. Knowing that he is probably suffering—

Hell.

This is hell.

September 15, 1944

They killed him yesterday.

They executed him along with Josef Wirmer, the lawyer; the lovely Chaplain Wehrle. Colonel von Üxküll-Gyllenband, and District President Michael Graf von Matuschhka. There were others, too. I just can't remember their names.

Fabiola said I screamed when I got the news.

I don't remember screaming. I don't remember anything but Fabiola's grandmother and mother putting me to bed and the grandmother and mother staying with me through the night, with the grandmother praying her rosary, praying to the Blessed Virgin Mary.

September 16, 1944

The staff knows Franz is gone. Murdered. They don't ask why. There is no need. It is war. A war that doesn't end.

September 23, 1944

Fabiola brought me some vegetable soup and some bread and sat with me while I ate it. I didn't want to eat in front of her. I didn't want to eat it at all but she's afraid I'll die in the hotel and that might make people ask questions. So I ate even though my stomach protested and we chatted and after she left I felt better.

September 27, 1944

Fabiola comes every day to sit with me to make sure I eat. She thinks I should walk in the garden with her, just a little bit as it is cooler outside in the courtyard, in the shade. My room is hot. It's sweltering. I don't want to walk but when I go outside with her, it is nicer. The stone walls of the courtyard have holes in them, exposing a garden on the other side of the wall. There is a headless statue in the neighbor garden. The head of the statue lies at its feet, the blank eyes of the goddess staring this way.

I can't look at her. I wish someone would move her head. Do something for her.

September 30, 1944

Fabiola is actually the daughter of the hotel owner, who died a year ago. She has been helping her mother run the hotel since her father was killed. She was supposed to be married by now but her fiancé went to war and never came home. There are no young men left, she tells me. Just little boys and old men who wish they were dead.

October 1, 1944

Fabiola invites me to dinner with her and her mother. The mother compliments my Italian. She said it is very good, and that I have almost no accent. I tell her that I have an ear for languages and worked for a while as a translator in Berlin. This seems to be the opportunity signora has been waiting for as she asks about my family in Germany, and why I am here, and not there.

I tell her I have no one in Germany. I tell her that my husband is German but I am actually an American and met him when I worked as a translator at the US embassy in Berlin.

"But the US is at war with Germany," she said.

"Yes."

"And the Americans have invaded Italy. Maybe they can help you."

"But I have given up my citizenship. I am now the enemy. If they capture me, I'd go to jail. A prisoner of war."

"Maybe that's not so bad if they sent you to jail in America, yes?"

We are still at the table but I start crying and can't stop. Fabiola is upset with her mother for upsetting me, but that's not why I'm crying. I'm crying because I gave up everything for Franz and Franz gave up everything—including me—for a coup that never had a chance.

But Fabiola doesn't know why I cry, and even though she is my age, maybe younger, she hugs me and rocks me, crooning comfort as if I'm a baby.

It's not until later I remember our conversation and her mother is right.

I need to find the Americans before the Nazis find me.

TWENTY-SEVEN

I can't sleep.

I am exhausted and overwhelmed and I wish I hadn't read the entire diary sitting at the restaurant, reading by candlelight. The words, the warm night, the flickering flame, the dull glow of light on the page combined to make it intensely emotional.

Even after returning to the hotel and climbing into bed I feel overwhelmed. Claustrophobic.

It's horrific, how Franz died.

It's horrific how Hitler had them hanged so that it was an excruciatingly slow death. Such an evil, evil man. I'm disgusted and angry, and lying in my room, which is too warm for me on this hot night, I feel disgust towards everyone and everything in Germany.

Why didn't more people do something? Why didn't more people rise up and act?

I understand that many were broken and afraid. I've read how there can be a diffusion of responsibility, part of something called the bystander effect, where people in groups are significantly slower to take action. They all figure someone else will do it. Or should do it.

Is that what happened in Germany?

Did Hitler seem good and helpful early on, and then later something of an egomaniac but for the most part, benign?

Did no one understand that Germans and Germany were in trouble before it was too late?

Surely there were people early on saying—hey, we've got a situation here.

Hey, this isn't right, isn't fair.

I cover my face with my forearm to stop the tears. It doesn't work. I fall asleep crying.

I oversleep in the morning. I've missed the breakfast buffet but I can get a coffee and some muesli and yogurt. It's hard to eat. My heart's heavy.

If I weren't going home tomorrow, I wouldn't go to the memorials today. I'd skip everything to do with the Holocaust and Third Reich and would make today a fun day. I'd go on a Spree River cruise, then visit the Bode Museum, and afterwards sit in one of the beer gardens that flank the river and listen to music and people watch.

I'd lift my face to the sun and breathe deeply and be glad for my health, and my family, and my life.

It's too easy to take good things for granted. Too easy to be lazy and spoiled and self-indulgent.

I don't want to be that woman who can't ever be happy, or be oblivious to her blessings—stability, security, peace.

I lost Andrew—and my Mom—but I'm young. Whole. Alive.

I have the present and the future. I can choose my thoughts. I can choose to hope. I can choose to love, and to give—like my Mom—and to believe.

Even if one is confronted by evil, one can still choose differently. We have free will. And a voice.

But I do leave Berlin tomorrow and I've promised Edie I would visit the Memorial to the German Resistance. I've promised to take photos for her and show her how they are finally honoring those who did try to do something—even if it took Germany twenty-eight years to recognize them.

Because I'm getting a later start than I planned, I swap the morning and afternoon itineraries and go to the German Resistance Memorial first, then Plötzensee Prison, break for a quick lunch, followed by an afternoon at Brandenburg Gate, Pariser Platz, and the Holocaust Memorial.

The man at the hotel reception desk suggests I either take the subway or a cab to the German Resistance Memorial Center at Bendlerblock, and then from there it would be another fifteen-minute car ride to the Prison's Memorial, should I cab it, but he isn't sure why I'd want to go. He thinks I might enjoy seeing all the award-winning new buildings at Potsdamer Platz—stunning, modern architecture—or visiting Berlin's Botanical Gardens or one of the many famous museums, and having been an art major, he can suggest a few. I simply smile and step outside where the doorman flags down a cab for me.

As my taxi travels past the Tiergarten and the soaring Victory Column, I feel a flutter of nerves. I'm not sure what I'll find at the memorial and I rather dread visiting the prison, but I go home tomorrow. I have a six a.m. flight out of Berlin, everything is wrapping up very quickly now. This week has passed fast. Hard to believe I'll be back to work at Dr. Morris' office in just three days.

At Bendlerblock on Stauffenbergstrasse—the government has renamed the street after Claus—I pay the cab driver, and approach the gray building that houses the memorial. The building is severe, and uninspiring, at least until I pass beneath an arch and enter a courtyard where I'm confronted by a statue of a naked man. I read the plaque, and its translation.

You did not bear the same
You resisted

It was here, on this spot, that Claus von Stauffenberg was executed.

I spend a few minutes just standing in the courtyard. It's quiet, too, despite the warm day. If I listen closely, I can hear cars and traffic in the distance, as well as warbling birds, but the high walls of the courtyard make it feel so very private here. Private and still.

As I enter the museum and pick up brochures, I scan the leaflets and handouts, hoping to discover something about Franz. Nothing jumps out at me, but at least I have his real name now. Maybe armed with his full name, I'll find a photo or mention. I really want to take pictures for Edie, so she can have something of him . . . a photo she can frame, a plaque she can read.

For an hour I silently tour the museum, reading each sign and studying the displays memorializing the individuals and groups who opposed the Nazis.

I'd read in one of the brochures that the memorial recognizes all who were part of the Resistance, that all who resisted—in whatever form—are given equal "respect," but as you wander through the memorial it becomes painfully clear that there were not enough of them who opposed Hitler. There was not enough organization and cohesion among the Resistance to be effective.

The memorial tries to put a brave face on the past, and the facts, but it strikes me that there are no heroes here.

There was simply not enough done.

Those who tried to do the right thing were smashed. The Germans with a conscience were ineffectual. Weak.

After an hour of reading signs and studying displays, I speak to the director of the Resistance Memorial, summoned for me by the man at the front desk, hoping he might help me find something on Major Baron Torsten von Franz here.

I start to tell him I'm friends with Major von Franz's wife, Edie, and the director interrupts. "Major Baron von Franz was married, but his wife's name was Elizabeth. She was born an American."

"Yes," I say. "Edie was American and she met him when she worked at the American embassy."

"That's correct, but if you check with the American embassy's records, her legal name was Elizabeth Doherty." He smiles at me. "Everyone at the embassy referred to her as Elizabeth. From what we've gathered through interviews, Torsten called her E.D.—short for Elizabeth Doherty. It was his private name for her. I don't believe anyone else used it but him."

He gestures for me to follow him and he leads me to a wall with a number of black-and-white photographs. In the bottom corner, and smaller than the others, are a group of women with children on their knees and playing at their feet. "There she is," he says. "With some of the other wives of the Resistance. They were, by all accounts, quite good friends."

I read the caption beneath the photo.

(LEFT TO RIGHT) Garden party, May 1943. Marion Yorck von Wartenburg, Clarita von Trott, Elizabeth von Franz, and Nina von Stauffenberg with four of the five von Stauffenberg children. The fifth, Konstanze, wasn't born until after her father's execution.

I scan the photo, counting heads, since Elizabeth—Edie—is the third from the left, and I've always thought of her as fair, but in this photo she's not blonde but brunette, her glossy dark hair rolled and pinned on the sides, the back caught in a loose, romantic chignon.

She's lovely and young and smiling. She had a regal profile even then—straight nose, firm lips, bright, clear eyes.

No wonder Franz loved her. No wonder she became his E.D. Edie.

My chest grows tight. My eyes sting. I smile at her. Lovely, fiery, independent Edie.

"Every one of these women lost their husbands, didn't they?" I say to the director.

"They did," he agrees. "And all of the wives in this photo, but Elizabeth, were imprisoned. Baroness von Franz was out of the country at the time of the coup and escaped prosecution."

"Not in the US," I tell him. "I've been told that on her return to the US in 1944, she spent a number of months in Texas at one of the German internment camps, before finally being released and allowed to join her sister in California."

"I wish we had more on Baron von Franz. After the war, some families shared their experiences, but many didn't, particularly those who lived in the Russian sector."

"From what Edie said, his family was on the East German side."

"This is the only photo we have of him." He leads me across the room to another wall and another photograph, this time of young officers in uniform, including Claus von Stauffenberg, in the front. The caption dates the photo to 1938. "Torsten von Franz is in the back row, far right."

I'd seen the photo before but the caption didn't mention Franz so I hadn't paid it more attention. It's a candid shot. The young officers are all smiling and relaxed.

I'm disappointed I can't see more of Franz but at least he is here, and he's included. I lean closer, studying the lapel of his jacket, the line of jaw, the high cheekbone and wide brow. I can see a bit of fair hair combed neatly back. He's not the tallest in the group, but not small, either. From the corner of his mouth, it seems as if he, too, was smiling. His arms are behind his back, possibly holding his hat. Franz. Edie's Franz.

The director tells me what I've already read, that after the July 20 assassination attempt, approximately seven thousand people were arrested by the Gestapo, with close to five thousand executed, even though very few of those were actually involved in the July 20 plot, carried out by Claus von Stauffenberg.

The high ranking officers, and those who'd agreed to serve on the new government once Hitler was gone, were hanged at the prison on meat hooks. In all, two ambassadors, seven diplomats, the head of the Reich police, three secretaries of state, two field marshals, nineteen generals, twenty-six colonels, and an unknown number of lawyers, teachers, aristocrats, and intellectuals were executed.

"Von Stauffenberg was executed here, the day after the attempt, in this very courtyard. This was once his building. His office. He was executed outside his own office."

The director accompanies me for the next fifteen minutes, telling me about the history of the memorial and why it took so long to get something organized for the Resistance. "It's only become acceptable to talk about the Resistance in the last forty years. Until then, most Germans believed that the members of the Resistance were traitors.

"Most Germans supported Hitler," he adds. "And they struggled with guilt after the war. They felt shame. Shame that Germans followed Hitler, shame that Germans plunged the world into war, shame that there had been an alternative and they didn't choose it. This code of silence is one of the reasons why widows of the executed Resistance members didn't receive pensions until the 1960s. They were being punished . . . They were wives of traitors."

And isn't this what Edie said?

"In fact," he adds, "there was no memorial, no tribute to the German Resistance until 1968."

I thank the director for his time and go outside to take more photos of the courtyard. I touch the ground with the bronze lines set into the cement.

This is where Claus and the other officers were shot.

This is where the men were lined up . . .

This is where the soldiers stood to shoot them.

I shudder and stop the thoughts by focusing on taking another half-dozen photographs to show Edie, and then leave as soon as I'm done.

I have to walk several blocks until I can hail a cab. It's another fifteen minutes until we reach Plötzensee Prison.

My heart falls as the car pulls up in front of the redbrick building. I don't want to do this anymore. I've had enough of the past, and the memories.

I will just take a few pictures for Edie and then leave. It is my last day here. I want to do something else besides feel so much sadness and pain.

I ask the driver to wait for me. He will but he'll keep the meter running.

I take pictures of the front of the prison. It's still a prison today, but the back "shed" used for the thousands of executions during the Third Reich has been turned into a memorial.

I don't feel any need to go inside the prison's memorial.

I don't need to see the meat hooks in the ceiling. They remind me too much of Andrew and his final moments.

I try so hard not to remember Andrew that way. I try so hard not to go there . . . but every now and then, I can't help myself.

Was he calm at the end, or in agony?

What was he thinking as he positioned the chair beneath the hall chandelier? Was he afraid as he wrapped the belt around his neck?

Did he think of me?

These are the thoughts that have haunted me late at night. These thoughts can still keep me from sleeping. And the only way I handle the thoughts is by believing Andrew was not alone at the end, that God was with him, and maybe an angel, whispering prayers, providing comfort.

I pray that angels were with Franz and Adam and Claus and Peter and the rest.

I pray that there is a reward for those who stand up and do the right thing. I pray that tortured souls get their peace.

I reach into my bag for Edie's diary, wanting to reread something she'd written about Franz here at Plötzensee, but when I dig for the diary, it isn't there.

I crouch down on the ground, and open my bag all the way up. I pull out my notebook, guidebook, map, wallet, everything. No diary.

I go through everything again. But the leather diary is gone.

I tell myself not to panic. There is no reason to panic. I must have left it in the hotel room. This morning I must have taken it out of my purse without knowing.

I return to the cab, giving the driver the address for the Mani, impatiently counting the minutes until we reach the hotel. After paying him, I hurry upstairs to my room. My gaze sweeps the bed, the dresser, the tiny nightstands. Nothing.

I go through my suitcase, search my carry-on bag. I look under the bed. I check my purse again. My heart is hammering now. I must go back to the restaurant where I ate dinner last night. Maybe I left it there. Maybe it fell out of my bag as I paid the bill. Maybe.

The restaurant doesn't have the diary.

I return to my hotel room. I search again, literally taking it apart—the bed, the sheets, the pillows, the shelves in the bathroom. I crawl around the tiny closet, patting every inch of floor.

It's not there.

I go back out, retrace my steps to the restaurant, looking in the gutters, checking trash cans, asking at nearby businesses if anyone turned in an old leather book, a journal, with a dark brown cover.

Nothing.

Nothing.

I'm supposed to fly home tomorrow. I'm supposed to be returning to Napa and work but I can't get on the plane. Not without Edie's diary.

Desperate, distraught, I return to the hotel and the front desk helps me dial Craig's number since I'm too upset to figure out the international codes.

TWENTY-EIGHT

⸻

C raig arrives in Berlin close to nine thirty, having caught a late-afternoon flight out of Pisa and then connecting in Frankfurt. He meets me at my hotel. He doesn't look the least bit rumpled.

I am waiting for him in the lobby when he arrives, pacing when I can't stay still on the sofa. I jump up as he walks through the glass doors. "Thank you so much for coming!"

He gives me a quick hug. "It's going to be okay, Ali."

"We have to find it. I'm not leaving without it—"

"We'll go look together tonight, but you can't miss your flight."

"I can't return without it, Craig."

"Let's take it a step at a time, okay?"

He leaves his leather briefcase and blazer in my room and we set out walking, retracing our steps from the Mani to the restaurant. It's a balmy Friday night and the streets are crowded, young people spilling out onto the streets with glasses of wine and beer. There is less traffic and noise on the narrower streets north of Torstrasse, and this is where I'd eaten last night, at one of the charming cafes with sidewalk tables beneath strings of light.

Craig enters every restaurant and store on the quieter side streets, asking about the diary, leaving his business card, and offering a reward if the book is found. We go up and down street after street making a giant circle that takes over an hour.

We do the same thing on all corners of Rosenthaler Platz before going down the stairs to the U-Bahn station below. Together Craig and I go through each of the garbage cans on the platform. The overhead light's a blinding yellow that casts a glare off the orange-tiled walls and columns.

"This was a ghost station for years," Craig tells me as we go through the trash filled with newspapers, discarded food, and worse. "The train wouldn't stop here because this section was in East Berlin, and this station, which had been here since the 1930s, only opened back up in 1989."

We're going through the last of the trash cans when a policeman descends to tell us we shouldn't be doing this. People are complaining. Craig tells the policeman what we're looking for, and the policeman is polite but insistent that we stop. We might be better off reporting the missing book to the nearest police station, and there is one not far from us, on Brunnenstrasse. He doesn't recommend us going down now. It's nearly eleven and the clerks for non-emergency reports have long since gone home. We should go home, or to our hotel, and file a report in the morning.

At the hotel we wash up. Craig speaks to the young man at the Mani's reception desk, telling him about the missing book. The young man promises to alert the hotel staff about the diary. Craig gives the young man his business card and says if it is found, there will be a substantial reward.

Craig and I face each other in the lobby. It's late. We're both tired. I fight tears. I feel horrible. I've failed Edie. This diary, this is all she has left of Franz.

"Don't cry," Craig tells me sternly. "It's not going to help."

I nod but I'm heartsick. I shouldn't have brought the diary. I shouldn't have taken it from the hotel.

"Let's go find some dinner," he says. "You'll feel better."

"You think we'll find something open now?"

"This is Berlin, and Berliners love to stay out late. Lots of places will be open until two, three, even four."

We return to my favorite side street, the one where I ate last night, but we go to a different restaurant where we're offered inside or outside seating. We choose outside, and have a corner table that's tucked beneath long strings of rose-colored lights.

"You obviously enjoy traveling," I say. "Tell me where you'd visit again if you could."

"Budapest," he says promptly. "And Ghent—"

"Ghent?"

"Belgium."

"Ah."

"Freiburg. Hamburg." He ticks them off. "Gothenburg."

"All Germany?"

"The first two are in Germany. Gothenburg is in Sweden." He pauses, thinks. "Innsbruck."

"Austria," I say.

He smiles. "Cinque Terra."

I raise my brows.

"Italy." Craig leans back, watches as the waiter uncorks the bottle of white wine and then fills our glasses. "Porto."

"Where's that?"

"Portugal. A beautiful little city, too." He lifts his glass in a toast. "To Ali on her first visit to Berlin."

I lift my glass. "How about to Edie, since she inspired the trip?"

"To Edie and Ali. Two of my favorite women."

We drink and talk and drink some more. Craig tells about the reality show he and his brother did for the Food Network several years ago. "We did it to grow our business, give us more exposure, and build our brand, and we did all that."

"So it was a good thing?" I ask, trying to relax, which means trying not to think about returning to Napa and telling Edie I'd lost her diary.

"It helped our business, definitely. But it wasn't good for Chad and me personally. Chad and I fought a lot more during the show. It strained our relationship and took a toll on our relationships with other people. But the winery prospered and we were able to step back after two years, and so that's what we did."

"Knowing what you know now, would you do it again?"

"Nope. No. And I'm pretty certain Chad feels the same way."

We order dinner and Craig orders a traditional Berlin appetizer called rollmops. I'm not sure I'm going to like them. The idea of pickled fish, even if it's pickled trout, doesn't sound appealing. Craig shows me how to eat it. He likes it without bread, some eat it with bread, and I try it (with bread) and it's okay, not terrible, but I do think it must be an acquired taste. I wash it down with wine, and then some more wine, since that is excellent.

I look up to find Craig smiling at me, as if amused.

"So how have you been?" he asks.

"I was great until I lost the diary." Just saying the words makes me feel as if I'm on a free-falling elevator, and I'm heartsick all over again. I thought I was being so careful.

"Shit happens," he says kindly.

"Not like this." I turn my glass on the table and watch the wine swirl. "This is her past . . . her life . . . her story of Franz." I glance back up. "Did you know his real name wasn't Franz? His real name was Torsten?"

"I actually know nothing about him, other than the fact that he was one of the German Resistance executed after July twentieth."

"You never wanted to know more?"

"She never wanted to share more. I'm amazed that she's told you what she has . . . It's something she refused to discuss . . . even with my grandmother or mother." He gives me another faint, crooked smile. "I guess she likes you."

"I wouldn't say she likes me. I think she tolerates me."

"My great-aunt wouldn't throw you a bon voyage party if she didn't like you."

My chest grows tight. I swallow around the lump in my throat. "That was her idea?"

"Yes."

And now I just want to cry.

Edie, I blew it. I'm sorry.

TWENTY-NINE

I lie in bed in the dark, waiting for morning to come so I can get dressed and grab my bags and head to the airport.

I don't know why it's taking so long for morning to come, but I lie on the edge of the bed, trying not to think, trying not to feel, doing my best to keep from acknowledging any of the crazy emotions bubbling inside of me.

This wasn't supposed to have happened.

I don't know how it happened.

Fleetingly, I picture our dinner together, and at no point did I consciously want him. At no point did I think, "I want to sleep with this guy." I wasn't sexual. I didn't feel romantic. I didn't feel anything that should have made sex an option.

Carefully, quietly I glance behind me to where Craig is sprawled asleep on his side of the bed.

He looks content. Relaxed.

I envy him. I would love to relax, and sleep. Instead I am quietly freaking out. I lie back down on my side, squeeze my eyes closed, my hands tucked beneath my chin, knees up to my chest.

I've assumed a fetal position. Never a good sign.

Eyes still closed, I see bits of our dinner and drinks flash through my mind. I try to analyze them without feeling . . . tricky. But without pulling it all apart, I can't quite figure out how we ended up in bed.

This wasn't part of the plan.

Craig wasn't part of the plan.

I'm angry with myself for letting things get so out of hand. It was one thing to call him after I lost the diary and allow him to fly in from Pisa and help me look for it—it was *his* great-aunt's diary, after all—but it's another to stay up until midnight and then cap it off with dinner and drinks and more drinks until I've lost my way completely.

I blame the three (four?) glasses of excellent Rhine wine, I do.

I blame the warm night and the bright sky and the easy conversation and laughter of those dining around us.

If Craig hadn't been such great company I would have wanted to return to my hotel room earlier . . . alone.

If I'd been unhappy I would have wanted to be alone.

I was upset about the diary, but I wasn't deeply, darkly unhappy . . . not the deep, dark unhappy I've been since Andrew died.

No, I was—if I let myself think about it long enough—exceptionally happy.

Relaxed and content, mellow from the warm night and crisp light wine. I could feel the warmth hum in my veins. It was the most lazy, indulgent of pleasures . . . a great meal, a balmy night, and the company of a man that was far too easy on the eyes.

I do not think of myself as superficial. I've never been a sucker for a pretty face. But Craig Hallahan dazzled me with his broad shoulders, shaggy dark blond hair, piercing blue eyes.

Yes, he is too handsome for his own good. Or more accurately, too handsome for my own good, because sometime between ordering dinner and finishing the bottle of wine, I wanted more of him than conversation.

I remember sitting there after midnight obsessively thinking that I wanted to test—taste—the distinctly male energy that vibrates around him, a shimmering force field of virility. Possibility.

I knew then the wine had gone to my head.

I knew then that I shouldn't want to test—taste—a man like Craig Hallahan. But I was too far gone.

Too drunk.

Too stirred.

Too stimulated.

Buzzed, and buzzing, I leaned across the table and kissed him. *I* kissed him.

It shocked him. It shocked me. But it didn't stop me from kissing him again, or stop us from returning to my hotel and making out for hours before we finally consummated the damn thing.

I was no longer drunk by the time his hips settled against mine, his hard body urgent against me. I was quite aware of what we were doing. I had to be. He asked me several times, *Ali, are you sure?*

I was sure. Because I wanted to know how it would be between us. I wanted to feel how it would feel with someone besides Andrew.

And it felt good. Really good. It was actually . . . incredible. Probably the best sex I've ever had. But that was also a bad thing.

Great sex with someone else means I'm not as frozen as I thought I was. Being able to feel good with another man makes it even harder to keep my vigil for Andrew. It means that at some point I'm going to have to move on.

Or even that I am already moving on.

If I move on, what happens to Andrew, my love?

What happens to me?

And so at three, when Craig held me after I'd climaxed once, and then again, I smashed my heart back into my chest and beat it down, even as I whipped my conscience.

Andrew isn't Craig. Craig isn't Andrew. Craig will never be Andrew.

And I don't know if that's bad or good.

THIRTY

I spend the flight from Berlin to Amsterdam telling myself Craig will be fine, that he's a big boy. He'll check out of the hotel, catch a flight from Berlin back to Pisa, finish the expo, watch his brother get married. He's okay. He travels a lot. He's gorgeous. He's smart. He's successful, wealthy, sexy . . . incredible in bed. He's got it made.

He doesn't need me.

I then spend the ten-hour flight from Amsterdam to San Francisco agonizing over how to tell Edie that I've lost the diary. I have no idea how to break the news. I dread facing her when I get home.

Do I blurt it our first? Do I show her my pictures first? Do I open the book I bought at the Resistance Memorial and leaf through it with her?

Perhaps I should have called her the moment it happened. Perhaps I should have prepared her before I came home . . .

Anxious and restless I glance at my watch, wondering how much longer until we land. Seven hours. We've only been flying for three.

I can't do this, agonize like this. I reach into my bag for the bottle of Ambien I brought to Germany with me. I don't take it often anymore, and didn't need it during the trip, but after Andrew died it was the only way I could make myself sleep. I pop an Ambien now, gulp down some water, and tell myself to stop thinking about everything. Nothing is going to change between now and landing. Worrying accomplishes nothing. Edie has been through worse. She's tough. She'll survive this.

And by repeating the mantra, Edie is fine, Edie is tough, Edie has been through worse, I relax long enough to fall asleep.

I turn my phone back on and as I head to the parking lot to get the car, voice mail messages and texts download.

Dad has left three messages. Craig has left two.

I know why Craig is calling—he wants to smooth things over, make everything okay—but I'm worried about Dad. Dad never phones me, and if he does want to get me a message, he'll send a brief text.

I call him as soon as I clear customs and am heading out towards my car.

"You've landed safely?" he asks.

"Yes. I'm walking through the parking lot now. Everything okay?"

"Yes," he answers, after the slightest hesitation.

I frown as I hit the elevator button. "What's going on?"

"Just come see me when you get home."

This isn't good. "Dad?"

"Drive safely. Don't rush. I'll see you soon."

Traffic is heavy leaving the city as the Giants ball game looks like it just ended. I fight back impatience and exhaustion. It's late at night in Germany right now and my body wants to be somewhere quiet and dark, probably sleeping.

Two and a half hours after leaving the San Francisco airport I reach Napa Estates.

I see Harold and Walter with a couple others in the lobby talking, and I wave as I head for the elevator.

Dad answers his door when I knock and he looks fine. Better than fine, he looks fit and tan and his brace is gone.

"What have you been doing?" I ask, giving him a hug. "Sunbathing?"

"I played a little golf."

"Balance was okay?"

"Not bad, but I couldn't walk the course. Rode in the golf cart but had a good time."

I set my purse and overnight bag, filled with books and maps and brochures for Edie, on the coffee table and sit down. "So . . . what's going on?"

He sits down, claps his hands on his knees. "You had a good trip, though?"

He's making me nervous. "I did. But what's up? What's wrong?"

"Edie passed away in the night."

It's the last thing I expected him to say and I give my head a slight, disbelieving shake.

"She died in her sleep," he adds. "The staff contacted her family, and Craig phoned this morning asking me to tell you. He knew you'd be upset. He tried to reach you but he couldn't get through."

That's why he'd called. Not because he wanted to talk about our night together.

Silence stretches.

I don't know what to say. There's nothing I can say. I went to Berlin for her. I went to take photos and get information that I could share with her . . .

"Does Ruth know?" I whisper.

"Ruth's aide was the one who alerted the front desk that Edie didn't show to meet Ruth for their Saturday morning breakfast. You know Edie. She never misses that breakfast. She's never late for anything."

My eyes sting. My throat aches. "I hate this."

"She was almost ninety-five. She lived a good life."

"Doesn't matter."

He gives me an odd half smile before looking away, but I saw the sheen of tears in his eyes. He's teared up—my dad who never cries. "She was a good old girl," he says gruffly.

That's when I break down and cry.

She was a remarkable woman.

I wasn't sure about her at first, but by the time I left for Berlin, she'd become a hero to me.

THIRTY-ONE

I've been in Scottsdale a week, and everyone at the office is glad to have me back, but it wasn't easy settling back in. There is to be a memorial service for Edie in late June, after Chad has returned from his honeymoon, and I've made Dad promise to keep me informed about details, but it's unlikely that I'll be able to be there. Dr. Morris is still experiencing significant nerve pain from shingles and so I'm trying to cover for him by putting in extra hours on Saturdays and staying later on the weekdays to try to see as many patients as necessary.

I think about Edie a lot. I only knew her a few weeks but somehow it feels as if she's always been part of my life. Maybe it's because I can still hear her voice in my head. I can see her standing next to her kitchen table, hands folded, shoulders squared.

And I ask her in my head, *Edie, what should I do about my house? Because I don't think I like my house anymore. It doesn't feel like home. Not since Andrew died.*

I hear her answer as clear as anything. *Don't ask me, Alison. Do what you want to do.*

Late June I put the house up for sale, and, taking the Realtor's advice, I have priced it aggressively. I want it to sell. Andrew and I put a lot of work into it and the house is gorgeous. I hope it'll be loved by a different family one day but I need to move on—literally—and I move into a one-bedroom apartment across the street from the mall. The apartment is small but it's new and clean with high ceilings and lots of light.

I tell myself I'll be happier in Scottsdale now. I just needed a new place for a new start, but as July wears on, I'm not sure Scottsdale is my home anymore.

I still love the desert and the red rocks by Fountain Hills and Mummy Mountain and Camelback Mountain, located above my neighborhood, but I miss seeing Dad. He and I found our own rhythm and relationship. It wasn't the one with Mom in the center, but it was one we both accepted, and found comfortable.

I miss Diana, too. I don't have any single girl friends in Scottsdale. Everyone I know here is either a couple friend I made with Andrew, or someone related to work.

But I need to have a life outside my job. And here I have a good job—a career—and let's face it, I'm a much better dentist than florist.

It's late Thursday afternoon on July 3, the day before the office closes for a three day weekend and the Realtor has called twice to let me know that we're going to get an offer on the house, and then, that the offer has come in and she'd like to present it to me later, once I'm off work.

I'm racing to finish my last appointment of the day—a crown—when Helene comes back to let me know there's a delivery for me and I need to sign for it personally.

"Can't you pretend to be me?" I ask, lifting my protective goggles.

"I didn't think of that. And now it's too late."

I sigh. "All right. I'll be there. I just need a few minutes."

Helene disappears and I finish cementing the crown, then carefully scrape away any excess cement. The crown looks good, and I ask my patient to gently bite down. I inspect her bite and the fit, and that looks good, too.

"Go easy for the first day," I tell her. "Avoid anything too hard or sticky for twenty-four hours but after that you should have no problem."

My patient is delighted. "That's it? All done?"

"Yep."

"It didn't even hurt today. You didn't even have to numb me!"

"If anything should bother you, or something doesn't feel right, don't hesitate to call the office and we'll get you right back in, okay?" I stand up and wash my hands, swapping places with the dental assistant who will finish cleaning up so the patient can leave.

At the front desk I ask about the delivery and Helene points to a dark brown leather book on the counter. There's a scratch on the lower right corner.

My heart does a funny double beat. *Edie's diary.* I grab it, open it, flipping through the thin pages, but they are all there. No stains. No tears. It's safe. It's back.

I hug it to my chest, and look at Helene, shocked.

She smiles at me, and points to the lobby. I open the door and exit into the waiting room, and there's Craig . . . lean and tan, a little rumpled, but still ridiculously handsome.

I should feel weird about our last night in Berlin, but I'm too delighted to see the diary to feel anything but pleasure. "I can't believe it," I say, hugging the diary tighter. "You found it. How?"

"Someone turned it in to that bakery on the corner of Rosenthaler and Torstrasse, but because they were closed when we were walking around, we never left a card there. One of the girls who works there was telling someone from the newsstand down the street about finding this old diary from 1944, written in English, and the man from the newsstand remembered us. He dug up my card and gave it to the girl, but the girl forgot about the diary for a few weeks. Eventually she came across my card again and e-mailed me a few days ago."

"Just a few days ago?"

He nods. "So I flew over and picked it up, and here I am."

Here he is.

My chest grows tight. "You just flew in?"

"Into LAX and then I caught a connection to Phoenix."

"I can't believe it. I never thought we'd see it again."

"I hoped we would."

I feel my lips tug and slowly curve up. "Such an optimist."

"Because it's you." He gives me a hug then, and kisses the top of my head. "I'm flying back out tonight, but Chad and I have talked, and we want you to have this diary. We both agree Aunt Edie would want you to have it—"

"I can't." I step back and look down at the diary. I'm so glad it's been found, and I'm very glad to see it, but it's not mine. It doesn't belong with me. "This needs to stay with your family. It's your family's history. It needs to go back in her boxes with her important papers—"

"No one will read it."

"Maybe not right now, but later, you and Chad will have kids and they'll want to know about this fascinating aunt of yours. And it'll be your responsibility to tell them . . . your responsibility to share Edie's diaries and letters with them."

I put the diary in his hands and for a split second I hold his hands and the book, but then I step away.

I kind of miss him as I step away. "I feel bad that you came so far."

"I don't. It's good to see you."

I can't help smiling a bit. "It's good to see you, too."

"Things going okay?"

"Working a lot, but I don't mind."

"Good."

I hold my breath, unsure what to do or say. It *is* good to see him. He feels a bit like . . . home.

He gestures to the door. "I better get going."

I suddenly don't want him to go. I want him to stay and have dinner with me and tell me about his brother's wedding and what's happening in Napa and if he's seen Diana or my dad or Ruth . . .

"Okay," I say, forcing a smile. "I'll walk you out."

"That's not necessary. I know you've got to work."

"I just saw my last patient." I walk to the door, open it, and squint against the bright sun as a blast of blistering heat reaches me. "Every day it's a shock," I say.

"It's hot."

"And yet it's only 106 today."

He laughs and we walk to the parking lot and he leads me to a sedate dark blue sedan.

"Nice rental car," I tease.

"You think Bruiser would like it?"

"Only if he could hang out the window."

He laughs as he unlocks the driver's door and reaches in to place Edie's diary on the console. "I'm not sure he'd love the heat, though."

"No, he wouldn't," I agree. "Bulldogs don't do well in the desert."

"I guess that means you have to come visit us."

"Yeah?"

"Yeah." He wraps me in his arms and hugs me, and for a moment I bury my face against his chest and breathe him in, and for a split second I'm tempted to give in to his strength and warmth.

It would be so easy to just lean on him . . . so easy to soak up his kindness.

But it wouldn't be fair to him. I'm not ready to love . . . not ready to give, not really even ready to receive.

I'm not and it kills me because if I were in a different place, Craig would be so perfect . . .

Perfect for me.

"I'm sorry," I whisper. "Sorry for how I left you in Berlin."

"It's okay."

"It wasn't okay. It was a terrible good-bye."

His hand reaches up to cup the back of my head before he runs it down, smoothing my hair. "I think the problem was the lack of good-bye."

But he's not angry. There's humor in his inflection. I can hear the smile in his voice.

I draw a deep breath and break free, and tip my head back to look at him, really look at him, and I see a tall man with dark blond hair and a bristly jaw and shadows and circles beneath his eyes.

He looks tired. Travel weary. And he did it for Edie . . .

Well, Edie and me.

My heart hurts, but it's a bittersweet ache because I feel things for him, but the timing is just off. I'm not ready to be open, yet, and he deserves a woman who can love him freely. Without reservation.

"Take care of yourself," I tell him.

"You, too."

And then I'm walking back to the office, hoping the frigid air conditioner will chill—or at least numb—the ache in my heart.

THIRTY-TWO

I work through the next few weeks of the hot summer, putting in significant hours at the office so I can see Dad at the end of the month.

I return again mid-August for the weekend, and Diana tells me she's bought tickets for a concert on the lawn Labor Day weekend and is hoping I can come back up and go with her. I hadn't planned on returning so soon but Dad offers to cover the ticket for me, saying it'd be nice to see me again, especially if I can join him "and the boys" for brunch. Dad hasn't bought me a ticket to any place since I was an undergrad at UW. I promise to come back up.

Labor Day weekend is really fun. I arrive Saturday morning and help Diana and Carolyn decorate the poles of a huge wedding tent with garlands of fresh flowers, and then meet Dad for lunch before joining Diana for the outdoor concert and picnic on the winery lawn.

I see Craig from afar with a group of people that includes his brother Chad. It looks like a couples event, with everyone paired up, and Craig's date is a petite redhead. I find myself watching him—them—and I'm curious. Okay, envious.

I'd like to be the one with him. I'd like it to be me that he leans in to, and me that he listens to, and me that he smiles at.

I'd like to be the girl that makes him laugh.

I'd like to be the girl he kisses.

Wait. I was the girl he kissed. And he did it really, really well.

I turn away then, not wanting to risk seeing him lean in for the kiss. I'm not curious anymore. I'm just plain jealous.

Resolutely I face forward and smile fiercely, determined to look happy. I'm going to have a good time if it kills me.

It's killing me.

"What's wrong?" Diana asks.

"Nothing." And then I slap the blanket. "No. Yes. Craig. He's here. He's on a date. With an itty-bitty redhead."

Diana wrinkles her nose. "I saw. I hoped you wouldn't see. Sorry."

"It's okay. It's not as if we had anything." *Well, we kind of did.*

I focus hard on the music for several minutes. I tell myself to savor it, and take it all in. After all, it's one of Edie's German boys, Beethoven.

And then, I don't know what happens. I don't know if it's the music or the warm balmy night, so much like that June night in Berlin, but I get to my feet and march across the lawn to the big plaid blankets where Craig and Chad and their friends are.

Chad sees me first. "Hello, Dr. McAdams."

Craig tilts his head back and looks up at me. He rises and steps around the others to kiss my cheek. "Didn't know you were here this weekend."

"Diana invited me."

He gestures to the group on the blanket. "You know Chad. Have you met his wife Meg, yet? And these are Meg's sisters—Kit and Kit's husband Jude, and Kit's fraternal twin, Brianna Brennan."

I say hello and shake hands all the while thinking—he's either on a date with Brianna, or they are both there as singles—but I'm not going to return to Diana without seizing the moment to ask Craig, "Feel like having brunch with me and eight or nine old men tomorrow morning?"

"I couldn't imagine anything more enjoyable."

My cheeks hurt from smiling. "Eleven work for you?"

"Perfect."

"Great. I'll see you then."

Brunch is good. Dad is delighted to see Craig and after the meal Craig goes with me to visit with Ruth, who is sure I'm her granddaughter and Craig is my husband.

I let Ruth hug me and hold my hand. It makes her happy, and I think it would make Edie happy, too.

Then Craig needs to go, as there's a private event at the winery this afternoon and he's promised to be on hand, since Chad is spending the weekend with his in-laws.

Monday morning I pack and go for a last run. I travel my favorite route down Poppy Lane, cutting down the dirt road, running past the farm with the horses and up the hill.

I don't cry as I run. I crest the hill and stand there, taking in the view.

It's beautiful and pastoral and calm.

I'm peaceful.

Content. Or at least, far more content.

I've been lonely this summer in Scottsdale, but I'm not lonely when I visit Napa. I feel as if I've got my own little community here. Friends. Family. One day maybe I could live here, too.

I jog down the hill, and stop to talk to the horses who come to the fence to see me. The white horse tosses his head, flicks his tail, and whinnies. I stroke his nose and then continue jogging along the path, dirt clouding around my ankles with every step.

The heat brings out the smell of the oak trees and tall, dry grass. Back on Poppy Lane I slow to a walk, my hands on my hips. I breathe in deep, great gulps of air. How far I've come in the past few months. The worst of the guilt and anguish is gone. I still think of Andrew, and feel sadness and regret, but most of all, I feel love.

I did love him. Dearly. And I will always love him. Just as I love Mom. And Edie.

I reach the first farmhouse, the one with the picket fence. The roses bloom, but today they're not the star. They're just part of a summer garden that's rioting with color.

Dahlias, zinnias, and lilies. Pinks and corals, reds, blues, crimson, purple. A sunny yellow dahlia with spidery blossoms peeks through the burgundy and orange dahlias and I smile at it. So bright, so insistent.

Beautiful.

I don't even realize I've said the word out loud until a straw hat rises from behind the picket fence and a woman smiles at me. "Dahlias are such show-offs, aren't they?" she says.

I can suddenly hear Edie's voice in my head.

Dahlias are such show-offs.

I nod, and smile, fighting tears. Good tears. Happy tears.

"I love your garden," I tell the woman.

"Thank you." She draws off a glove and stretches her hand across the fence. "I'm Lulu London. And you're the woman living at 33 Poppy Lane?"

I start to answer that it's my dad's house and I just stay there when I visit him, but for some reason I can't say it. Instead I nod, and shake her hand. "I'm Alison McAdams."

"You're Dr. McAdams' daughter, the dentist."

"Yes."

Lulu smiles. "So nice to meet you after all this time, and I'm so glad you're living here now. Your father's so much happier when you're around."

"You know Dad?"

"I'm George's daughter. He's at Napa Estates, too, and is a friend of your father's."

We chat for another moment and then say good-bye. And as I walk the rest of the way home, I keep seeing Lulu's smile beneath her straw hat.

I see the dahlias.

I hear Edie's voice. *They're such show-offs, aren't they?*

And suddenly I know I want to live here. I'm ready to move here. I'm ready to call Napa home.

There is no reason I can't look for a dental practice up here. There has to be something, somewhere, even if part-time.

I wouldn't mind part-time, because then I could still work a couple days a week at Bloom.

Or I could just spend my free time with Dad, watching golf with him on the TV and learning to play a really mean game of bridge.

Dad would be happy.

Maybe Craig would even take some bridge lessons with me. It'd be fun to spend more time with him. Get to know him slowly, properly.

Maybe even have a real date now and then, or another dinner date where we'd sit outside in his garden beneath the strings of lights, and drink wine and talk quietly while Bruiser snores at our feet. I really like Bruiser.

And Craig.

It could work.

And even if it doesn't, it's okay. I'm going to be okay. In fact, I'm okay right now. Maybe even better than okay.

I smile, slowly, realizing it's working out already. I'm good.

Life is good.

It's You

DISCUSSION QUESTIONS

1. What do you think brought Ali and Diana together into a fast friendship?
2. Why is Ali so insistent on her dad moving in with her despite the fact that they can barely talk to each other?
3. When the novel begins, Ali and Andrew's family are still deep in grief over Andrew's suicide. Do you think the suicide of a loved one is something someone can ever move beyond?
4. At first, Ali does not realize that becoming a dentist in Andrew's father's practice may not have been Andrew's wish. Why does it take so long for her to reach this conclusion?
5. Halfway through the novel, the reader is introduced to Edie's backstory, which adds a new time, place, and even narrative style to *It's You*. How did this inform your reading experience?
6. What helps Ali realize she needs to forgive Andrew?
7. Berlin plays an important role as a turning point in Ali's emotional journey. What city would you pick for a similar soul-searching mission?
8. Did you see any significance in Ali's losing the diary in Berlin? How did that moment alter her course afterwards?

9. Edie's journals allowed Ali to experience some of what Edie went through, and also allowed Edie to relive her past. Do you keep a journal, and would you share it with someone else?

10. How does Ali's relationship with her father evolve throughout the novel? By the novel's end, do you like where they stand?